JOURNEY TO THE KINGDOM

OF SOUL

Written By: Everlazt

Zahara .

The Making of A Queen

Chapter 1

Planet Muzena

Pakisound   1996 O.W.

A misty rain swept through the land, covering the already wet Industriarmy, as they stood shoulder to shoulder. Spots of flambeau light sparkled in the distance from the top of the 30 foot wall that surrounded the small town of Pakisound, illuminating the vicious stares from the legions of foot soldiers as they patiently waited for their command to attack.

The fear within the walls of Pakisound could be felt throughout the small city as the towns people ran to and from preparing for the inevitable battle. "Are the archers in position?" King Steven asked his general at arms.

"Yes Sire". General Rock answered as he looked over the people scurrying for cover.

"Allow me to interject Sire." St.Eagle eagerly said from the Kings side. "I believe we can come to an understanding with Tmus, before the Industriarmy advances in their quest."

King Steven cut his eyes at his spiritual consultant, "St.Eagle, we are beyond the stage of agreement with Tmus and his mad band of blood thirsty barbarian's…I refuse to surrender Pakisound to him."

"Very well Sire." St.Eagle's four foot long, eight feet wide wings spread open and lifted him up into the air. After hovering in the air for a moment, St.Eagle flew out of the castle war chamber and headed down the long corridor to see where he would be needed at.

"Rock", King Steven got his generals attention. "You have been my most trusted friend and confidant. I want you to promise me, if Tmus seizes the city- killing me in the process you will vow revenge on Tmus and the Industriarmy." King Steven sincerely asked.

"King, what makes you think I will live, if the Industriarmy kills you?" Rock asked.

King Steven smirked", Because, Tmus may not know what lies within the walls of this land, but I know what lies within your heart. It's a strength the people will always follow once I am long gone."

The reflection of the bubbling fire in the fireplace danced in the King's eyes as he continued, "Rock, I'm getting old, and I feel like this is my last stand. But you have years of leadership ahead of you".

If Rock knew how to be affectionate this would have been the moment when he would smile and embrace his King, but General Rock was groomed from birth to abstain from all forms of emotion that did not involve the love for his army, and the defense of his beloved Pakisound. This is why General Rock never married, because he could never be a successful lover to one woman, like he was successful in the army.

His rocky dark skin, that seemed impenetrable through the many battles General Rock had been in, made the stocky man a rising force in the King's army. Rock was blessed with the natural ability to lead winnable campaigns against the small assault that came upon the city during his years of leadership.

However, this time it was different.

Tmus and his powerful army had assembled outside the walls of Pakisound, ready to make a bold statement in the world of Muzena. Either convert to the powers and lifestyle permitted by the Gods of force. Or be forcefully industrialized by Tmus and his Industriarmy. Pakisound never stood face to face with a foe as large as the Industriarmy.

"Sire, we will come out of this battle the same way as all the other ones...Victorious!" General Rock boldly predicted as he raised his sword high into the air to stress his conviction. King Steven admired his general's confidence, but deep down inside he felt his reign was coming to an end.

The side door to the chamber opened and Queen Taila quickly sashayed over to the King with Nalani, her personal housemaid in tow. "Steven, do you think it's time to send the children down to the castle's shelter?" The Queen asked with a worried look in her eyes.

Taking in the Queens beauty, King Steven admired how his wife has always been a breath of fresh air for him. That was one of the many reasons it was easy for him to take her in as his new wife after his first wife died.

"In a moment my love", King Steven said, looking down at the defense map of the city. Queen Talia stood back and stared at her husband.

King Steven stood at a towering 6'4' height, matched up with an intimidating body presence that commanded respect, even if he wasn't the King of Pakisound. His salt and pepper beard mixed well with his bald head and dark brown skin, giving him the look of a man who possessed infinite knowledge and wisdom.

Queen Taila was full of swirling emotions as she watched the King and Rock strategize for the survival of their city. Taila flashed back to how she was handpicked by a special committee to be groomed and given to the King for marriage, if he chose to marry again. Once Steven lost Ophilia, the mother of his first child, the committee quickly swung into action to fill the void. A void Taila was more than happy to fill. So long as the coca brown slim beauty, with long flowing bronze color hair, could love the King on her own accord.

When Taila birthed the King's first son, their bond became more solid, which was the envy of the King's mistresses. The almost 25/year age difference between King Steven and Taila never mattered to the couple. As long as Taila was ready to step into her position and help work to keep the city on the continued path of constant elevation, she and the King would get along just fine. Which they did, but now all of that work was in jeopardy.

After taking one last look at the map, the King said", General Rock, I will join you at the second line of defense once I secure the Queen and the children."

"Yes Sire", The General responded, before slightly bowing his head, and leaving the chamber.

"Come my dear", King Steven said as he led the way into the adjoining room. Cutting through the room, they made their way down a narrow pathway and walked through another room where they were greeted by the Queens housemaid.

"Nalani is the princess ready?"

"Yes my Queen", Nalani answered as she stuffed a few small items into her carrier.

Steven and Taila walked into the next adjoining room and found their two children busy at work putting away their prized possessions that could go with them to the city shelter.

"It's time", King Steven said, and then slowly walked over to his daughter. At the age of 17, Princess Zahara was growing into a spitting image of her late mother. With her deep chocolate skin, hazel eyes, and a head full of waist length curly locks, the King found himself in a flash back to one of the happier moments he shared with Zahara and her mother many years ago.

Queen Taila walked over to their only son Prince Steven III. Knowing that he was about to be separated from his father for an undetermined amount of time, the young prince wasn't in the best of spirits. Taila stood before him as he sat Indian style, on the floor, at the foot of Zahara's straw bed.

"Come Steven and give your mom a hug", Taila said with a warm smile that melted her son stone face. At 10/years old the young prince felt he was old enough to fight at his father's side, but his mother had to burst the young man's bubble by saying", The only one in this room that will be fighting by your father's side is me." With that said the discussion was over before it even started.

"Will you join us father?" Zahara asked in a somber tone.

"When I can my dear", The King said. "But it won't be in the shelter. This time you will be leaving Pakisound."

"Leaving? And go where?" Zahara asked with a surprised look on her face.

"For your protection, you will be going to the Kingdom of Soul. Queen Mary Jane will gladly receive you", The King said.

"The Kingdom of Soul?..Isn't that another world?" Prince Steven asked.

"He's right Steven. Isn't that a long journey for them to be traveling?" A surprised Taila asked. Usually the Queen knows about a change in the plan like this, but the look on her face told the real story today.

"Yes it is that is why you will be going with them", The King said. "With your guidance they should reach the Kingdom of Soul safely."

"I'm sorry my dear", Taila began. "But I am not leaving you here".

"Me neither!" Prince Steven boasted, sticking his little chest out for emphasis.

"Taila don't fight me on this, our children safety is our priority right now. If Pakisound is going to have any kind of future after this war, then we must protect the future monarch of this city", said the King, but the Queen would hear none of it.

"Steven, I agree with you about protecting our children. But my undying loyalty is to you, and I will not leave your side. Like I said I wouldn't before the people of this city. So if you stay, then so will I", Taila stated firmly.

The room was silent as the King let her words mill over in his mind.

BOOM!

A loud explosion rattled the night sky, interrupting Stevens thought's.

"Nalani, you go with the children", Taila said quickly taking control of the conversation.

"Yes Madam", Nalani agreed.

"Zahara and Steven come with me", Taila ordered bringing the children through the side door and into a small chamber. The special chamber was used by the King and Queen as a spiritual parlor. Nalani stood in the doorway, as King Steven held his sword ready for anything.

Queen Taila, walked over to the altar, and picked up a large brown book that had the Pakisound insignia on it. She put the book into a carry bag. Then she grabbed a gold necklace with a glowing heart dangling from it. Zahara, Prince Steven, and Nalani never laid eyes on the glowing heart.

"What is this?" Zahara asked as the charm was placed around her neck.

"This is the heart of Pakisound...Its powers are unlimited, and sometimes uncontrollable." Taila said. "But, something is telling me you are the right person to finally learn how to use the heart for its intended purpose."

The King stepped into the room to add his insight. "When the heart was first found by your mother, we all thought she would be the one who could channel its powers into the soul of land."

"But, what happened?" Zahara quickly asked feeling like this would finally be the moment when she will hear about her mother's sudden death.

"Like Taila said, the heart possesses very strong powers that no one has been able to control. Not even St.Eagle... And St.Eagle is the most powerful priest in Pakisound." The King said, trying his best to keep the old tale short.

"Did it kill her?" Zahara asked, causing everyone to turn to the King for confirmation.

He slowly nodded his head and said, "We believe so my child."

"But that doesn't mean you will face that same fate", Taila quickly added. "They say the Kingdom of Soul possesses many answers to very complicated questions. You may discover answers in the Kingdom we could not find here." She told Zahara with an affectionate look of honesty in her eyes.

Zahara silently nodded, then tucked the necklace into the silky green wrap she was wearing. Taila kissed Zahara's forehead and gave her a big hug. Then Taila handed the Prince the carry bag with the sacred book in it.

"With this book you will forever be the people of Pakisound future ruler. In this book there are spoken and unspoken spells and gifts that were used to build our beautiful city."

The young Prince took the bag and slung it over his shoulder. "Protect this book with your life my child." The Queen said, before taking his face into her hands and kissing him on his cheek.

The King stepped up and kneeled down in front of his son. "This is the first sword my father gave to me when I was about your age. And now it is time I pass it down to you." He handed his son a foot and a half long sword, the Prince took it, admiring the Pakisound insignia on its thick silver handle.

A huge smile crawled into the corners of Prince Steven's mouth, as a surge of power flowed threw his body the moment his hand gripped the handle.

"Always defend the truth of Pakisound, and always stand by your sister." The King firmly said, staring into his sons eyes.

"Yes father", The Prince said. Steven helped his son strap the sword's case over his back, and gave him a big hug.

"Nalani, I'm trusting you to bring the children to The Kingdom of Soul safely", Queen Taila said sternly to her housemaid.

"Yes madam, I will."

Taila handed Nalani a small carry bag. "If you run into any adversity along the way, all you have to do is reach into this bag. Everything you shall need to successfully complete this journey is in this bag".

"I understand madam, and I want to thank you for trusting in me with such a meaningful task for you and the King", Nalani humbly said as she bowed her head slightly.

There was no doubt in Taila's mind that Nalani would get the children to their destination safely- by any means necessary. Taila had spent most of her adult life with Nalani as her housemaid, and now she considered Nalani a friend.

Another loud explosion rocked the castle, as a loud scream echoed through the halls.

"Sire! Sire!" Bounced off the walls as the King and Queen began to scramble.

"Nalani quickly, take the children through the royal passage way." Taila ordered, as she rushed them to a hidden doorway in the corner of the stone wall. Taila moved a stone and a big portion of the wall shifted, then pushed inward. Inside revealed a staircase that descended into the lower depths of the castle. The King passed Zahara a torch and gave her a hug for what everyone believed would be the last time.

"May the Gods of song bless you my child", The King told his daughter. Then he turned to his son. "Remember, you are the future of Pakisound."

"I will remember father", The Prince bravely said.

"Come young Prince", Nalani ordered, taking charge of the emotional scene.

Zahara lead the way down the steps, with the Prince hot on her heels. Before Nalani followed the children down the steps, she turned to the King and Queen, and gave them what she hoped wouldn't be a final hug.

"Travel safely Nalani."

"Yes Sire", She said with a reassuring nod- took one last look over to the Queen, who was now crying – nodded then vanished into the darkness.

King Steven quickly closed the wall back as one of his aids barged into the room. "Sire, they're storming the main wall!"

"Then let's go and greet them", The King announced looking over to his Queen. She gave him a firm look and nodded, silently letting him know she was there until the end.

✳✳✳✳✳

Tmus sat patiently on his black stallion, with his black hood over his bald head. Silently he let the excitement coming from the depths of his army build inside of him. The sounds of the hungry Industriarmy hummed from a low murmur into a loud roar once Major Zor raised his four foot long sword into the air. Zor looked over to Tmus and waited for him to give the final order.

Tmus stared at the city of Pakisound and he could feel the rhythm of the war drums beating from within the high walls of the promising metropolis. Pakisound was one of Tmus' biggest challenges to date as he continues on his campaign of Industrial dominance of the entire Muzena.

As in the previous takeovers, Tmus sent in a committee that came bearing gifts, a proposal that promised a stronger economic infusion into the city, as well as raw material that could be used to build better and stronger homes. The proposal also promised a more ecological system that would give the soil a better richness, and help the land produce food for the people at a much faster rate. Of course access to the Industriarmy- who will protect the city from future plots and attempts – was part of the package.

These lopsided negotiations have always ended with the King or ruling monarchy feeling insulted by these heavy handed demands.

Even though the committee would not make an outright declaration of a destructive campaign coming to town, word always traveled throughout the land about how Tmus was not taking no for an answer.

When the committee returns to Industriland with a negative response from the sought after city, Tmus would then send in an army of pain inflicting soldiers, always lead by the ruthless Major Zor.

Major Zor has been hands on in the building process that made the Industriarmy into the force it is today. The troops respond to Major Zor with a mirror like brutality they witness their leader administer to the enemy numerous times. With his forearms and hands covered in impenetrable gold, the Major has been known to rip his victim's limbs out of socket.

Usually Tmus would send Major Zor with a sizable army to take over a city, but the seizure of Pakisound was different.

He thought back to when his great uncle Boliy almost died in a famous battle against Pakisound. It was a defining moment in Muzena where many states erupted into war for that state's independence. Watching his uncle come back with only a third of his troops and a defeated look made Tmus vow to win any war he was to lead in, especially one against the land of Pakisound. To industrialize Pakisound would be a powerful victory on Tmus' resume.

The troops worked themselves up into frenzy, as Major Zor awaited the signal. Tmus' horse sneezed and shifted in his stance. The rain drops grew thicker with the wind picking up speed.

"Begin..." Tmus said without taking his eyes off of the lined up archers atop of the parameter wall.

Major Zor quickly pointed his sword to Pakisound, "INDUSTRY!!!"

RRRRWWW! The army roared as the front line charged the wall.

*****

General Rock kept his eyes on the mass approaching sea of foot soldiers, who kept their shields in a protective position. "Steady!" Rock yelled over the loud war drums.

"Steady!"

The sea was within 300 yards.

"FIRE!"

On General Rocks command, the archers released a hail storm of poisonous arrows through the night sky. Even with their burning torches, the Industriarmy could not see the venomous arrows raining down on them.

'AAAAWWWW!'

"Shields Up! Shields Up!"

Orders began to circulate through the ranks, as the wounded fell to the ground. The hundreds of surviving soldiers dropped down to one knee and put their shields up over their heads. When a break came, the soldiers hopped back up to their feet and continued to charge at the wall.

"FIRE!"

The heavy sounds of catapults releasing big firey balls of destruction into the air, along with another barrage of poisonous arrows lit up the sky, shining light on the entire flatlands.

The furious pace of the war drums thumping a hard rhythm was so intense; King Steven could feel it in his teeth when he joined his general at the command post. The King stayed in the back ground, with the Queen by his side, watching his general coordinate their line of offense.

"FIRE!"

"AAAAWWWW!"

The air assault hurt the approaching enemy, but as they reached inside of 100 yards of the city, fewer soldiers succumbed to the onslaught.

"They're On the Wall!" Someone called out.

"Release The Kettles!" The General ordered.

Big bowls of molten hot tar were tipped over the side of the wall, stopping the determined attackers in their tracks. Screams rang out as the lead ranks fell off of the ladders that made it to the wall.

The second line of attack quickly stepped over their fallen comrades, picked up the ladders and proceeded to climb up into the waiting hands of desperate Pakisound defenders.

BOOM!--BOOM!--BOOM!

King Steven kept a straight face as the rattling of the front portcullis vibrated through his body. 20 to 30 men wheeled a large tree bark back, then wheeled it up against the portcullis sending debris flying.

A strong second effort is what the Industriarmy used to get over the ledge, and the hand to hand combat began.

BOOM!--BOOM!--BOOM!

"RRRRAAWWWWW!" The Industriarmy soldiers roared out in triumph as they made a big crack into the front gate.

"Hit it again!" Someone ordered.

The large battering ram was wheeled back and rushed forward. BOOM!

"AAAAWWW!" Some of the soldiers working the battering ram cried out in pain as another hot kettle of tar was poured onto their heads. Hand to hand combat is General Rock specialty. Once he witnessed the first sign of the enemy coming over the ramparts, he quickly unleashed his sword from its holster and ran straight for the first person who looked like they would make it over the ledge untouched.

Whoosh! General Rock swung his sword chopping off one of the attackers arms. Then he kicked him back over the ledge. The war was officially on.

St.Eagle flew in and landed beside the King, "Sire". The front gate has been breached", he said with nervousness in his voice.

"Then make sure they don't make it into the castle without a fight", The King ordered.

"Yes Sire", St.Eagle said before flying off to go help the troops in the front court. King Steven stood erect, taking in the struggle between his troops and the Industriarmy, until he felt it was time for him to release his own share of fiery.

"Taila I want you to protect the people in the shelter", The King ordered.

Taila was hesitant to leave her King's side, and he felt it. He looked into Taila's eyes, then kissed her for what might be the last time. "Don't worry my Queen, we have the Gods of Song on our side. Now go!"

The assuring words were enough to motivate Taila to go tackle her task without any arguments. "Yes Sire", then she quickly ran off.

King Steven stepped out of the post and jumped right into the battle, swinging his sword with a purpose as the Industriarmy soldiers began to come over the wall like ants.

"Let's go." Tmus calmly said to Major Zor, and with a security team consisting of 50 foot soldiers and 50 knights, They galloped to the front gate under the horrifying sounds of bones being crushed by the horses, and rushed right through the destroyed portcullis.

The court yard was full of men engaged in hand to hand combat. St.Eagle flew around over the soldiers' heads releasing spells on the invaders. Tmus admired the all white wizard with wings. He saw St.Eagle as an asset to his army- only if he could convert him.

Tmus pulled down his hood, letting the rain water run down his porcelain white bald head. His eyes turned into a dark red as he locked his sight on St.Eagle. A sound wave powerful enough to crack stone vibrated through the air knocking down everyone in its path.

St.Eagle's wings froze on him and he crashed out of the sky on to the muddy court grounds.

"Seize him!" Tmus ordered Zor.

Major Zor and five of his men dismounted their horses and surrounded St.Eagle, who was squirming around on the ground in a confused state. "Toss the net." The Major ordered, but St.Eagle gathered himself, "Wark!" He spat and turned the net into a pattern of snakes. "Wark!-Mark!" The snakes rose off of the ground then flew at the soldiers like daggers.

Some of the snake daggers hit their intended targets, but were stopped before penetrating the knight's armor. That did not stop the snake daggers from taking down the soldiers who were struck on their hands and faces.

Tmus smiled, "Bravo sorcerer, but it's not enough". A second later two strong rays shot out of Tmus' eyes. St.Eagle quickly lifted off of the ground just time. The two rays shot by him and slammed into a wall sending debris sprawling everywhere.

St.Eagle fired two hard fire balls out of his hands at Tmus. Boom-Boom…

Tmus chuckled as the flames bounced off of his protective shield that formed around him like a bubble. "Silly fool", Tmus hissed, then shot out a secession of eye rays.

St.Eagle ducked and weaved, but two of the rays clipped his wings. His feathers caught fire, causing St.Eagle to panic and fall out of the sky. "EEEEKKKK!"

"Now, seize him!" Tmus barked as he zapped St.Eagle with a knockout blow. Tmus rode his horse through the courtyard, toward the steps that lead up to the castle, with a blood thirsty entourage hot on his heels.

King Steven found himself fighting back to back with General Rock, as they cut, slashed, and smashed anybody that came within five feet of their circumference. Sounds of swords clinking together, mixed with war cries and pleas for help echoed throughout the yard. A fire raged in the background, as men ran to and from helping out fallen comrades in the battle.

A horse's whine caught Steven's attention, causing him to turn toward the main stairway. The King was shocked to see Tmus emerge on his black stallion with red demonic eyes.

"Tmus", King Steven blurted out to himself. Then he slowly walked out into the courtyard to do battle. Tmus hopped off of his horse, as his troops swarmed the area, over powering the Pakisound soldiers.

"Last chance King...You can save the rest of your people if you simply industrialize the city", Tmus said, with a wide smirk on his face.

King Steven's blood began to boil, as his body seemed to grow two sizes bigger. His anger vibrated into his grip, causing his sword to glow in the dark. "You'll die where you stand before I allow my people to be enslaved by you."

"Okay, have it your way", Tmus said, and produced a four foot sword.

Sizing each other up, the two rulers faced off under the back drop of thunder and lighting. Industriarmy men flooded the court yard with a force of 2 against 1. Rock felt the overwhelming pressure the army was putting on his men. Knowing he had to do something, Rock held his breath and his entire body turned into a black rock. The General curled up into a ball, and steam rolled into twenty Industriarmy men, causing bodies to fly into the air.

King Steven charged at Tmus swinging his sword at Tmus' head. Tmus quickly blocked the blow. When the two swords connected a bright flash lit up the night sky.

Clink, Clink! The two rulers swords could be heard across the court yard, as they war danced with each other in the gloom of the down pour. Tmus swung his sword in a slashing motion connecting with the King's sword, giving off an impact strong enough to shake the ground beneath them.

King Steven got up close on Tmus and struggled with the evil leader as their blades grinded up against each other. Steven kneed Tmus in his gut, then elbowed him across is chin.

Tmus staggered backwards, and spat", that's all you got?"

The King swung his sword, and when their blades connected, they created another deafening boom that echoed through the night. Steven dipped down and spun around brandishing a dagger in his free hand. Tmus could sense a trick reaction with the King's spinning move. He caught the King's hand in mid air, stopped the dagger before it struck, but paid the price from the Kings sword which slashed Tmus on his arm.

"Enough of this!" Tmus barked and his entire body lit up into a bright flash of light. Steven jumped back and shielded his eyes with his forearm, pitching his dagger at Tmus to stop him from running at the King with a quick offense.

"AAAWWW!" Tmus cried out in pain as the dagger struck him in the shoulder. Tmus shot a ray of light out of his eyes and socked the King in his chest, rocking Steven off of his feet.

The King tried to scramble to his feet, but Tmus was faster than him. Tmus swung his sword with such force that it cut right through Steven's sword. Deeming the sword useless, Steven tossed the rest of his sword then rushed at Tmus with his bare hands. The King grabbed the dagger that was sticking out of Tmus' shoulder, but Tmus was swifter then Steven expected.

Tmus side stepped the King's advance and shot out another round of rays out of eyes hitting Steven in his chest again. Steven flew off of his feet again, then Tmus came down hard with his sword chopping Steven's arm clear off. The King's scream was caught in the back of his throat as Tmus delivered a death blow that froze every fighter in the land.

"NNNNOOOO!" Rock cried out. Letting his shock turn into rage, Rock began to bull rush every enemy in sight. Rock used his rock solid hands to smack anyone within reach, breaking jaws and eye sockets.

Major Zor arrived just in time to witness his leader hand King Steven his death sentence. This gave Zor the motivation to destroy the King's second in command with the same viciousness he just witnessed Tmus hand Steven. The Major's arms turned a bright yellow, as he punched Rock in his face. Stone fragments flew off of Rock's face and turned into damaged flesh as soon as the chipped pieces hit the ground. Rock spit out chipped pieces of his teeth, and smiled at Zor.

General Rock blocked Zor's second effort, then threw an uppercut to Zor stomach; Lifting him three feet into the air. Rock chopped down on the winded Major's shoulder and almost knocked Zor's arm out of socket.

Major Zor collected himself and punched Rock in his knee cap. Rock cried out in pain as he stumbled backwards, then Zor jumped up and ceased Rock by his throat.

Major Zor growled as his arms locked on and squeezed the rocks around the General's neck, sending stone chips flying in all directions. Rock took the open opportunity to punish the Major's mid-section by punching Zor in his stomach in a quick succession-connecting twenty times within ten seconds.

Zor loosened his grip and dropped to one knee. Rock swung a left hook and connected with a blow that was strong enough to take

Zor's head off of his shoulders. Zor crumbed to the ground and Rock went in for the kill.

Sensing his Major was in trouble. Tmus shot a paralyzing eye ray at Rock and struck him in his back. Rock cried out in pain as he fell down to his knees and Zor capitalized off of the unexpected moment of assistance.

The Major hopped to his feet and summoned all of his inner strength which went into his hands. Zor grabbed Rock by his head and spun it out of socket. The General fell to the ground and his body slowly began to transform back into General Rock, the human being.

The surviving Pakisound troops, witnessing their King and military leader fall by the hands of Tmus and Zor, threw down their weapons and surrendered to the Industriarmy.

After pulling the dagger out of his shoulder, Tmus felt a little weaker than expected. A minor injury from a dagger usually would not affect Tmus, but for some reason he wasn't feeling like himself.

"Find the royal family, and bring them to me", Tmus ordered, before climbing back on his horse.

A huge scramble ensued as knights and soldiers searched the castle to find the surviving members of the destroyed city.

✳✳✳✳✳
———————

Down in the shelter all was quiet as the women and children tried to listen for any signs of a victory for the Pakisound people. Queen Taila stood by the door with two other mothers preparing themselves for anything.

"What do you think is going on my Queen?" Thea nervously asked.

Taila looked over to her and quickly noted that Thea always looked presentable, even in the time of war. Taila found herself wondering if Thea would get dirty in her shady blue village dress if she had to.

"I don't know Thea, but we are ready for whatever it is", the Queen firmly stated, raising her tone a little higher then Thea's whisper.

"I don't hear the war drums anymore", Ruby pointed out in the tension filled shelter.

Moments later footsteps and voices could be heard on the other side of the thick wooden door. Taila put her fingers up to her lips giving everyone in sight the signal to be quiet.

"There's a door back here!"

"Check it out", another voice echoed down the corridor.

The door handle rattled, but that's as far as the secured door was going to budge. "It's locked."

More footsteps were heard coming down the corridor, and then the handle rattled again, followed by loud banging. 'BANG- BANG- BANG!'

Queen Taila, Thea, and Ruby jumped at the sound of the banging.

"Seems like its sealed shut."

"Here comes the Major", another voice said.

"What's in there?"

"We don't know Major Zor. The door seems to be sealed shut."

Queen Taila listened intently to the conversation, and then motioned for her small group of mothers and wives to arm themselves. The women quickly grabbed some clubs and sticks, while the Queen's weapon of choice was a foot long dagger. Thea picked up a club with nails sticking out of it. The pounding started again, but this time the hinges began to rattle.

The women tensed up as they positioned themselves on either side of the door. BANG- BANG- BANG- CRACK!

A gold plated fist came through the middle of the door, and then pulled back. An eye and half of face appeared in the hole.

Queen Taila saw a free shot and took it.

AAAAWWWW! One of the men on the other side of the door cried out in agony as he grabbed for his bleeding eye.

All of the women in the shelter felt a surge strength from their Queen's potent blow with her dagger. The children huddled together in the next room feeling nervous about the loud banging, and the horrible cry from the injured man. The younger ones began to cry, but were quickly shushed by the others.

"Stand back", Major Zor ordered. His gold fist lit up the dark corridor as he pulled back and began to punch the wood door like it was feather stuffed pillow. Splinters flew into the room, sending a chill through the large room.

When he made the hole big enough, Major Zor violently reached into the door and with all of his strength began to rip the door off its hinges.

The women readied themselves as huge chunks of the door was ripped away and discarded as scrap. BANG- CRACK- POP!

The remainder of the door was ripped in half and ten Industriarmy soldiers rushed in. The women jumped right into action with their sticks and clubs. The women caught the first wave of soldiers off guard as cries of pain echoed through the lower depths of the castle.

Queen Taila and her group of mothers were far from killers. With the life of their children on the line, the women quickly went for death blows. Taila went straight for face and neck shots, cringing every time she connected.

Thea on the other hand kept a straight face as her billy-club connected with one of her attacker's faces.

AAAWWW! AAAHHH!

Grunts, cries and screams echoed through the room as the Major watched the brawl from the doorway. The confrontation was looking more brutal then Zor would have expected in a fight with a bunch of women. More soldiers hustled by Zor and ran into the room over whelming the women.

Major Zor stepped over two dead bodies and walked up behind a bronze colored fighter, whose weapon of choice was a foot long dagger.

The Queen was engaged in a one on one struggle with a soldier who was trying to disarm her. "Let go!" Taila cried out as she tried to snatch her arm away.

Major Zor punched Taila in her back with enough force to crumble her, but not enough to kill her.

"Secure the prisoner!" Major Zor ordered as he took control of the room. The first order of business was disarming the feisty female fighters. Zor then made his way into the second chamber, which was large enough fill one wall with a stock pile of food, and water jugs.

On the other side of the room then Zor came face to face with a group of children, ranging from ages 2/to 14.

"Shut Up!" "Stop That Crying!" Soldiers yelled at the frighten children.

Major Zor watched the chaotic scene from the back of the room, paying special attention to each child's face. None of the brown and honey complexioned faces gave Zor the impression of being royalty. "Round them up and take them out to the court yard", The Major ordered, then stepped back into the adjoining chamber.

"You heard him! Move it!"

The strong Thea sat on the ground, holding her injured arm, as tears rolled down her cheeks for her slain friend. "Ruby", Thea mouthed in a low tone, as she looked into Ruby's cold stare.

Major Zor walked over to Thea and grabbed her by the injured arm. He lifted Thea up off of the ground and looked into her eyes with one of the most ruthless stares she had ever seen. "Where is the royal family?" Zor asked with a voice full of death that matched his eyes.

The pain Thea felt was enough to make the average person pass out, but Thea refused to let any man from the Industriarmy feel superior over her. Tears streamed down her face heavier than ever, but Thea did not let herself cry out.

The procession of children was marched out into the room to witness the Major's brutality on one of their most celebrated protectors. Whimpers and cries vibrated through the group causing Thea's blood to boil. The innocent spirit and soul of the children was one of the most guarded ways of raising them in Pakisound, and the Industriarmy was here to destroy it.

Thea spit in the Major's face.

He smiled as the green mucus rolled down his dark brown cheek. "Fine, have it your way", Zor said, and with his free hand he chopped Thea in her wind pipe. Zor let go of Thea and she crashed down to the ground gasping for air.

Queen Taila felt a sudden ping of guilt knowing that Thea just died for trying to protect her from a more brutal enslavement, due to her status as Queen of Pakisound. The heat coming from the eyes of the remaining women were burning holes in her face. The thought never crossed Taila's mind to come forward and confess her status to the Industriarmy.

Taila felt extremely sadden for what all of the women and children had to witness, but she felt she would be more of an asset to them alive than dead. Making her remained silent.

"Okay, so no one knows where the royal family is? Huh?" the Major said in a matter of fact tone. "Well, if they are hiding somewhere in this city, they will burn up with the rest of it", he concluded as he wiped the spit off of his face, and walked out of the shelter.

"Let's go! Move it!" One of the soldiers barked as they herded the women and children prisoners out of the chamber.

"Burn everything down!" Zor barked as he led the way out into the bloodied court yard.

A scene filled of horror, shock, and defeat was rampant throughout the land as soldiers on horseback rode around torching anything that wasn't made out of stone.

Chapter II

The woods opened up into another world during night fall in Muzena. The more timid animals crawled into their safe houses, while the night hunters combed the land in search for food. Sounds of the night surrounded Nalani as she held onto Prince Steven's hand, and lead the way through the trails. Growls and howls echoed around them as they moved as quickly as possible without running into unwanted guest.

"You sure this is the right way?" Zahara asked trying to keep pace with her brother and their new guardian.

"Yes my lady...Now please keep moving", Nalani said with a nice blend of respect and authority.

Nalani knew the children had to be walking nervous wrecks like herself. Traveling into the forest, in the middle of the night, and unprepared was not Nalani idea of a quiet evening. She wasn't going to show the children their creepy surrounding was rattling her as much as them.

To ignore her fears, Nalani blocked the night dangers out of her mind, and pressed on through the woods, with her heart set on getting the children to their destination safely. They walked for what seemed like an eternity until they came to a large clearing. Stepping cautiously through the two foot high grass, the sounds of running water let Nalani know they were by the Nire River. As the after rain breeze blew through the land, the half moon shined a nice glare of light across the river.

"I'm thirsty", Prince Steven said.

"We'll be able to get water at the Golona village", Nalani said feeling a slight ping of relief now that they were out of the woods.

Wanting to sit down, Zahara asked, "How far is it?"

"It shouldn't be that far from here my lady", Nalani answered.

Zahara sucked her teeth, "Well I'm thirsty too... Why can't we drink that water?" She asked pointing to the river.

"Because my lady, if the salt in the water doesn't kill you, then one of the many hungry water lizards will reach out into the night for you", Nalani said.

Zahara knew it would get her nowhere to continue on with the back and forth with Nalani. Even though Zahara knew she could have easily ordered Nalani to get the Prince and her water, she knew it would be unwise to go against an elder's words. Especially, those who have been outside the gates of Pakisound.

Zahara never ventured this far outside of Pakisound and her inexperience showed as she tried to maneuver through the night, bumping into bushes and jumping every time an owl hooted or a coyote howled. Sticking as close to the side of the river as they could without falling in the three travelers avoided the thick forest on the other side of them. Nalani prayed to the Gods of Song to keep the moon light strong enough to help guild them through the night.

"Nalani, my feet hurt," the young prince whined.

"Don't worry young one, it won't be long now", Nalani confidently said.

"How can you tell?" Zahara asked.

Nalani had been around the princess most of her life. Princess Zahara had always been a free spirited child who always had something to smile about, bringing an air of laughter to the castle whenever she was around. From the moment, the King told her she and the prince would be leaving their home from birth, Zahara's entire demeanor had been one filled with disorientation, mixed with flashes of sadness.

Nalani could tell from the way Zahara snapped every time she said something that being out of her comfort zone was really affecting the young princess. Nalani knew she would have to get Zahara to the Kingdom of Soul as soon as physically possible, before the Princess had a nervous breakdown in the woods.

"We've always had good relations with the Golona people. We've always kept our distance--" Nalani paused in mid-sentence, and flexed her head as if she was listening for something.

"What's wro—?"

Ssshhh! Nalani quickly quieted the prince as they stood stock still in the middle of the trail.

Faint sounds could be heard coming from the right side of the woods, prompting Nalani to slip her free hand into her bag. She gripped Prince Steven's hand even tighter to give him a sense of security in what may be their first confrontation.

The Prince did not know his position yet on this journey, and at ten years old, he was far from seasoned on how to deal with danger out in the wild. Some things did not need to be taught, the Prince thought to himself, as he went for the oversized sword his father gave him.

'No!" Nalani snapped, yanking his hand away from his sword.

A dark figure slowly made his self visible. Stepping out into the clearing, the five foot tall man aimed his bow and arrow at the Princess.

"We come in peace." Nalani said, still gripping the Princes hand, while her free hand locked around something in her bag.

"Why you travel the path of the Golona people?" The man asked, as he continued to aim his arrow at them.

The man became more visible the further he came out into the clearing. He wore colorful war paint on his face and upper part of his body. He was dressed in a traditional green and brown Golona people fabric that covered his lower body down to his knees.

"We come from Pakisound. We were attacked tonight by the Industriarmy, and--"

"Pakisound?" he asked looking interested.

"Yes Pakisound", Nalani answered as she watched him analyze their clothing. A sure way to distinguish ones tribe or statehood is by their dress.

"The Industriarmy invaded the land?" he asked, loosening his grip on his bow and arrow.

"Yes."

He stared at Nalani for a moment then turned to the woods and said something in his native tongue. Slowly three other men began to appear out of the darkness. They conversed amongst themselves then the first man said, "You come with us… to Golona village... to see high priest."

Nalani smiled. "Yes, thank you", "Come my lady", she said as she took her hand out of her bag and began to follow the men.

No one spoke as they made their way down a snake trail. Zahara could smell the difference of the forest as they ventured further into the woods. She did not know if it was the surrounding vegetation or if the unusual scents were part of the approaching village. Whatever it was, it was making her hungry.

The forest began to open up as they stepped into the sleeping village. Two of the men ran off to a short hut, as the spokesman said, "We wait."

Nalani, Zahara, and Steven sat down on a large log and patiently waited until an older man hustled out of the hut with the two escorts following close behind him.

Nalani recognized the gray bearded man immediately and stood to greet the high priest. "Stooler, thank you for accepting us into your village", Nalani said with a bright smile and a hand shake.

The High Priest took her hands and said, "Anything for dear friends. Now tell me about the invasion", he said with a concerned look in his eyes.

"Yes of course." Nalani said. "But, first I would like you to meet the royal Princess Zahara and Prince Steven." She led the man over to the exhausted looking prince and princess.

A large smile spread across his face, "Ahh, yes, the young royals. Welcome to Golona village", Stooler said as he took Zahara's hands then Stevens, bowing his head to complete his greeting.

Zahara blushed hard, even though she was used to being catered too. It felt special being greeted in a servitor manner by a spiritual leader. "Thank you for having us", Zahara said with her customary smile.

Stooler's face twisted up as he turned to Nalani and asked, "What about the King and Queen?"

A somber look crept up on Nalani's face, "They ordered us to leave the city, to avoid capture by the Industriarmy".

Stooler did not like the sound of her story. He turned to the men that brought them into the village and ran down a list of things he wanted them to do. One by one, they disappeared to go carry out

their task. When he was done he turned back to Nalani and said,"
We prepare a place for rest."

"Can we have some water?" Steven asked, not wanting to be
sent to bed with a dry throat.

"Yes my Prince. All will be made", Stooler said. He turned
back to Nalani, sat down next her on the log, and asked her to fill
him in on what took place in Pakisound.

As they spoke amongst themselves, sections of the village
slowly began to come to life. A small reconnaissance team was put
together and sent up to Pakisound to assess the situation up at
Pakisound. A few women were woken up and ordered to prepare two
huts for their guess. Then they were shown to their huts.

Zahara and Steven were placed in a large hut with a thick hay
bed. The young prince laid down and was lightly snoring within two
minutes. Zahara on the other hand laid down and kept her eyes
focused on the strong bamboo roof. Thoughts of how much her life
had changed since her mom's death was all Zahara could think
about. She hadn't thought about her mom in a long time. Now that
Zahara was resting in a foreign land, on the run from one of
Muzena's most deadliest beings she had the deep longing to be up
under her mother right now.

A strong vibration murmured on Zahara's chest reminding her
of the priceless necklace she was wearing under her blue and green

shawl. Zahara pulled the heart of Pakisound out and it lit up the hut like it was a torch.

Zahara sat up and stared into the heart. Every person in the world was on a quest for answers to very complex questions, and Zahara was no different. She silently wanted the heart to speak to her. To tell her about its existence, and what part does she play in it. The main question that floated through her mind was if this was the mighty heart of Pakisound, then why didn't it protect them from being invaded by the Industriarmy?

While she was growing up Zahara had heard about the heart of Pakisound. However, like the rest of the city, beside the royal elders and priest, Zahara had never laid eyes on the gem.

Like most legends, it was told the most powerful article in the royal sanctuary was the Book of Pakisound. The book is the written testament to Pakisound's beautiful history, and spells. Zahara knew her deceased mother wrote a few of the spells in the book, but she was never awarded the privilege to view the book.

The same went for the heart of Pakisound once it was discovered. It was labeled a powerful treasure that could only be held and viewed in the royal sanctuary. Unlike the book, the heart was a hushed subject amongst the people, especially, after Queen Ophilia's death.

Now that Zahara possessed the heart, and she was feeling its powers flowing through her body, she could not understand why the heart had not preformed the way the people expected it too. What was its real purpose? Why did it feel so energetic to her touch? As if, it was meant for her to have.

A thought came to Zahara as she sat there staring at the heart. When Queen Taila took it out of its velvet resting place on the altar the heart seemed like a regular piece of jewelry. That is until it was placed around Zahara's neck. That's when the heart came alive.

That had to mean something, right? Zahara thought to herself. The questions continued to come until her eyes became heavy. She slipped the necklace back into her shawl, then laid down next to her brother. Maybe the answers will find their way to her, or maybe she will find herself traveling to the answers. Only time will tell, she told herself before she drifted off to sleep.

Chapter III

The hustle and bustle of the Golona village woke Zahara out of her sleep. She quickly sat up and looked over to her brother. The prince was still sound asleep. Zahara wiped her eyes and tried to decipher the Golona people's native tongue, as a group of voices conversed right outside her hut. She quickly gave up on what was being said and shook her brother.

"Steven...Steven, wake up".

The prince stirred, looked around the hut as if he had no idea where he was, sucked his teeth and whined, "Why? I'm still tired."

"So am I, but we have to move, we cannot stay in this village", Zahara said and then stood up. Frustrated by the short height of the hut, Zahara sucked her teeth and got down on her knees to talk to her brother.

"Why not?"

"Because father wanted us to go to the Kingdom of Soul, and that's where we're going. Now get up and let's go", Zahara said with her big sister authority.

Steven mumbled something under his breath, and said. "Alright" with all the attitude he could muster before he got up.

The Golona village looked like a totally different place than the deserted place from the night before. Children ran around the yard laughing and playing a game Zahara did not quite understand. A few small fires, bubbled pots of various morning dishes, and all were attended by women.

A congregation was gathering around what looked like the high priest's daily governing station. Stooler sat on a chair Zahara would consider a regular seat in the castle, but since the Golona people were no more than 5 feet tall, there was no need to have big chairs in the village. Zahara recognized the men that escorted them to the village standing amongst the congregation.

Prince Steven joined his sister and was amazed at the movement of the people who were no taller than him. Steven thought the men from the night before were young like him, or short for some other reason. When he laid eyes on the people of the village, Steven realized the Golona people natural size <u>was</u> his size. He burst out laughing causing his sister to give him the evil eye.

"Come on", Zahara said as they made their way over to the group.

Nalani was sitting on a chair next to Stooler. When she saw Zahara approaching them, Nalani quickly rose to her feet. "My lady. How did you sleep?" Zahara looked like she had been up all night.

"Okay, I guess."

"What about you Prince?" Nalani asked as she attended to him like he was a baby.

"I'm still tired."

Nalani picked the loose sticks of hay out of his hair, then brushed off his smock and trousers. The prince's brown cheeks turned red when he noticed everyone was watching him be attended to. "Nalani", Steven whined. She ignored him, and when she was satisfied, Nalani looked over Zahara with the same care. Zahara wasn't as embarrassed as her brother, because a true princess did not walk around with sticks of hay in her hair.

"What's going on?" Zahara asked Nalani once her check up was done.

"They sent some men to have a look at Pakisound", Nalani said in a melancholy tone.

"And what happened?" Zahara asked, looking from Nalani to Stooler.

Stooler hopped out of his seat and said, "We're sorry Princess, but your land was destroyed".

Zahara learned from her father many years ago to never show defeated emotions in front of people who were lower in rank and stature. At this very moment, Zahara was ready to abandon the rule, break down and cry in front of everyone.

"I'm sorry my lady", Nalani said, as she looked over to Steven. The young prince stood fully erect and showed his ability to maintain his composure in the face of adversity. "Are you okay young Prince?"

Steven wore one of the saddest faces Nalani ever saw him wear. Like his older sister, Steven was taught royal etiquette by his father. Biting his lower lip, Steven stood firm as he slowly nodded his head.

"Yeah, I guess we have to make it to the Kingdom of Soul, like my father said we must", Steven said. He then shared a look with his sister. Zahara knew her brother was hurting inside, but she would have to wait until the right time to comfort him.

Zahara felt really bad for Steven because he just lost both his parents in one motion, while she lost her mom many years ago, and was able to grow up with her father. Steven will be without both parents for the rest of his young life, which will be hard.

"That's right Nalani, can we leave as soon as possible?"Zahara asked.

The tragedy that just transformed their lives was much deeper than people could imagine, sending thoughts of Zahara's status through Nalani's mind. Zahara had now inherited the matriarch title Queen of Pakisound, and it was more important than ever to get the royal children safely to the Kingdom of Soul. Looking into Zahara's eyes, Nalani knew the young woman was trusting in her to get them to their destination, like she promised the King and Queen she would.

"Yes my lady, just let me gather up a few things and we can proceed on our journey", Nalani said. She went over to a small group of village women.

"I will send some men", Stooler said.

"Thank you", Zahara said, and watched the high priest give orders to a group of men.

Zahara walked over to her brother and silently congratulated him on a job well done. She put her arm on his shoulder and walked him away from the rest of the gatherers.

"Don't worry Steven, it will be okay. Nalani will get us to the Kingdom of Soul safely."

"I know", Steven said confidently. "My mom would not have trusted her with us, if she didn't believe in Nalani."

Zahara smiled. "That's right. Now let's try and find some food."

To protect the royal children and their guardian Stooler picked three men to go with them on their journey. Their guide to the Kingdom of Soul was an elder man named Tusi. Tusi was a fast thinker and very familiar with the path to the great city. Being a man of Golona tradition, Tusi never learned Muzena's universal language, sometimes making his communication with non-Golona people near impossible.

Gond the youngest Golona to go with them would be their translator was well versed in both languages. He was also a respected fighter and hunter. Unlike Tusi who was a dark brown complexion, Gond was the same caramel complexion as Steven. Being close in age with Zahara, Gond silently was nursing a crush on the princess. Gond would never have the heart to express his affection for the princess, especially because she was royalty and Gond was a village peasant.

The real brawn of the trio was a dark brown Golona named DanDan. His size and strength gave him many advantages when it came to close range combat.

Each Golona wore a pack on their backs, packed with an array of supplies made out of hide. Tusi and Gond also carried poisonous arrows and other small, but deadly weapons. While DanDan carried a sword, he picked up in a battle in the woods with a group of random scavengers.

Nalani got a nice helping hand from some of the women in the village, who packed some fresh fruits, bread, and a flask of water for the travelers. They also packed two canvases that could be set up in the rain and other cold nights in the forest.

The forest was better traveled during daylight times, making all travelers want to take advantage of those hours. Tusi lead the way, with Gond right behind him to relay messages Tusi might want sent to Nalani, who kept Steven close to her side, and Zahara right behind her. DanDan brought up the rear as their back guard, making the group a tight knit unit on the move.

The 40 foot trees provide them with a nice umbrella to shield them from the sun, but left them open to the large mixture of wild animals that roamed the forest living off of the vast fusion of Muzena's best vegetation. In the distance, calls from different species of birds echoed through the trees. To put the group's mind at ease Zahara hummed a sweet melody, giving them all their own sense of peace on the trail.

When it came to song Zahara still saw herself as a student of the rhythm, even though she was born in Pakisound, the place known throughout Muzena as one of High-Hop's traditional cities. Zahara had been attending feast and festival's in Pakisound from before she could remember, and all of that culture still offered a wide range of endless harmonic possibilities. Knowing she will be missing out on all of that stuff made Zahara sad, and when she was sad Zahara usually sang to herself to kill the ills.

For centuries, the indigenous ones and visitors of the city have always been heavily influenced by the soulful rhythms in Pakisound. The culture of High-Hop gave the people of Pakisound the power to stand together and the strength to become one. Joyous memories of good food, dance, love, and hope have always been staples of a Pakisound festival. A vibrant city known for embracing all, coming for a dose of festive affection with their brothers and sisters.

Now that Zahara was Queen of Pakisound, she would be looked at as a teacher of the sound and flow that will band people together under the scriptures of High-Hop. With a voice like Zahara's she never had any problem's serenading any listeners, but it was different now.

"MMMmmmuumm/ All for you/ We will defend for you/ HHuuummm/ We will befriend in the name of you/ Ooh Pakisound/

We will see you again, land of the strong child." Zahara's voice was soothing, nicely blended with some motivation from one of her favorite songs.

They walked for a quarter of the day before Tusi said something to Gond over his shoulder. Gond in turn translated Tusi's message to the rest of the group.

"Tusi say, a little city is up ahead."

"How far away"? Nalani asked ready to take a break.

"Not far", Gond replied over his shoulder.

"Will we be welcome?" Nalani asked.

Nalani had ventured out of Pakisound only a few times with the King and Queen, but never on a journey all the way to the Kingdom of Soul. Nalani was worried about the receptions they may receive at the different cities they will have to stop at.

"There should be no problems", Gond said in a nonchalant tone.

The group was 30 yards away from the approaching city when a voice suddenly called down to them from the trees. "Who goes there?"

Every one froze in their tracks.

"I ask again. Who goes there?" The question traveled through the thick vegetation.

Gond looked at Nalani and they silently debated with each other on who would do the talking.

"The Queen of Pakisound", Zahara yelled up to the trees, quickly ending their debate.

There was no response, as everyone in the group looked at Zahara with admiration. This was the first time Zahara publicly acknowledge her position as the Queen. The most alluring part about her statement was Zahara said it with a Queen's confidence. Something she would need in the future.

The trees began to ruffle as a few camouflaged warriors made their way down some vines. The group was lightly surrounded as the men dropped down brandishing bows and arrows.

"You say the Queen of Pakisound?" One of the warriors asked, sounding like the man with all the questions a moment ago. He was caramel in complexion, wearing green and black paint on his face and different parts of his body. He only wore one piece of clothing, a piece of cloth that covered his thighs and privates.

"Yes, and we don't mean to intrude on your land", Zahara said.

The man wore a puzzled look on his face, "But he's Golona", he said pointing to DanDan.

"Yes he is. They were sent with us on our journey by their village as our protection", Zahara said, giving the sentry as little information as possible. "So if it's possible we ask permission to pass through your land".

He looked over to two of his brothers, and said, "We must see Naji first".

"Who is that?" Gond asked Tusi answered him in their native tongue. Tusi may not speak the universal language for his own personal reasons, but he understood it for the most part.

"Oh."

"What did he say?" Nalani asked.

"He is their leader", Gond said.

"Yes, now come with us please", the warrior said, as his back-up continued to aim their weapons at their unexpected guest.

They walked out of the thick woods, and stepped into a clearing. Zahara, Nalani, and Steven marveled at the sight of the small village. All movement within the community ceased when the visitors were escorted in by the first line of defense. Small children scrambled to be within arm reach of their mothers, while the men put their weapons in the ready position and spread themselves out.

A young boy, who looked to be in his teenage years, ran ahead of the pack to a hut that was situated in the middle of the village.

Zahara tried not to stare at the women, who were lightly dressed in the same piece of cloth the men wore, on their bottom half, while they wore nothing on the top. The children on the other hand ran around the village freely with no cloth at all.

The huts were identical in texture to the huts in the Golona village, but that's where the similarities ended. The huts were made for taller people and looked stronger.

"What is the name of this place?" Steven asked, sticking close to Nalani.

"Hawlaw. Welcome", a coco skin colored man said, as he stepped out of the center hut. A woman slightly darker than the man came out and took up her place by his side. Two guards eased their way over to the man and woman, but tried not to look imposing.

The man walked up to Nalani and said with a bright smile," Queen, thank you for blessing our village with your presence".

Nalani pecan colored cheeks turned rosy red, "No, I'm sorry, but she is the Queen of Pakisound".

The leader looked embarrassed, "But she is so young".

"Hello my Queen. I am Kanette, and this is my husband Naji", the woman stepped up and took Zahara's hand.

Zahara blessed them with her winning smile. "I am Queen Zahara and this is my brother Prince Steven. That is our guardian Nalani".

"Oh, please forgive me for the mix up", Naji said, trying to show how humbled he was by the mistake.

"There is no problem Naji."

"My guard's say you wish to pass through our land", Naji said with everyone in the village watching the exchange.

"Yes, we are going to the Kingdom of Soul, and with your permission we want to pass through your land to continue on our journey." Nalani said.

"Yes, but why doesn't the Queen have a bigger?" he waved his hands as if to pull the word out of the air.

"He means a much bigger group, like most traveling royalty", Kanette said with enough grace to let the average observer know she has been finishing her husband's sentences for years.

"Pakisound was attacked by the Industriarmy", Nalani said. The mention of the brutal army changed the loose demeanor of the village into a place of worry and fear.

"Are they following you?" a big guard standing next to Kanette asked.

"No. Not that we know of", Nalani answered.

Naji looked over to his wife; whose facial expression was also one filled with worry and firmly stated, "They cannot stay", she silently agreed with him.

Many days Naji welcomes his wife's input on the daily activities in the village. When it comes to the safety and security of the people in their village, the decision rests solely on Naji's shoulders. Kanette never questions him on it.

Zahara felt the meeting was taking a sour turn. "Ah, forgive us for intruding Naji. If it is possible, we would like to rest for a little while before we continue on our journey", she asked.

The frown on Naji's face showed everyone his mind was already made. "I'm sorry Queen, but I will not put my people in harm's way. If I allow you to stay, the Industriarmy will penalize us for it. So please leave our village," he firmly stated. He then clapped his hands twice and the entire village began to transform. The men scrambled, taking up position inside and outside of the village. The women grabbed up their children and ducked into their huts.

"Okay. We will leave", Gond said, catching the eye of everyone in his group.

"Thank you for having us anyway", Zahara said in a defeated tone.

"Come my lady", Nalani said. Putting her arm around Steven's neck, they followed Tusi out of the village.

A few of the village men followed the travelers at least one hundred yards out of the village, before turning back and going home to prepare for any more unexpected guest.

"I don't understand. What was said to make them send us away?" Zahara asked with bewilderment in her voice.

"You will see that a lot", Gond said. "Many people are in fear of the Industriarmy."

"Yeah, but we said we weren't being followed", Steven said with the same disappointed tone as his sister.

"This is true young prince, but people will not want to take a chance, not knowing if we are lying", Nalani said.

Tusi said something over his shoulder.

"He says we can rest a little, and continue on until it gets dark", Gond translated.

Everyone began to entertain their own thoughts and forget about the scared village. Zahara was left wondering how they will be received in other villages they have to pass through. Will they be embraced, once they reviled they were coming from Pakisound, or will they be shut out like they were in the village of Hawlaw?

Industriland   .

The best jewels are stolen from other's.

Chapter IV

Industriland was a city full of evil energy that descended down from the depths of the gray clouds hovering above the 200 acre city. Industriland was controlled by its spiritual leader Tmus, who was taught at an early age how to encourage the followers of High-Hop, to denounce the Gods of Song, and embrace the words that speak only through him from the Gods of Force. Gods who will spare the lives of those that allow their city to be industrialized under a new way of life willingly.

In turn, they destroyed the cities that resisted the Industriarmy and Tmus' advices. The Gods of Force encouraged Tmus to speak to the people in a forceful voice filled with the ability to take their soul. Feeding the soul of a loyalist of High-Hop to the Gods of Force gave the dark skies over Industriland the strength to supply Tmus with the power he needed to march on to the grand prize…The Kingdom of Soul.

Industriland was built in the 1970's O.W. (Old World), by the late King Boliy to appease the Gods of Force. Their powerful existence flows from the forceful taken of people souls. Converting the loyal followers from High-Hop, focusing on the smaller cities that were only miles away from Industriland, easily convincing the people to abandon the old High-Hop traditions, and adopt the Melody of Domination that was handed down to him directly from the Gods of Force. Boliy never had true success when he ventured out to larger cities like Pakisound. His presence was definitely felt throughout the entire world of Muzena once word began to spread about the forceful changing of culture.

Tmus first teacher was his uncle King Boliy, who was the original speaker of industrialized rhythms and traditions of mental dominance. King Boliy prayed to the Gods of Force, to pledge his only living descendant eternal devotion to industrializing the entire Muzena. In return, he asked that the Gods grant his nephew cities and riches beyond his wildest dreams.

King Boliy knew the work he had to accomplish would take a life time and only the Gods of Force could bless Tmus with the power to build an army that flowed to their dark rhythms, savagely laying down a trail of blood, and taking prisoners once Boliy passed on to the afterlife.

As a young boy, Tmus learned from his great uncle Boliy how to plot and plan an attack on a city. Then Industrialize it. Tmus also learned from King Boliy short comings. This made the growing leader plan his attacks with precision, and give his major free reign to be as brutal as he pleased.

The taking of Pakisound just allowed Tmus to rewrite history. King Steven was a well respected leader in Muzena, who defended his city with decades of success. Even though Tmus just destroyed the vibrate city of Pakisound, he still wasn't satisfied with the victory. He was determined to make his presence felt in the entire world of Muzena.

Tmus sat on his throne absorbed in the silence of his torch lit chamber. A cold wind blew lightly over the stone floor and walls, blowing a mist of dirt particles around the chamber. Hand size creatures searched the corners for food, while trying to stay out of eye shot of the dark ruler who likes to shoot anything moving around in his chamber.

Tmus played back the taking of Pakisound and one thing continued to bother him. Where were the royal children? He knew King Steven had a teenage daughter and a young son, but they weren't identified. They must be with the Queen, Tmus thought to himself. A Queen who also wasn't found. He will have to tell Major Zor to turn up the pressure on the captured people in the dungeons. The royal family must be found at all cost. If they're not Tmus knows it may come back to haunt him in the future.

Tmus was a strong visualizer, who liked to sit in the confines of his chamber with his eyes closed, and call on the Gods of Force. They in turn provided him with the strength and power he needed to carry out the will of the Gods of Force. Their will was to capture the soul of the people, thus Industrializing them. Striping the people of their culture and traditions.

Then Tums fed the dead souls to the Gods of Force. Behind his closed eye lids, Tmus is able to venture off into the future. No one is allowed in Tmus' chamber when he is locked into his rituals and trances.

Anyone watching Tmus go through this exercise would witness his pale white face twitch and twist, as his eye lids thumped like a drum line. All of his visions ended with Tmus being victorious in his campaigns. Tmus did not get this far in his quest by being foolish. He knew the Gods of Song worked just as hard for the opposition as the as Gods of Force worked for him and his army of destructive soldier's. The culture of High-Hop had deep roots in Muzena. Causing many to die for what they believed in.

A light tap rapped on the thick wooden door snapping Tmus out of his trance. Tmus' red eyes popped open and he stared across the large room at the door.

"Enter." Tmus said with little effort.

The large door was pushed open by one of his guards and Celius floated into the chamber. The door was closed behind him and the two spiritual evils were left alone.

"Tmus, I must congratulate you on a very important victory." The Sorcerer said, as he floated eight inches off the ground up to the throne.

"Yes...But more must be done", Tmus stated dryly.

The glassy white Celius the Sorcerer is Tmus' spiritual adviser. Celius is a powerful instrument in Tmus' connection to the dark side, and is the only being in the world of the living besides Tmus who can be a conduit to the Gods of Force. Celius' long white beard matched his waist length white hair, and was the only color he will put up against his long black robe.

With his powers, Celius floated through Industriland instead of walking the walkways. Very few people in the city had contact with Celius, and only Tmus, Major Zor, and a few high ranking officers were able to hold a conversation with the Sorcerer.

Tmus resided in the highest tower in Industriland, where as Celius lived in the lower depths of the castle. No one- but Tmus- is allowed in Celius' part of the castle. Legend had it that those who disobeyed the order to never cross the Sorcerer's threshold have either return back up the dark stairwell cursed, or they never returned at all.

"Ahh...Yes, more must be done", Celius said looking up at Tmus, who sat comfortably on his three step throne, with his black hood low to his eyes.

"I believe we are strong enough now to travel to the Kingdom of Soul." Tmus threw out there to see what response he would get from his spiritual adviser.

Celius put his head down and floated back and forth as if he was pacing. "This may be so...But you have to keep in mind the Kingdom of Soul is three times the size of Pakisound. Their army is more developed and trained for a brutal war", Celius said." The Kingdom of Soul is a totality different beast".

Tmus smiled, "I know, that is why I am preparing a campaign that will be a traveling Industry".

"What do you mean?" Celius stopped his pacing.

"We pack up the entire Industriland, and as we travel to the Kingdom of Soul we overcome every city in our path", Tmus said, toying with the idea as he went along.

"Yesss... But isn't that what you've been doing?" Celius asked not seeing the goal.

"Yes...But we have always returned to Industriland with our prize. This time I say we continue on until we reach the Kingdom of Soul. Occupy it as the new Industricenter". Tmus said with a little light in his eyes that told Celius the great leader was on to something.

Tmus was the only one to accomplish the feat of taking over the Pakisound, and becoming the sole possessor of the Soul of the people made his ice cold vein's boil with excitement.

Celius thought about it. This could be a defining moment in Industriland history. World supremacy was what they lived for, but the Sorcerer needed a little time to give his blessings on such a big move, and have to answer to the Gods of Force if the army was to fail.

Tmus was the supreme leader and did not need Celius' approval to place one of his plans in motion, but he did value Celius' words and judgment. Giving Celius voting power in meetings only the two of them attended.

"I say you allow Zor some weeks to ready the army. Then we set out for what should be Industrilands greatest tour-de-force", Celius said.

Tmus took in this wisdom, slowly nodding his bald head, as he continued to stare at the torch that burn next to the chambers door.

"You have something on your mind", Celius said, feeling a vibe coming from Tmus.

"The royal family from Pakisound is missing", Tmus said without taking his eyes off of the burning flame.

Celius did not like this announcement. "How is the royal family missing? I was informed King Steven is dead".

"He is...But his wife and children are not".

"What about the powerful heart Pakisound possessed?" Celius asked, figuring they were able to at least cease the energizing gem.

"It burned in the fire", Tmus said.

"Are you sure?"

"Yes I'm sure!" Tmus snapped. The dark leader was not one to be questioned about anything that would end up making him look incompetent in the eyes of the Gods of Force.

"I sent a search party out to find any signs of the family making it out of the city. If anyone is found, they are to be brought to me...Dead or alive".

"No word yet?" Celius asked.

"No."

"I don't have to tell you how important it is to find those children", Celius said, replaying a moment in time when Tmus' father made the mistake of allowing the child of a town leader to live and avenge his father's death. He killed Tmus' father in one of the most one on one battles in Industriland history. Which happen before Tmus was old enough to walk and talk.

"I'll be in my chambers", Celius concluded in his low drawl. Then he floated off to the door.

Tmus watched the Sorcerer leave allowing his final words to linger in the air. 'I don't have to tell you how important it is to find those children'.

"No you don't", Tmus said to himself, then closed his eyes and went into a deep state of meditation . The royal family will be found Tmus assured himself, as a picture behind his eye lids began to take shape. The death and destruction Tmus and his army thrived off of began to speak to him. His face twitched and his head spasm to the side as the future played out just how the Gods of Force told him it would.

With Industriland victorious.

Whenever the guards wanted some action they would simply crack open one of the holding cells, reach in and extract someone to entertain them. It did not matter the age of the woman. All they cared about was violating her until she pledged her undying loyalty to her captors.

Taila shared a cell with twenty other women. The women lived in consent fear of who would be the next victim of the late night violations, all the while worrying about their children, who were being held in another wing of the dungeon. Cries for help could heard faintly traveling through the dark halls. Whenever a cry seeped through the thick walls, the women in the holding cells would fall into an emotional tailspin that was full of shouts, curses, and cries of their own. But it all was for nothing, because the bored and drunk guards got a rush off of the thick cloud of fear they breathed into the cells of the dungeon.

The women section of the dungeon had six large holding cells, with scattered hay on the ground for the prisoners to lie on. In the back corner of each cell was a hole in the ground for them to relieve themselves in. Making the entire dungeon smelled worst than the hog barn.

Once a day bread, and cornmeal is brought in for the day meal, and water was brought in twice a day. The prisoners are to distribute the food and water as they see fit in their cells.

Even though the women were from different parts of Muzena, they all shared the same horror story of how the Industriarmy came into their city and destroyed their lives. The army showed no mercy on those who would not convert willingly.

The current conditions were way below anything Taila had ever been under but that did not stop her from holding her head high. If not for her own sanity, Taila did it for the women from Pakisound that kept her identity secret. Who silently looked to their Queen for the strength to continue on, and Taila did not disappoint them.

Taila shared encouraging words of one day meeting freedom again, and being able to rebuild Pakisound when this was all over. This gave the women hope. Whenever one of the women needed a shoulder to cry on, Taila was there to comfort her.

Her hardest task came up every time the guards raped one of them than brought the battered woman back down to the dungeon— which was rare. Taila could sense some of the women put themselves on the line to protect their Queen, and they silently tried to keep that invisible barrier firm around Taila. Because once they let them animals violate their Queen, then all hope for them was lost. Whenever the gate popped open the women would put up a fight, keeping Taila behind them until one of the others was dragged out of the cell kicking and screaming.

Taila prayed to the Gods of Song many nights to keep the guards away from her cell. Some night's her prayers would be answered, but others would bring sadness into her heart so heavy that Taila would go days without eating, electing to give her portion away.

"Taila, how long do you think we will be down here?" Nahir asked snapping Taila out of her day dream. It had been settled back in the shelter in Pakisiound that no one will refer to Taila as 'Queen', to keep her safe from Tmus.

"I don't know Nahir...But I have been thinking of a way to get us out of here", Taila said in a near whisper.

"Really?" Nahir asked to loudly, prompting Taila to shoot her a stern look. "I'm sorry", Nahir looked around to see who was watching them.

Once she felt their privacy wasn't compromised Nahir leaned in closer to Taila and said," You know I'm with you on anything you want to do...But whatever you plan, please make sure it is a triumphant one", Nahir pleaded through her eyes.

Taila took the woman's hand and said, "Nahir, you have my word, the first chance we get, I will give all of my life to help us get free".

A tear slid down Nahir's cheek as she finally felt that rare drip of hope. "Thank you", Nahir mouthed in a sincere whisper.

Taila nodded, then hugged the coffee complexion mother who lost a lot of weight in the dungeon, but still looked a little healthier than majority of the women down there with her.

Taila felt the spirit move through her and she let it flow out of her threw her voice, "Mmmmuumm"

The dungeon began to quiet down, as the magical sound rolled through the air like a refreshing cool breeze.

"I share your strength //...To our last breath...//Even if we are all we have left// I'll keep Pakisound with the heart in my chest// Ooh—uh-- Ooh-- uhh// Stay strong with me sister...//And we'll get through this// We must lean on each other ...// In order to be victorious!!!...//MMmmuummm"

Some of the women in the dreary dungeon sat back with their eyes closed trying to flash back to more pleasant time in their lives. While others simply stared off and let the Taila's beautiful voice fill a void within them.

Taila continued to hold Nahir's hand as her feelings of hope generated to the other women, and she silently made a promise to all of them to lead them back to freedom one day.

Chapter V

A gang of horses trotted down the pathway, as the sun began to descend behind the thick row of huge mountains. The lead horse carried the commander of the ten man team that was sent out to find the royal family.

Usually Commander Vance would have turned his search part around and headed back to Industriland. Tracking down runaways was not his idea of a worthy kill, because a runaway is a coward. He stayed on the trail after passing through the Golona village and getting an eerie feeling, the short people were hiding something. They weren't hiding it in their village, but they were hiding something.

The high priest of the village denied having any unexpected visitors come through Golona, but the Commander sensed something wasn't right. He thanked the high priest for his cooperation and the group rode out of the center of the village. Once they reached the furthest sentry stationed on the outside perimeter, Vance ordered one of his men to fall off of his horse and they all gathered around him as if concerned. When the Golona sentry got curious enough to approach the group, they seized him.

The brutal hunters tortured the Golona sentry until he pointed them in the right direction. Once Vance was satisfied, it was the royal family that traveled through the village, the Commander had the battered man put out of his misery.

When the sun began to set, Commander Vance ordered his men to pull over and set up camp. That is until one of his men saw smoke rising over the tall trees, "Commander, I see smoke", the man said pointing in the northwest direction.

One of Vance's men rode up ahead to scope out the area. The horse cried out in pain as it stepped into a trap and broke its leg. The soldier was violently thrown from the horse, landing in a thorny bush.

Commander Vance and the rest of his group immediately stopped in their tracks, hopped off of their horses, and went into attack formation. "Down! Down! Spread Out!" Vance ordered.

"OOOWW!" One of his troops cried out in pain as an arrow glided through the air and lodged itself in his chest.

"Who goes there?" Vance barked, trying to get a better idea of who they were dealing with. "Show yourself!"

The night was quiet as each side held their position. Darkness was quickly approaching giving the protectors of the pathway the upper hand. Vance knew this, but he didn't want his men to make any sudden moves and give their attackers a clean shot.

"We are just passing through", the Commander said into the trees.

"You can't come through here! Turn around and leave!" A voice answered from above.

Commander Vance weighed his options. "We come in peace! And we can't turn back!"

"Where do you come from?"

"We come from Flatlands", Vance said. Everyone in Muzena knew Flatlands was neutral territory.

It was quiet for a moment as the injured horse whimpered in the dark. Some of the trees began to ruffle, causing Vance and his men to brace themselves for a close encounter.

Seven warriors slid down the dangling vines and approached the intruders with caution. Vance could see the approaching bodies in the moons silhouette, itching to attack them. The Commander let the discipline in him, tell him to be patient, they will show themselves. The Commander slowly rose from his crouched position. "Who approaches?"

"The guards of Hawlaw", the man said, standing five feet away. "What's brings you this way?"

Two soldiers eased up on Vance's side, as he said", our land was attacked and we're traveling to find a new settling".

The Hawlaw warrior looked over to his left and let his eyes talk to his brother in arms, before turning back to Vance saying, "Attacked by whom?"

"The Industriarmy", Vance said.

The vocal man looked at his tribesmen again and this time he got a silent nod from one of them. "You cannot go through our village. You have to go around", he told the commander.

Vance returned a nod in agreement. The Hawlaw men had a lot of things in their favor and Vance had no problems living to fight another day. If this would have been daylight, the commander would have tried his luck against the Hawlaw men.

"Okay, we'll go around", Vance conceded, then slowly climbed on top of the horse. His troops followed suit as the soldier who lost his horse hopped onto his fallen comrade's horse. "Have others from Flatlands come through here?" Vance asked.

"No .Only people from Pakisound. They also were attacked by the Industriarmy".

Commander Vance smiled to himself. "Okay, if anyone else from my homeland comes this way, can you assure them of our safety. Let them know we are traveling northeast."

"Yes, go in peace", the Hawlaw man said, as he and his tribesmen faded back into the shadows.

Commander Vance rode into the darkness mumbling a deadly promise under his breath. No one threatens members of the Industriarmy. When Vance returns to this part of the forest he will make sure the Hawlaw people pay for their mistakes.

As night began to fall, Tusi suggested they stop and set up camp. Everyone was designated a task, as the days fatigue began to set in. Zahara and Steven put up one canvas, while Nalani got a hand from Gond and they put up the other canvas.

When everyone was done, they all sat around the fire and warmed up some dried out jerky and bread. A cool breeze floated through the forest making their surrounding feel like a place of peace. Small talk about their day and the road ahead flowed freely over the fire and food.

"Why do you think they reacted the way they did? We told them what happened to us..." Zahara said out loud.

"Because they're afraid", Nalani said.

"She's right", Gond agreed. "The army has many villages afraid."

"People no wanna get involved," DanDan said.

"Yeah, but it's not like the Industriarmy is following us. Besides I would never put their people in danger". Zahara said. She felt hurt that Naji and Kanette seemed willing to welcome them with open arms, and then suddenly turned on them.

"We know you wouldn't my lady". Nalani said. "But not everyone has a good heart like you."

When Nalani said that, the necklace around Zahara's neck began to vibrate on her chest. Zahara dug into her smock and lit up the night with the heart of Pakisound. Everyone was mesmerized by the beautiful light. Especially the Golona men, who did not know Zahara was in possession of such a priceless jewel.

"What is that?" Gond asked.

"The heart of Pakisound", Zahara proudly said.

"Do you feel any powers from it?" Steven asked his sister.

"Sometimes", Zahara said looking into the glowing glass heart. It seemed like the colors within the heart would change according to Zahara's words or mood. "Nalani, do you think I will ever learn how the heart works?"

"Of course you will my lady." Nalani confidently said. "Once we get to the Kingdom of Soul I'm sure you will receive some form of wisdom and guidance from the Queen of High-Hop Soul.

"Have you ever been to the Kingdom of Soul Nalani?" Steven asked.

"Yes I have young prince". She said with a warming smile. I was part of a caravan that traveled with your mother and father a very long time ago."

"What is it like there?" Zahara asked with a glimmer in her eyes. Everyone shifted their focus from the heart to Nalani's words.

"I used to think Pakisound was the most beautiful city I've ever breathed in, but when we arrived in the Kingdom." Nalani grinned, savoring the enchanting memory. "I was in love like never before."

The three Golona men sat back and enjoyed the tale of the largest city in Muzena, as Steven and Zahara continued to tag team Nalani with more questions.

"Are there festivals like in Pakisound?" Steven asked.

"There you go, always thinking about food", Zahara said rolling her eyes.

Nalani laughed, "No young prince. Their festivals are much bigger than the ones in Pakisound."

"Really?" Steven excitedly asked.

"Yes. There is dancing in the streets and courts of food to choose from." Nalani said.

"What about the music and flow?" Zahara asked knowing how important the rhythms were at a Pakisound feast.

"Oh... the Queen MaryJane sang a song that was so soulful, I saw people in the room with tears in their eyes."

"For real?" Zahara asked in awe.

"Yes, the only person in Pakisound I ever witnessed with that much vocal power was your mother". Nalani said to Zahara. "But that's a story for another day. Now let's get you two ready to get some rest."

Steven sucked his teeth, "Ah, come on Nalani. I want to hear more about the Kingdom of Soul. Like what kind of army do they have? Does the King lead them into battle like my father does? And"…

"That's enough Steven". Zahara said, cutting her energetic brother off. "You heard Nalani. We'll hear more about the Kingdom soon enough. For now we have to get some rest."

"Yes, we have a long day". DanDan added, as everyone stood up and went to their respective places for the night.

The next morning the small group started on their trek to the Kingdom of Soul. After walking for half of the day, Tusi said something to Gond, and he in turn relayed the message to everyone else.

"Tusi say, up ahead should be the falls."

"The Krava Falls." Nalani said, as the memory of the long stretch of river cascading down the tall mountains began to flash before her.

"You've been there before?" Steven asked.

"Yes everyone has to go through Krava Falls."

"Does anyone live there?" Zahara asked.

"I don't think we ran into anyone, but you never know". Nalani said as the faint sound of running water could be heard.

They stepped out of the woods and Tusi pointed to the water falls, which were reflecting off of the hot sun. "Can we drink that water?" Steven asked feeling the dryness in his mouth.

"Yes young Prince. There are also some good fish around these parts". Nalani said as they walked over to the edge of the large river.

"We take a break." DanDan said, causing everyone to use the water to either quench their thirst or wash their face.

"Wow Zahara. Look!" Steven said pointing into the clear blue water. Zahara looked down into the water and saw scores of colorful fish swimming in droves down the river.

"They are beautiful". Zahara said with a huge smile.

"We fish". Gond said to Nalani, who was washing her face. DanDan and Tusi pulled out their fishing equipment and got right to work. DanDan stepped into the shallow water and patiently waited with his spear aimed and ready.

Steven never witnessed how fishing was done and he didn't want to miss any of the action. He eased up on Tusi's side and watched, as DanDan stood stark still. Then with speed and force of a poisonous snake, DanDan jabbed his spear down into the flowing water. When he pulled the spear out of the water, an eight pound fish was wiggling back and forth trying to free himself off of the sharp point.

"Wow! Did you see that?" Steven exclaimed with excitement.

Tusi smiled at the young prince, nodded his head, and collected the fish from DanDan. Then DanDan went back into the water and performed the same process all over again.

"Do you think we should set up camp here?" Nalani asked Gond.

"Yes, we eat, then travel until sun set". Gond said, before he wandered off to go gather some wood to build a small fire.

DanDan caught three fish before curiosity over came the young prince and he asked if could he go next. The three Golona men agreed in letting Steven get his feet wet in his first taste of hunting, but the protective Nalani wasn't enthusiastic about the Prince stepping out into the flowing river.

"If he's going out there, then you're going to hold his shirt". Nalani stated, and stared at DanDan with an eye that told him nothing better go wrong.

"Yes I hold". DanDan said, as he led Steven out into the waist deep water.

"You hold like this". DanDan told Steven as fixed his grip on the spear. Then he guided Steven into a stabbing position. "Now you wait".

Steven nodded, and stared down into the flowing water like he watched his instructor do. A few small fish fiddled around their legs, but nothing was worth the shot.

Zahara watched from afar, while Nalani stood right next to Tusi. Her mind was already made up. If the action called for it, Nalani was mentally prepared to dive right into the river, even though she wasn't a good swimmer.

Steven tried to focus once he saw some bigger fish swim by. Then he took his shot.

All of the fish spread out into different directions. When he yanked the spear out of the water, the tip was empty. Steven sucked his teeth, and DanDan encouraged him to go again.

The Prince took a deep breath and waited. Slowly the fish began to feel comfortable again. First the small fish, then the much bigger ones.

Steven took another and stabbed his spear into the water again. When Steven yanked his spear back this time, he had a prize on the end. "I did it! I got one!" He boasted.

"Come". DanDan said then lead him back to shore.

"You see it Nalani?" Steven beamed.

"Yup and we're going to eat it too", she joked, as Tusi took the spear from him and the freshly caught fish with the rest of them. The fish wasn't as big as the ones DanDan caught, but they all we're still pleased with the young Prince first kill.

Tusi showed Steven how to skin the fish without destroying it. Gond built a small fire, while Zahara and DanDan veered off into the woods to look for some fruits and berries that grew wildly in the forest.

"DanDan, do you think the next village we come to will turn us away like the last one did?" Zahara asked.

DanDan was inspecting a bush that was growing blackberries, "I don't know. Maybe they let us rest. Maybe they send help with us. I hope no turn away."

Zahara was a little frustrated from not knowing the unknown. She would rather be prepared for what they may be faced with on their journey, than walking into unwelcoming cities.

"DanDan, do you have a wife?" Zahara asked, changing the subject to a much easier one.

He picked the berries with care, making sure, he didn't pick any sour ones, but her question made him stop in mid-reach, "A wife?"

Zahara smiled, "Yes a wife. You know. Someone that loves you."

"Yes me have a wife", he said returning the smile. DanDan never knew he would be having a conversation like this with someone with Zahara's stature.

"Yeah? Do you have children yet?" She asked giddy about how the two unions of love, and family were made.

"One boy. He name Fama. It mean young warrior", he said proudly.

"That's great". Zahara thought for a moment. "I guess now that I am Queen, I'm expected to build a new family."

"You find a King in Soul?" he asked, as they continued with the task of finding good berries. Then he moved on to pick some root.

"I don't know DanDan. I never thought of being the Queen before. I always thought my father would be around". Zahara said staring off into the thick vegetation.

"Me sorry about you father", he said as he gathered up their pickings.

"Thank you DanDan", she said taking one of the bags of fruit from him. The sadness of losing her father hit her, and she knew it would always be there.

"We have enough". DanDan said, and led them back to camp.

Nalani had the fish grilling over the fire, and the aroma sent hunger pains rambling through every ones stomach. Tusi was showing Steven how to use his sword, while Gond stood off to the side like he was a coach.

"No, he's saying to fix the feet". Gond translated for his partner.

"Like this?" Steven asked as he positioned his feet.

Tusi showed him how to follow through with his swing and be one with his sword. Steven knew with some good coaching on how to defend himself and engaged in strong strategic combat he could be as good a swordsman as his father, the King was. These thoughts made him want to get the teachings down even more.

"Nalani that smells good". Zahara beamed as they brought their pickings over to her.

"I wish we had some herbs my lady". Nalani said with a slight frown.

"We have root". DanDan said, handing her the fresh part of the plant which smelled like cinnamon.

Nalani washed off the root and instructed Zahara to wash off the berries, while DanDan went over to observe the Prince's training.

Zahara was amazed at how Nalani put together their mid-day meal with virtually no tools, but what the forest had to offer them. "Nalani, how did you learn to make do with so little?"

"My mother. Who learned from her mother. That's how it's supposed to be. Traditions are handed down so the next generation can hold on to the ways of their bloodline", Nalani said. She put a piece of fish on a flat plate the Golona's carried in their packs.

Zahara thought about this. "You know I don't think I learned any traditions from my mom".

"I know. That's because you were so young when she passed." Nalani paused to look at Zahara, "I'm sorry you never had any time with her. Your mother knew so many things".

"Were you and her close?"

"Not as close as me and Queen Taila, but I believe that's because your mom was a high priestess. That made her a very private person".

"So she wouldn't talk to everyone like Taila would?" Zahara asked. She felt that with the little information she could gather about her mother, she could put it with the things she already learned. Then maybe she could come up with a good picture of how her mother conducted herself in public.

"Well, yes and no", Nalani thought back for a second. "Like when there was a festival, or when we received a royal visit your mother was one of the best hostesses I've ever seen, but when she would retreat into the royal sanctuary. Sometimes it would be for days".

"Do you know how she died?" Zahara asked, figuring she can finally get one of the elders comfortable enough to want to tell her the tale they always shielded her from.

Nalani weighed the question, as she continued to work her magic on the food. "To tell you the truth my lady, we weren't really sure... We know it had something to do with the heart."

"Why would you think that?"

"Because, the same way the heart lights up to your touch, is the same way it would come alive for your mother", Nalani said, handing Zahara the makeshift plate with fish, cooked root, and a side of berries. "But no one else could get a response from it. Not even St.Eagle, and he's one of the most powerful beings in Muzena. After her death, people began to talk and blame was focused on the heart."

Zahara thought about this as she ate her food. She felt blessed and cursed at the same time. On one hand, it was an honor to possess her powers. Even though she didn't exactly know how to use them yet. However, on the other hand isn't that the same power that took her mother away from her? Would this same power suddenly turn on me? Will she figure out how the heart actually works? Or will it remain a glass heart that shines under her touch?

So many questions ran through Zahara's mind, as Nalani gave out the food as it finished cooking. When Nalani finished she fixed her plate and sat down next to Zahara.

"Nalani, do you think I will get the answers I'm looking for?"

"The answers to what. The heart?" Nalani asked in between bites.

"Yes. Do you think there is a spirit in the Kingdom of Soul that will know about the heart and tell me how am I supposed to use it to help our people?" Zahara asked.

"Maybe. We will see when we meet with the Queen. She may be able to help us", Nalani concluded. They finished eating so they could get back to their journey and Zahara's quest for her answers.

✳✳✳✳✳

"It's still fresh", one of the commander's men informed him as he investigated the burned bush the traveling group used to build a fire.

"Check the rest of the area". Vance ordered. Then he and his troops fanned out to see if there were any traces of them being on the right trail. The area where the two canvases were put up gave the Commander some insight on the place being recently occupied.

"Commander, we found some waste over there behind that bush", one of his men said pointing to the far west end of the wooded area.

"Is it human?"

"Yes sir".

The Commander stood still and looked around the area as if he was trying to feel the presence that just left that morning. He took a deep breath to smell area, and then closed his eyes.

His troops gave the Commander his space whenever he preformed this ritual. Commander Vance was a good tracker because he used the interrupted sections of the forest to tell him a story. The old fire, the interrupted section of the forest bed, and the human waste behind the bushes, were all a testament, and Vance never ignored the testaments.

"They were here. We are on the right trail". Vance said to no one in particular. "Let's go", the Commander ordered before hopping on to his horse and leading the way out of the old campsite.

Commander Vance and his troops covered a lot of ground by being on horseback. He knew it was only a matter of time before they caught up with the royal family, because they were traveling on foot. Vance and his men got to Krava Falls mid-day and he was not surprised to run into the ruins of another recently abandon campsite.

Anyone traveling on a long journey will stop on the side of Krava Falls to rest. The trackers investigated the ruins and found the remains of fish and fruit. "We're getting closer", Traver said as he walked up on the side of the Commander. Traver was the only soldier out of his unit Vance felt he could depend on to complete a task without Vance breathing down his neck.

"Yes, let the horses drink from the Krava and we will rest." The Commander said observing the area. "Tell them to gather some food and get the nets ready for some fishing".

"Yes sir". Traver said, before going over to the rest of the troops to relay the Commander's message. The men quickly spread out and took on different task to ensure they would have food to eat.

Vance wandered off alone and took in his surroundings. "Yes. You definitely were here." He mumbled to himself. "You can run, but you can't for too much longer", he said with the taste of death in his mouth. It was nothing like chasing down some worthy prey.

Chapter VI

To appease the noble citizens of Industriland, Tmus ordered a feast be enjoyed by all of his loyal followers. Before they pack up the large city and go out on Tmus aggressive takeover of Muzena.

The Industrial castle main hall was large enough to fit up to one thousand people in it. Equipped with rows of tables, covered in crisp white cloth tables. With each set up to seat ten grown people and two children. A band played only industrialized rhythms from the melodies of domination, and plenty of room in the aisles so the help could get around, making the hall grand in its look and feel on this special day. Now that Tmus followers helped him secure a great victory, they were rewarded for their assistance with plenty of food and drink.

Only Industriland's governmental elite, high ranking military officers and members of the socialist society's country folk of high standards were invited to the feast. Otherwise, the working class, soldiers, and Industrilands slaves were allowed to celebrate in the main court yard and the streets.

Inside and outside of the hall the atmosphere was festive and full of ease. A tone that was not allowed in Industriland on a daily basis. Industriland was all about work – morning, noon, and night – to satisfy their ruler's thirst to collect the souls of the followers of High-Hop. Their blood, sweat, and tears are what allowed the devoted followers of Tmus, and his industrializing the world doctrine to live comfortably, and it showed at today's celebration.

Off to the side of the hall ten tables were packed to capacity with food from all sectors of the food chain. The elite dinned on dodo bird, duck, ostrich, steamed six foot long snakes, roasted pig, freshly picked vegetables, and hot breads baked with goat cheese. The drinks were plentiful and flowed with ease. The help were instructed to keep the wine pitchers on the tables full at all times, and the guest were free to drink as much as they liked.

A four foot platform, at the front of the hall, is where the exclusive members of Industriland sat on top of the platform sat one straight line of tables, laced with a silk red table cloth. Food, flowers, candles, and drinks where spread out nicely for the elite to dine freely.

Tmus blessed the table with his presence at the center of it. Even though he would rather be in his cool chamber, Tmus blocked the relaxing thought out of his mind and let his dark eyes roam around the hall.

Major Zor sat on his leaders' right hand side, with one of Industrilands socialites that he would forget about after tonight's events. She only spoke to Zor when spoken to. Even though Trina was popular amongst the underlinings of the city, none of that mattered when you are in the presence of Tmus, Major Zor, and Governor Solomon, who sat on Tmus' left side with his wife Debbra for his date.

Governor Solomon was a short round man who wore thick glasses, and was the lead architect in writing the language for the government rules of conduct for the scared people of Industriland. His salt and pepper hair was balding in the center of his pale white head. Solomon's daily focus revolved around how many ways he could make Tmus happy, and how divine his wardrobe must be. Debbra, the Governor's wife, like her husband, paid full attention to her wardrobe. Pleasing Tmus and trying to stay alive under the daily pressures of being in the government was a full time job.

Debbra was five inches taller than her five foot tall husband, and at the tender age of fifty five, she continued to maintain her slim build well. Debbra was a flaunter who always showed off the heavy jewelry her husband furnished her with. Debbra was one of the best dressed- woman in the city always wearing a loosely flowing gown, which were produced with the silkiest fabrics so not to irritate her milky white skin.

Debbra was only attracted to Solomon's powerful position, which showed every time she was allowed in Tmus' presence. Debbra usually used these rare moments to smoothly throw herself at their ruler, but not to aggressively where it put a blemish on her gold record of being a woman of an exquisite manner.

"Honey, you have not touched your turtle soup", Solomon said. His wife's attention had been wandering past him all night, and he could sense what she was up to. "Debbra. Did you hear me?"

"Huh? What's that dear?" Debbra asked, snapping out of her trance.

"I said you haven't touched your soup. Is it not up to your standards? Would you like something else? Maybe something more. Unique?" Solomon asked.

"I ah, no I'm fine". Debbra stumbled over her words. "I'm just enjoying the dance", she lied. Debbra turned her focus to the dance floor where an array of attendees were engaged in an Industriland favorite dance called the swing.

Tmus was not much of a socializer but he knew his presence was needed at this event. He sat back in his maple wood throne, which was draped in red and black fabric made of chenille. Tmus black hood came down low on his eyes so people could not tell if he was resting or enjoying the festivities. Either way Tmus did not care, as long as no one in the hall disturbed the serenading ballad being sung by the most beautiful voice in Industriland, Nipoly.

Tmus was well aware of Debbra's constant staring. It never bothered him, because he was used to people staring at him. Being the brutal ruler of such a large city, Tmus had the option to pick threw the litter of wives who always through themselves at him. However, none of that mattered to Tmus when Nipoly sung in his presence.

"Would you like for me to have her sent up to your chamber?" Major Zor asked, following the direction of his leaders line of vision.

Tmus stared at Nipoly's milky brown skin glistening under the bright lights. She stood in the middle of the hall's dance floor and let her voice carry out into the court yard. Her voice was hitting nerves inside of Tmus' body. He had to have her to himself later.

"Yes", Tmus said without taking his eyes off of the song bird.

"I will take care of it your Excellency". Major Zor said, causing Solomon to silently curse himself for not thinking of the idea first.

The government system Tmus put in place gave the people of Industriland a sense of being part of a free society. Government officials were paraded around the city as the ones who make the laws and calls the army off to war. What the people didn't know was Tmus made every decision concerning the development of Industriland. All laws, rituals, traditions, and calls for war were made by Tmus and the Gods of Force. Which were then were relayed to Major Zor and Solomon. They in turn fed the orders of the day to the other government officials. All are to do what they are told, or suffer dire consequences.

The government is chaired by Solomon and the army is lead by Major Zor. Even though the two parts of the Industriland system had two powerful structures functioning under Tmus' guidance, there still was a rivalry silently battled between Major Zor and Solomon. With the latter always jockeying for Tmus' recognition.

Major Zor smirked when he looked past Tmus and noticed the disapproving frown on Solomon's face. Solomon might be the most powerful mortal man in Industriland, but what he failed to realize is

Tmus did not care about the Government and its official's. The Government was Tmus' puppet and would never be more than that.

The army was Tmus' muscle. The Industriarmy were the ones who went to battle for him whenever he called on them to do so. This made him hold them in a higher regard than the other mortals in his city.

Solomon regrouped, then tried to show Zor he could do better than the little display of kissing up he did, "Your Excellency, all of your plans are in place, just as you asked them to be and I have taken the liberty of hand picking the best stone and granite worker's myself for the journey."

Tmus was lost in Nipoly's words. Whatever Solomon was talking about was unimportant to Tmus.

"I swing...for thee// what you ask for me// If I care to dream// What you say for me// Its all there to see// Let's go take the seeds// A page that's all a scene...

Tmus sat there questioning himself about what it was Nipoly was trying to say right now. Is she talking to me directly or is she just singing a song? He asked himself, this while his eyes stayed locked onto her body movements. Sexy.

"Come and take from me// You can have the cream// The signs// Can you read// Its not all a dream...

Her voice had Tmus hypnotized. Nipoly was the only person in Muzena who ever held his attention in such a fashion, and he liked it. No one should have so much power over the ruler of the strongest land in the world.

As Nipoly sang, the crowd of people on the dance floor moved in unison with the rhythm of the beat and her mesmerizing voice. Even in a dark city like Industriland, the coordination of the people was a work of art.

"And I also handpicked the best musicians", Tmus heard Solomon say.

"Yesss. The musicians are supposed to be a compliment for the Industry for travel", Tmus said. Anything dealing with music caught his ear whenever Nipoly performed.

Feeling the response from his master, Solomon got a new surge of energy, "And we will take the best singers".

"What do you mean we?" Tmus asked, shooting the look of death at Solomon as he snapped out of his trance.

"I'm. I. I'm sorry Your Excellency. I thought you would want me to go on-"

"No one from the high government is to leave Industriland. Is that understood?" Tmus said in a tone that was far from a question.

"Ye...Yes your Excellency", Solomon said, and kept his mouth closed until Tmus was ready for him to talk again. Upsetting Tmus was an easy thing to do. Solomon was a witness to what was done to those who upset the supreme leader of Industriland, and it wasn't a pretty sight.

"You will remain the administrative body until I return", Tmus said, turning his attention back to the night's entertainment.

"The main course your Excellency", a waiter said as he leaned in between Tmus and Solomon.

Solomon knew Tmus would ignore the waiter, so he used this opportunity to restore a piece of dignity for himself to whomever was in ear shot of him receiving the tongue lashing from Tmus. "Yes... Put them down... And make sure you bring a fresh pot of wine and cakes." Solomon ordered.

Debbra rolled her eyes at her husband's hollow attempt at dictating the service at the executive table. A plate of roasted python was placed on the table, along with fresh wine and dough cakes. Debbra picked at her plate as she consumed glass after glass of wine. Solomon on the other hand had no problems digging into his roasted python.

Tmus' plate sat untouched, while his eyes stayed locked on the action on the dance floor. He felt his inner arousal begin to take shape, and without warning Tmus rose from his seat. "Major Zor, I expect my company within ten minutes", he said, and then walked away with two of his personal knight's men.

Major Zor stopped eating long enough to give one of his message men the order to have Nipoly brought up to Tmus' chamber. Then the Major turned back to his meal. The soldier walked across the dance floor, ignoring the questioning eyes that followed him.

Nipoly saw Tmus leave his seat and immediately knew why the soldier was approaching her on the dance floor. Knowing she would have to cut her performance short, Nipoly began to whine down the song as the soldier leaned in and spoke into her ear, "Your Excellency would like to see you in his chambers." He stepped back and waited without saying another word.

Nipoly finished her rendition, then gave the band the signal to continue on with a solid rhythmic sound that the people could continue to enjoy. Many were not to happy about Nipoly being escorted out of the hall in the middle of her performance, but they all knew it was for a private show for Tmus. No one would voice their opinion about that, running the risk of being heard and disciplined.

At the executive table, Debbra sucked her teeth, causing Solomon to quickly look over to her, "Is there something wrong Debbra?"

She looked at him with her drunken stare and said, " Yesss, theress something wrong! I'm ready to leave", Debbra snapped.

"But the night is still young", Solomon whined, with a piece of dough in one hand and a glass of wine in the other.

Major Zor couldn't believe how soft Solomon was. Especially when it came to controlling Debbra. Zor shook his head in disgust and felt a wave of relief that he wasn't married. He felt that marrying a woman gave her too much power. This is why women never lasted longer than two dates with the Major.

"And you're not". Debbra said aiming at the governor's age. "Now, are you going to take me home or do I have to find another escort?" she asked with a slight slur.

Zor knew this would be the moment where he would show her who the man of the house is but not Solomon.

"Okay...okay", he said in frustration, before stuffing his face with the last piece of dough cake. Debbra always found a way to make a scene whenever they we're out enjoying a festive night. Solomon then stood up and helped his drunk wife out of her chair.

"I can walk damnit!" Debbra snapped as she swatted his hand. She lost her balance in the process and almost fell on a council member who was sitting next to her. Solomon caught his wife at an awkward spot on her poplin dress and the soft fabric ripped.

"Aww!" Debbra cried out, as she fell into the council member lap. The shoulder portion of her dress tore down to her right breast revealing her nakedness.

"You idiot! Look what you've done!"

"I'm sorry honey. Come, let's get you out of here." Solomon fumbled with his wife trying to grab her arm.

Debbra snapped, "Don't touch me!"

She stood up, with the councilman's help and she quickly stomped off toward the exit. Solomon looked around to see who was watching the spectacle he and his wife just put on. The majority of the diners were to busy enjoying their food, drink, and music to worry about another humiliating display by the head of the governor's classless wife.

"I'm sorry. Please excuse us", he said, trying to follow his wife out of the hall, but was stopped short by Zor.

"Why don't you let her accompany the procession to the Kingdom of Soul". Zor asked.

Solomon stared at Zor, then looked around to see who was listening to their conversation. "Why would I do that?"

"Because, may be you will be able to rule Industriland in Tmus' absence much better, without having to take care of someone that doesn't care if you exist." Zor said with a sinister smirk on his face.

Solomon knew Zor had a trick up his sleeve. "That would be like you helping me out now, wouldn't it?"

"If you want to believe that, then yes. My only concern is the well being of Industriland in Tmus' absence. As long as you and everyone else that is left behind can competently control the city, I have no questions about your household", Zor said low enough for only Solomon to hear. "But if you feel like you will have too much on your plate governing the city and trying to control your wife, then why not send her on the trip?"

Solomon felt Zor was trying to question his manhood. "I know what you're up too Zor, and I'm not going to give you the satisfaction of telling Tmus you are a better fit for my position."

"Now why would I want to do that?" Zor asked with the same smirk on his face. "We both know you can govern the city better than me. I was just making a suggestion about how you can finally give yourself peace of mind. Look at it this way, she will be playing an important role in the takeover of Muzena. Giving you a stronger position in Tmus' good graces."

"And what kind of role are you talking about?" Solomon asked, not buying what the Major was selling.

"Whatever role Tmus calls upon her to fulfill", Zor said. "She could be in charge of the entire body of women who feeds the army or she can be a part of the negotiating committee that convinces the Queen of the Kingdom of Soul to surrender."

He might be right, Solomon thought to himself. Even though Debbra could not hold her wine and she turned into a crazy woman whenever she did drink, she still was a great organizer. Being that this trip will need the city's best organizers on hand it might be a good idea for Debbra to go.

Moves like this would also give Solomon free reign to do few things in Debbra's absence. Things he would never attempt to do while she was around. Mainly because Debbra had a violent streak that Solomon knew he needed a break from.

"You know something Zor, I know you have a trick up that gold sleeve of yours, but it will be good to govern the city without any added distractions. Especially Debbra". Solomon swallowed hard, and wiped his forehead with a napkin. He couldn't believe he just said that, and in front of Zor of all people.

"That's all I care about. As long as you have a clear head, things should remain stable around here", Zor said.

Always the thinker, Solomon asked, "What if she doesn't want to go?"

Zor patted the man on his back, and Solomon cringed as he thought the gold arm would break his shoulder blade. "Solomon don't worry yourself with such minor details. She will go with the army." Zor said with an air full of confidence.

"Okay, I'll go and ask her."

"No Solomon. You go and tell her she's going with us regardless of how she feels." Zor said then stepped out of the man's way. "It's all for the people of Industriland. You make sure she understands that".

Solomon nodded his head, and ran off to go find his drunken wife.

Zor sat back down and silently thought of the victory he just stole. Solomon had always been Zor's quiet competition, and Zor was finally tired of the who can impress Tmus better game. Zor knew Solomon was worthless in his physical form, but when it came to intelligence there was no question Solomon was one of the smartest governors in Muzena.

If Zor eliminated Solomon, or better yet if he eliminated himself, then Zor would be able to convince Tmus to allow him to run the government, as well as lead the army. A vision he had been flirting with for some time now.

*****

The torches in the chamber crackled as Tmus meditated with his eyes closed. He replayed the visions of the night's events in his mind to see if he missed anything. Whenever Tmus found himself surrounded by his city officials and other underlining's at one of the many gatherings they held in Industriland, afterwards he would retreat to his chamber and review. A tap on his door brought Tmus back to the present.

"Enter".

The door swung open and Nipoly strolled into the chamber. "You requested me?"

"You sang beautifully tonight", Tmus said staring at her slender physique as Nipoly's caramel skin glistened under the dim lights.

"Thank you."

From the distance, Tmus appeared to be in a more composed mood than usual, but Nipoly knew better. She made her way up to the throne reflecting on the many times she witnessed Tmus inflict his worst pain on people for the most minor offenses.

Many times Nipoly tried to use her prowess of song and sexual persuasion to save people from Tmus' rage. It worked many days and back fired on others.

Nipoly was born in a small town that was invaded by the Industriarmy, and she was taken with the rest of the women and children to be forced into a new life as a slave for the army. Slowly word began to spread that there was a young girl who possessed the voice of an angel, and Nipoly was forced to sing for the sound committee of Industriland.

Nipoly wowed the committee and one day was summoned to sing at one of the Industriland festivals. A festival Tmus was reluctantly attending, but once he heard the songstresses voice, he privately felt a surge of pleasure no one has ever given him. These were feelings Tmus would never allow to be showcased to the general public, for fear of the people seeing their ruler having feelings like them under his murderous demeanor.

Soon after the discovery of the beautiful song bird, Tmus began ordering these private performances. Tmus used these sessions as a tool that would allow him to meditate into a deeper zone.

Nipoly on the other hand saw the private meetings as a gateway to use her prowess to persuade Tmus to loosen up his grip on the population of Industriland. If she couldn't get him to release some of the slaves, Nipoly felt she could at least get Tmus to give the people better rights. A more relaxed people, can be a more productive people. Convincing Tmus of this was not a hard task, being that the city's leader only cared about the advancement of his projects and the building of his new industry.

"I've been thinking on how you must join the army on our journey to the Kingdom of Soul", Tmus threw out there to test Nipoly's reaction.

"I'm not a warrior. Why must I participate in a campaign, that I'm pretty sure will require me to be as brutal as the rest of the army?"

"Because, you are the army's inspiration. With you as a part of the operation, the soldiers will perform at a higher level", Tmus said.

"You give me too much credit", Nipoly said with a slight smile.

"That I do, but that doesn't mean you don't motivate the people of this city". Tmus said without a smile.

"I always thought the ruler of the city was the motivator of this city, and not the songstress." Nipoly said.

"So it's settled. You will join us on our journey", he said, making the decision for her.

"Yes your Excellency, and what will be my duty to the army?" Nipoly asked.

"It will be the same as it is here in Industriland. You are the voice that drives this city to continue on with its development towards a more harmonizing future. One that will be more fruitful once more of the people see my vision of success", Tmus said in a low tone.

"And what makes you think the people don't believe in your visions of advancement?" Nipoly asked.

"Nipoly, if the people believed, then I would not have to keep them in bondage", Tmus said in a matter of fact tone.

Nipoly saw an opening and decided to step through it. "Well, you know if the people were given a choice, in a more negotiative capacity then it would be a more comparative society. Instead of -" she stopped in mid sentence and stared into Tmus' red eyes.

Tmus could feel her unwillingness to be honest with him because of the way he ruled his city. No one in Industriland ever questioned Tmus or his ways of ruler ship. If anyone did they would face an unimaginable wrath from Tmus or a member of his army.

But through the time they had spent together, Tmus had grown to value Nipoly's opinion. Her insight on how to motivate the people was taken into account whenever Tmus wanted things to move in a more productive atmosphere. Especially at a time like this.

"Go on", Tmus encouraged her. "Tell me what you need to say Nipoly. How is the state of Industriland viewed in the eyes of the people?"

Nipoly shifted her weight from one foot to the next, then looked down at her bronze feet. "I think the people feel. They believe that no matter how much of your vision they accomplish for you, they will never be free to live in a land they can call their own."

"Industriland is their home", Tmus said.

"But not by choice and you know this Tmus", Nipoly said with her eyes full of sorrow.

"Everyone in Muzena is not capable of making choices on their own", Tmus said in a flat tone.

"You are right Your Excellency, but will the people ever have a voice in Muzena?" Nipoly asked, almost pleading with him.

Tmus thought about this. He had been ruling with an iron fist for so long that he didn't know how it would feel to be more empathetic to the people's wants or needs.

"I will be able to answer that after we secure the Kingdom of Soul".

Nipoly felt defeated. She thought he was going to open up and finally embrace the thought of letting the people function a little more freely. Maybe even establish a new state for some of the loyalist and hardest working slaves. A place that would give them some hope. The people would want nothing more than a chance to work toward a future, and taste of independence at their end of the tunnel.

Tmus knew this, Nipoly reasoned with herself. But he was a tyrant, who would never be satisfied enough to let the people walk Muzena on their own. Tmus fed off of the people's misery and he looked forward to capturing their souls.

He has to see the passion in my eyes, Nipoly told herself. He knows how much she has the people's best interest at heart, and he showed no mercy as she presented her feelings in the people's name. Then he coldly closed the door on her when he was done listening.

"Now sing to me", Tmus said in his dark voice.

Nipoly let her argument rest as she closed her eyes and started off her ballad in a low hum that built itself up into a verse of deep words.

"Mmm, oh share// oh share// it's my gift to you// let me take your fear// give you strength so you can rule// it's Industrious// sealed with a kiss// no one love the lust// I picture one day they'll have love for us// A love we can trust..."

✱✱✱✱✱
_____

The holding cell keys rattled causing the dungeon to suddenly go silent.

"Alright ladies. Tonight is your lucky night", the guard said as he stepped out into the open. He was the first person to appear in hours and the women down in the Industriland dungeon were not to enthused to see him.

Queen Taila had watched the dungeon population shrink in the last few days, which gave her a small sense of relief. Whenever one of her cellmates was released out into the city it felt like a moment of freedom for all of the prisoners. What worried Queen Taila is what were the women being released into? Would one of the townspeople take her in? Are the women shipped off to another place far worse than the one they are released from?

Many unanswered questions ran through Taila's head as she tried to keep up her cellmates' spirits. She knew opportunity would come knocking, and she wanted he women to be ready. Positive energy was contagious, and by showing the others she believed they would make it out of there alive was the motivation they would need to remain strong in the dungeon.

Every woman in the six holding cells began to crowd the cell bars, as a group of women – flanked by armed guards – swarmed the dungeon carrying trays of food like they were waitresses.

Conversations began to erupt in every direction as some of the women carrying the food were noticed by their country women who they left down in the dungeon.

'Tap! Tap! Tap!'

"Alright ladies, calm down!!! Calm down!!! I know you're hungry. That doesn't mean you have the right to ask your feeders what's the weather out there", the short, rotten tooth guard snapped as he open up the first cell.

The caged women were so happy to see familiar faces that they ignored the guard and continued on with their barrage of questions.

"Did you see Harry?"

"How is it out there?"

"Did you see the children?"

"Will you come back and feed us again?"

"Do the men know we're down here?"

Some dug into the platters of roast pig, smoked turkey, sweet cakes, sour bread and fruits, while the others continued on with their onslaught of questions.

"Why are they serving us so much food?" Taila asked one of the recently freed women.

Della stepped closer to the bars and said, "They're having some type of going away festival. They say the Industriarmy is going to forge an assault on the Kingdom of Soul".

"Oh no", Nahir said, as she stepped up next to Taila with a sweet cake in her hand.

"When are they leaving?"Taila asked.

"Within the next coming days and I think we're going to be forced to go along", Della said. Then she looked over her shoulder to make sure the guards weren't watching her.

"Well, if they do take you, make sure you tell the women of Pakisound I said to remain strong and don't give up hope", Taila said. Then she leaned in closer to the bars and said, "And if they get the chance to run, take it."

Della looked into the eyes of her imprisoned Queen and felt the true embrace of a leader who was willing to put the happiness of her people before her own. At that moment, Della knew if she got the opportunity to free her Queen, she would. Della's conscious would never let her rest knowing that she left such a loving, caring, and compassionate leader behind without attempting to free her if she had the chance.

"We won't leave you Taila", Della said with a tear hanging on the corner of her eye.

"Yes you will", Taila forcefully said in a suppressed tone. "You must save yourselves, and the children of Pakisound. You understand?"

"Alright ladies, visit is over! Let's go!" The rotten tooth guard barked at them, as he and his partners began to push the tray carriers out of the dungeon.

"We will not leave you my Queen", Della said before one of the guards took hold of her arm.

"You heard the man! Let's go!"

"Please, do as I say", Taila helplessly said, as cries rang out in the dungeon.

Women began to sob and shout plea, while others stood by silently and watched their friends get forcefully hustled out of the dungeon.

"Do you think they're going to take us on the trip too?" Nahir asked Taila once they were back in the corner of their cell.

Taila slowly chewed on a piece of turkey. "I doubt it Nahir. I think if they were, they would have released us from down here already".

"So what do you think is going to happen to us?" Nahir asked with her eyes full of uncertainty.

"I don't know, but I do know if the majority of the Industriarmy is going on this trip to do battle with the Kingdom of Soul, then there won't be as many guards here patrolling the city", Taila said, as she gave voice to her thoughts out into the open.

"Will that be when we'll make our move?" Nahir asked, feeling a surge of energy flow through her body.

"Yes, so everyone must be ready", Talia firmly stated before she took a bit of some sour bread.

"Don't worry my Queen. We will be ready". Nahir assured her, then faded off into her own thought's of escape and happiness on the other side of Industriland.

The Brook .

The heart of Muzena beats
within these walls…Welcome .

Chapter VII

With a week of travel by foot under their belt's the small royal party was exhausted by the time the Brook territory came into view.

"Tusi say, the people of the Brook will embrace us", Gond said over his shoulder.

"I hope so, 'cause my feet are killing me", Steven whined, causing everyone to let out a chuckle.

"Don't worry little brother. If we're lucky, we might be able to get a few horses to use for the rest of our journey", Zahara said as she rubbed Steven's head.

"That sounds like a plan me lady", Nalani agreed, as they made their way up the grassy hill.

The Brook territory is a large expansion of land, with the main portion of the metropolis resting atop a hill, making the Brook hard to attack, but easy to defend. With its twenty five foot high stone wall surrounding the entire city, and armed guards posted in strategic positions to keep a watchful eye on all sides, the Brook has never had any invaders make it pass their stone rampart.

The Brook territory had a long and deep history that was filled with a rich culture of life, music, mysticism, and a profound love for its people. The humans of the Brook were very vain people, who took pride in the work they put in to keep their dark skin moisturized and always smelling good. The different fabrics and color coordination used to make their garments always separated the Brooknite's from the rest of the city's population in Muzena.

Another dimension of the Brook that made the strong city stand out in Muzena were the unusual inhabitants, called the humanals (an animal with human traits and functions). The special living arrangement with the city mystified friend's who visited and enemies alike who tried to invade the city.

The Brook's chief leader, Poppa Big, always stood his ground with the will of his people against invader's who usually retreated from the Brooknite's after not being able to conquer the first leg of their attack. Whenever the element of the steep land didn't stop them, the humanals would step up and secure a victory for their people.

The alliance between The Brook and The Kingdom of Soul was made many centuries ago, through the secrets and power of their universal culture- High-Hop. Outside of these two cities no one understood how a people could be so different in life, but have such a powerful love for each other allowing them to communicate with each other through the Gods of Song whenever necessary.

The front portcullis of the main wall opened, and two men atop of horses, rode out of the gate and down the hill. They met the royal party halfway up the hill.

"State your business", one of the riders commanded. His large sword hung from his hip making his burly size more threatening from his high position.

"We only wish to stay over for a few days before we continue on our journey to the Kingdom of Soul", Zahara said, matching the serious stare the guard gave them.

The two guards exchanged a look, then looked back down to Zahara, "If you are traveling to the Kingdom of Soul, then why are you traveling by foot?"

"Our land was attacked", Zahara said with nothing but hurt flowing from her eyes. "We never had time to gather horses or even supplies for that matter".

"What land?" the other large guard asked, as he rested his left hand on the butt of his sword.

"Pakisound". Zahara said, watching as the two guards exchanged another look.

"Pakisound was attacked? By whom?"

"The Industriarmy", Zahara said, trying to keep it together until they made it into the city.

"What about the King and Queen of Pakisound?" The guard asked.

Zahara looked down to her feet, then looked back up into his hard eyes and said, "My father, the King, died in battle".

"Oh, forgive us princess."

"Yes, please follow us to the castle", the two guards quickly rode back up the hill to inform the others of the arriving guest.

"I guess he was happy to see us", Zahara said, her smile helped the rest of the party relax a little after their unpredictable encounter.

"Well let's not disappoint them", Nalani said, leading the way up the dark green hill. The sun steadily fell behind the horizon, giving the land a red glow. Thoughts of finally being saved from having to walk under the hot sun motivated Nalani to walk a little faster than she did all day.

"Come on young Prince", Nalani snapped over her shoulder.

Steven sucked his teeth."I'm coming Nalani", he whined, as he put a little pep in his step.

When they made it to the open portcullis, a small welcoming committee was slowly taking form at the front gate. The talk of visitors quickly began to spread with the excitement and activity of nothing short of rolling out the red carpet for the arrivals.

"Welcome to the Brook!" A man as brown skin man, with a wide smile greeted the royal party. He was dressed in blue and silver flowing fabric that mirrored the traditional dress of an old Brooknite.

Zahara matched his 5'7 height as he stepped up to her and extended his hand, "I am Diop".

"Pleased to meet you, I am Zahara, Queen of Pakisound", she said returning a smile.

"Pleased to meet you Queen. We are preparing some rooms in the main castle for you and your retinue", Diop said looking over the rest of the party.

"Thank you. If it's possible I have a few request, and I would like to speak to the King of your land", Zahara said. "But if it's any inconvenience to you and the sovereign, then..." Diop quickly interjected, "No...No, of course there's no problem. Poppa Big has already informed us to bring you to a prepared dinner, hosted by the King himself."

"Okay." Zahara said, as Diop lead her onto the back of a carriage. Once the carriage was packed with the new arrivals they took a short ride through the vibrant city up toward the main castle.

People waved as the strong smells of food being prepared floated through the air. The heavy sounds of drums mixed with the rocking of maracas danced all around them.

"Look Nalani!" Steven exclaimed in awe. Nalani looked over in the direction he was pointing in and she was also amazed to see a panther having a conversation with a woman, who looked to be buying vegetables from him.

"Is that a panther talking?" Nalani asked.

Diop chuckled, "Yes Madam. You will see a lot of that in The Brook".

"Oh", Nalani said under her breath as if embarrassed.

The Golona men were also impressed as they conversed amongst themselves in their native tongue. The energetic activity of men, women, and humanals taking place in the streets of The Brook was a sight to see. Zahara nibbled on a piece of dried cinnamon bread, looking off into the distance of acreage that was a colorful blend of city and jungle. The fruits that hung from trees made her mouth water, as she flashed back to the beautiful fruit and vegetable trees that used to blossom back in her homeland.

The main castle was surrounded by 70 foot tall trees, and an array of shorter dense thicket that gave the place a feel of being protected by the tropical vegetation. Colorful pieces of cloth hung from the machinations like they were flags blowing in the wind. From the outside of the castle looked to be a place that was full of spirit.

Zahara leaned over to Nalani and said, "It's beautiful."

"Yes it is", Nalani said returning the smile to the young Queen.

The carriage came to a stop and a small group gathered at the back of it to help it's riders off. The Golona men hopped out first and quickly scanned the area, with the prince hopping down next. The two women were helped off last and were welcomed with a small boutique of flowers.

"Are the rooms ready?" Diop asked.

A woman dressed in a long flowing red and yellow damask garment answered with a, "Yes sir", and she took up a position next to a line of women that stood shoulder to shoulder holding baskets of fruits, bread, linens and pitchers of water.

"Queen, this is Santoya. She will head the group for your hospitality", Diop said introducing the honey complexion woman to the Queen.

"It's my pleasure Queen", Sontoya said with a slight bend at her knees and a head nod.

"Thank you Sontoya", Zahara said. "This is my brother Prince Steven and our guardian Nalani. These men are from Golona village. They are our personal guard".

Everyone exchanged pleasantries as Zahara leaned over to Sontoya and asked, "Is there some place where... I can... You know". Zahara was feeling a little embarrassed to be speaking about her personal hygiene in front of a group of people.

"Of course my Queen", Sontoya quickly said, sensing Zahara's need for some privacy. "Everything is waiting for you inside".

The visiting group was taken up to the second level of the castle. "This wing will be yours for your stay", Diop said as he lead the group through the halls, which were buzzing with activity.

"Would you like to share or would you prefer separate rooms?" Sontoya asked Zahara, referring to her and Nalani.

Zahara smiled, "Yes, we will be sharing and my brother can have his own. Unless he wants to be with the Golona men", she said looking over to Steven.

Not wanting to be left alone in a strange building, the young prince easily agreed to be with the Golonas, "Yes, we can stay together".

"Okay, it's settled. The women will be in here, and the men will be across the hall", Diop said, as he pointed and shouted orders to the women who ran from room to room getting things ready for the guest.

"Dinner with Poppa Big will be served in 2 hours, so we will be back for you then", Diop said, and he escorted the men to their room.

"I will be staying with you Queen", Sontoya said.

"Sontoya, please call me Zahara, if you're going to be hanging out with me".

Sontoya chuckled, "Yes ma'am". Then she led the way into the large room. Big feather stuffed pillows and large blankets, laced with colorful patterns were laid out in the far corner up under an open face window with a color filled cloth blowing in its wings. The strong smell of freshly lit incense filled the room, over powering the smell of fresh bread and baskets of fruit that rested on a table at the far end of the room. A large tub, with a flowing sheer curtain around it was filled with hot water. Off to their right was a small selection of garments laid out for the women to choose from.

"Your bath is ready. Do you need anything with it?" Sontoya asked, as she tested the water temperature.

"No. Is there another bath for Nalani?" Zahara asked looking around the room.

"Yes, in the other room. Come Nalnai, I'll show you", Sontoya said, and then escorted her into an adjoining room.

Zahara undressed, then eased her body down into the water. Her body slowly began to relax as she rubbed the soap onto her cocoa skin. Once she was satisfied, Zahara rested her head on the edge of the tub, and let fragrances from the soap and incense release the held up tension in her body.

Zahara could tell that after the bath and a hot meal she was going to sleep like a baby. She realized this trip had her whole body aching. She closed her eyes and decided to rest them.

"Queen Zahara?" Sontoya said in a soft voice.

Zahara opened her eyes and was confused for a moment about where she was.

"I'm sorry for waking you".

"Oh, no that's alright. How long have I been sleeping?" Zahara asked rubbing her eyes.

"Not for too long", Sontoya said with a smile. "Are you ready?" she asked holding out a fuzzy cloth for Zahara to dry off with.

"Yes", Zahara stepped out of the tub and Sontoya wrapped the cloth around her.

"What patterns would you like to wear?" Sontoya asked, walking over to the laid out garments.

"She should wear the colors of power and prestige to give off a strong presence, for her first appearance", Nalani said as she strolled into the room looking like a new woman. Nalani was dressed from head to toe in a sky blue and black wrap. Her black hair was still wet and curly from the half way point down to the ends.

"Nalani, you look beautiful", Zahara said with a bright smile.

"Thank you me lady", Nalani blushed, and went over to pick out a wrap that would help Zahara make a statement at the dinner.

"What colors were you thinking about?" Zahara asked.

Sontoya handed Zahara a bottle of oil that smelled like roses. "Use this Zahara to moisturize your skin".

"Okay. Thank you".

"You'll see". Nalani said over her shoulder.

Zahara rubbed the oil over her naked body and was immediately captured by its scent. "This smells great".

"Now this will give you the high ranking appearance you will grow into and at the same time give your first major audience the impression of you being comfortable and confident in your position", Nalani said with a warm smile. She held up a fire red and green patterned two piece. The material was soft chiffon, making Zahara feel like she was being wrapped in lace. Sontoya wrapped Zahara's still damp hair in a matching pattern. Then the two women stepped back to view their creation.

"Now that's a work of art", Sontoya said. She looked over to Nalani and the two women shared a chuckle.

Zahara blushed, "I feel like it", she told them. Zahara put the heart of Pakisound around her neck, and took a deep breath. "Okay, I'm ready now".

The women went across the hall and found the Golona men clean and ready to go. "Young prince are you ready?" Nalani asked, as she rushed over to him straightening out his black and silver jerkin.

"Yes. Can I bring my sword?" Steven asked. Nalani looked over her shoulder to Zahara.

"What you think me lady?"

Zahara thought about this for a moment, then stepped further into to room. "Yes, and bring the book too". She looked around the room as the Golona men and Sontoya waited in the hallway. "They seem like nice people, but we have to be ready at all times, just in case we have to run in a moment's notice".

The three of them looked at each other and a telepathic feeling came over them. From the moment they left the safe confines of Pakisound it has been them against the world, and even though they were welcomed by fellow allies, this wasn't the time for them to let their guard down.

The corridor was once again hopping with activity as word quickly spread that the royal visitors were making their way down to the dining hall. Diop met the procession half way to the dining hall, looking energized and happy they had guest from one of the major civilizations in Muzena.

"People are already buzzing around the hall. Poppa Big and Lady Light will be joining us shortly", Diop said with a bright smile.

"Lady Light?" Zahara asked in a low voice, but the attentive Diop heard her.

"Yes, she is very excited to meet you Queen." Diop said as he led them around a series of white clothed tables, which had either a basket of fruit or fresh bread on top of it.

"You sit here Queen, and the Prince shall sit here", Diop said directing the seating arrangement.

Once Zahara sat down, the opportunity to finally take in the hall presented itself. The room was flowing with electricity, and she knew everyone would be staring at her as she tried to seem interested in the bowl of fruit in the center of the table.

People made their way into the large hall to the blend of bongos, tom toms, and a pair of lyres rolled through the air waves. Conversation rumbled like low hums, as head nods were exchanged. Inquisitive eyes gazed across the high city council table at the guest of honor tonight, as freshly dried breads were placed on the tables. Prince Steven wasted no time and went right to work on a set of cinnamon flavored rolls.

Nalani fussed over Steven to get her mind off of all the people that were staring at them, while the Golona men sat at the next table over and conversed amongst themselves.

"They will bring in the black bean soap first, then the fish meal, and finally wild turkey with tomatoes", Diop said with much enthusiasm.

"Oh, when will Poppa Big be joining us?" Zahara asked ready to get this first meeting underway. Zahara did not know there were going to be so many people there to witness the royal meeting. She would have preferred a humbler reception, but the smile on her face told the story of a young queen that was very grateful for the one they were receiving.

Diop was giving them the run down on the production of the night's events when he spotted the King. "Ahh, there he is".

Zahara looked over to the set of double doors on the east side of the dining hall as they were held open by two guards and thought she was dreaming. She watched a 6 foot 8 inch tall black bear walk fully erect into the hall. His paw was in a hand lock with one of the most beautiful light skinned women Zahara had ever seen.

"Ladies and gentlemen! Please rise!" Diop said, grabbing the attention of the entire hall with his booming voice. Every person in the hall rose out of their seat and began to applaud.

Zahara looked around the crowd of close to 500 attendees and slowly began to realize a large number of animals and humanals were sprinkled throughout the seating arrangement. Loud cheers greeted the royal couple, as Poppa Big escorted Lady Light over to the table with a large red tiger trailing them.

Zahara was knocked off of her feet by the couple, but when she got a good look at the rare tiger, she was in awe. Legend had it that there was only one red tiger in Muzena, but no one really believed that tale unless they had the opportunity to come to The Brook.

"Queen, welcome to our land", Poppa Big said, as he took Zahara's hand and kissed the back of it.

Zahara blushed. "Thank you for having us".

He nodded. "I am Poppa Big, the crown of the jungle city and this is my wife, Lady Light", he said stepping over so the two women could have a better face to face greeting.

The red and green wrap complimented Zahara's chocolate skin and bright smile very well, but Lady Light took everyone in the room's breath away decked out in a pink and blue sari. Her long flowing black hair looked as soft as silk and the stone encrusted tiara was only out shined by Lady Light's smile.

"Nice to meet you Queen?" Lady Light asked as if not sure Zahara was the right person to address.

"Yes, Queen Zahara of Pakisound," she said returning the smile. "This is my brother, Prince Steven, and our guardian Nalani. The three Golona warriors are our personal guards given to us by their high priest", Zahara held her head high as she took pleasure in introducing everyone.

Lady Light's eyes dazzled as she stepped closer to Zahara. "Your necklace is magnificent," she said as the heart of Pakisound slowly glowed to life. Lady Light could feel its power without having touched it.

"Thank you".

Poppa Big was also intrigued by the heart, but he was more interested in what they were having to eat. There would be plenty of time to inquire about the glowing gem. Poppa Big introduce D.Tiger as his second in command and the red tiger surprised Zahara by bowing it's head and saying, "Please to meet you my Queen".

"My people of The Brook, I would love for you to welcome our friends from Pakisound, Queen Zahara and Prince Steven", Poppa Big announced causing the hall to erupt in another round of applause.

"Now please, enjoy your food and drink, and let's show our friendly visitors a good time", Poppa Big said, as he sat down indicating to the rest of the hall they had permission to sit.

The black bean soup was passed out and Poppa Big jumped right into his bowl. He did not do this to ignore anyone at the table. He wanted everyone more interested in their food then in the conversations taking place at the head table. The way he saw it they would have plenty of time to ask the most important questions of what brought them to The Brook in such a disturbed state.

"How was the receiving committee?" Lady Light asked.

"They were wonderful. That was a breath of fresh air", Zahara said, sounding truly pleased.

"I'm glad. Whatever you need, they will provide it for you", Lady Light said, as she looked around the hall for one of the food servers. "How long is it for the next course?"

"In one minute, Miss. Lady", one of the servers said and quickly ran off.

Zahara sipped on her soup until the plate of snapper fish, with an array of green and yellow vegetables finally arrived. Lady Light seemed pleased they bought her something she could eat, because black bean soup wasn't one of her favorite dishes.

"How is your fish Zahara?" Lady Light asked. She was sitting on Zahara's right at the circular table which was full of an array of different dishes.

She chewed on a piece and gave a pleased grin, "This is delicious, and these greens are extremely tasty".

"I'm happy your pleased", Poppa Big said.

He looked around at the festive crowd, which was seemingly lost in good food and the steady flow of the music, and decided this was a good time to speak with Zahara about her travels.

"So tell me Zahara, what brings you to our Land?" Poppa Big asked in between bites of his snapper.

"Our city was attacked by the Industriarmy, but before they stormed the wall, my father sent us out of the city through a secret pathway, and we were instructed to go to the Kingdom of Soul", Zahara said.

"I've heard the Industriarmy was stepping up their campaign to industrialize the entire Muzena", Poppa Big said. He then thought carefully about his next set of words. "So Zahara, you say you are the Queen now. Does that mean the King and Queen of Pakisound did not make it through the invasion ?"

Zahara looked down at her plate, then back up into the eyes of the black bear sitting across from her and said, "We spent the night in the Golona village and the high priest sent a small committee back to Pakisound to see if there were any survivors".

Her silence after that statement told Poppa Big and Lady Light volumes about what they must have went through in the last hours of being in their home land. "Were sorry to hear this", Poppa Big said in a sincere tone.

Zahara stopped twirling her salad and put her fork down. "We wanted to stay with my father, but he insisted we leave the city. It was as if he knew this battle was going to be different", she said, feeling like she somehow failed the people by leaving in the middle of a fight for their right to live under the loving umbrella of High-Hop.

Sensing she was feeling down about the decision her father made, Poppa Big pushed his plate over to the side, "Your father made the right choice to sneak you and your brother out of the city", he said looking into her eyes. "Trust me, if I was put into his position, I would have made the same decision for my son".

Surprised, Zahara asked, "You have a son?"

Poppa Big and Lady Light chuckled, "Yes we do. You'll see him".

"That is, if you stay around for a while", Lady Light said, finishing Poppa Big's thought.

"You've been so kind to us. We don't want be any kind of burden on you and your people", Zahara said.

"Child don't be silly", Lady Light playfully said. "You are welcome to stay here for as long as you need. We are here to help you, not rush you off after one dinner."

Zahara chuckled, "Thank you Lady Light. Which reminds me…Poppa Big do you think it's possible for us to gather up some horses to use on the rest of our journey?"

"Of course, I was wondering how you made it this far on foot", he said with a hardy chuckle.

"I've never walked so much before in my life", Zahara said with a bright smile.

"Well, you don't have to worry about that anymore", Poppa Big said returning the smile. "I will also send a couple of soldiers to accompany you on the rest of your journey".

"Oh no, that's not necessary".

"No, please. Let us do this for you", Lady Light said. "That will put our minds at ease knowing that we can help you in areas that are well needed, like your security".

"Also, our people know the faster and safer trails to the Kingdom of Soul", Poppa Big added.

Zahara thought about this and the prospect of having more allies with them on this long journey began to appeal to her. "Okay Poppa Big, I will accept your personal escort."

His smile was wide as he stood up and said, "Good. Now we will entertain you and your people to a taste of The Brook flavors".

"I hope you enjoy it", Lady Light said as she also rose out of her seat.

Zahara didn't know what to say. She thought they had already witnessed the night's entertainment and after their meal, the night would be over. But as the activity around the band began to change it was clear the night was far from over.

The music began to shift from the mellow mood of serenading the dinner crowd while they ate, to a more uptempo beat that began to grab everyone's attention.

"People of the Brook, since we have special guest to join us tonight Poppa Big and Lady Light would like to share a melody with them, and you too, to show our universal sign of greetings", Diop announced to the crowd.

Applause erupted as all eyes once again focused on the guests sitting at the high council table, causing Zahara to blush. Lady Light's soulful voice slowly began to boom from her five foot, six inch frame as all eyes turned back to where the band was set up at. The tom-toms thumped as the maracas rattled under the influence of three horns.

"La..Laa..La La La—La Laa.... Here to be together// Be down for whatever// The love we share// Can only make us better//"

Poppa Big sang, " Uhh- Words that talk// Dance before your eyes// It's no surprise// How we stand by each other's side// I've been known to smother a few cries// Emotions on the rise// Poppa-// The tough one// The list// The most proper// The crown jewels consist of gems// There's nothing hotter// We in the gritty land// The city of jungle bands// The beats and sounds// The flows are through the hands// We are the proud people// All created to stand equal// Blessed by the Gods of Song// To keep pressing on// Speak, and let your word be born// I feel the truth as it seeps out of the gold horns..."

Lady Light – "Here to be together// Be down for whatever// The love we share// Can only make us better// Laa..Laa..Lalala-Lala...Laaaa!"

Poppa Big – " It's all about the back up// You got mine – I got yours// Never have to look over your shoulder// In the midst of war// Our roots are rich// And the bloodlines are thick// Hope to be here forever// The generational grip// Let the knowledge run free// To the

young in line// Share our gift of the hard beats and smooth rhymes//
Visit distant lands// They say Poppa you too kind// Try to shower the
big bear in fruits and sweet wines// The first Lady by my side// She's
full of diamond lines// The envious don't understand// That their
stares are a crime..."

Lady Light – "Here to be together// Be down for whatever//
The love that we share// Can only make us better// Laa... Laa..
Lalalala – La La..."

The entire hall was in a frenzy as people and humanals danced
with each other under the heavily influenced High-Hop vibe. Zahara
was clearly marveled by the performance as she sat back clapping
her hands to the beat. Nalani and Steven stood up and began to dance
with each other, as the Golona men laughed and clapped their hands
to the beat.

Poppa Big and Lady Light looked like an ideal team –
musically. Feeding off of each other's words and energy, keeping
their audience in a joyous mood.

Zahara had witnessed some great festivals and feast in her
homeland, but there was something very special about the one she
was now attending. She knew the welcome feeling the people of The
Brook were showering them with was turning into an extraordinary
experience she was proud to be part of. Zahara did not want it to
end, because it felt so right from where she was sitting.

Zahara laughed to herself thinking anything will feel right after the hectic weeks they had just been through. More food and drinks were brought out as another woman stepped in and took over the job of serenading the people with her voice. Everyone enjoyed themselves well into the night. When Zahara finally laid down on the comfortable hay filled comforter her worn out body relaxed and her mind floated off into a heavy dream state.

Today was a good day were the last words she remembered telling herself.

Chapter VIII

One of the night guards on his post at the perimeter wall surrounding the jungle city stared out into the moon covered forest and watched as a small speck of light hopped through the woods. Slowly it made its way toward the huge clearing that separated The Brook from the forest. The guard did not know what to make of the dancing light, so he stood idle and waited before he alerted anyone about what he was seeing. The last thing he wanted to do was cause a ruckus and it turn out to be nothing.

The light stopped short of the clearing for a moment, and it emerged out of the forest. The guard motioned to the nearest person on patrol and the other guard quickly jogged over.

"It's two of them".

"Man the gates!"

A group of five well armed men converged on the front gate, and patiently waited until the two riders was in close range. "State Your Business!" one of the guards barked from behind the closed portcullis.

The two riders stopped their horses, and one of them responded. "If it's possible, we would like to rest for the night in your city".

"Where you come from?"

"We come in peace. We're coming from Flattlands. We are on our way to GreenWater", the bearded man said as his horse wandered into the light bouncing off the wall.

"Hold on!" the guard said, and walked away from the gate.

The two riders waited in silence for a few moments. A crackling sound snapped through the dead air, followed by the squeaky sounds of the rising portcullis.

The two riders rode their horses up the rest of the hill and into the front entrance. "Whoooa", the bearded rider said, hopping off of his horse. "Thank you", he said as the guard approached them.

"What is your name?"

"I'm Wak, and this is Mosie", the bearded man answered with the butt of a chew stick hanging out of his mouth. The night sky made his dark skin look darker then it was, but the clear whites of his eyes gave him the aura of a man that is always alert. The large sword he carried on his hip is what the Brook guardsmen focused on as they sized up the two visitors.

Mosie hopped down off of his horse to join Wak's side, making himself look peaceful and approachable. Mosie was a lighter shade of brown then his partner. Standing at 6feet, 11inches tall, Mosie weighed close to 240 pounds, and the long cut he had on his right cheek made him look more menacing then he appeared to be. Wak was a few inches shorter and weighed 50 pounds less, but he was the more vocal one out of the two.

"Well, the captain of the guard has given you permission to rest until you continue on your journey tomorrow", the guard said to the two visitors.

"Thank you. We will be leaving mid-day tomorrow. Is there a place where we can water our horses?" Wak asked.

"Yes, wall guard Evan will escort you to the horse stables. Then take you over to the main hall so you can get something to eat for yourselves".

Evan nodded with a welcoming grin, "This way gentlemen".

Wak chatted lightly with Evan as they walked toward the east of the city. The streets were lightly illuminated by a few torch lamps, which enabled the two traveler's eyes to roam the area intently, but not so much where they looked like they were re-conning the city.

Wak had heard about the Brook as being a possible place Tmus might want to be in control over in the very near future. What always hindered Tmus' advancement was inside knowledge of the jungle city. Before he gave his men the green light to attack the city again he was going to need more insight on the terrain, as well as other things about the city.

Wak was feeling a rush flow through his veins because he was gathering vital information for the Industriarmy, and if he completed his mission he would be in a good position to finally make the rank of Commander in the army.

They walked into a huge barn that had tall trees on both sides, and a huge clearing behind it where the horses could go to graze at. A lone torch burned in the center of the barn, giving the place a nice taste of light, but also giving it a dangerous feel from it being surrounded by the loose strands of hay at the same time. They put the horses in empty stalls and unloaded their carry sacks. Once the horses were free of the baggage, they made their way over to the buckets of water and apples that were placed in front of each stall. Evan then took the visitors over to the main hall where they could grab something to eat for themselves.

The heavy tom-tom beats and sharp harp vibrations overwhelmed them as Wak's eyes scanned the hall in amazement. He didn't know what kind of scene they were walking into, but once they stepped inside surprise took over Wak and Mosie as people and humanals danced before them. A scene neither of them had ever witnessed before.

The rhymes coming from the right side of the hall made Wak turn and he saw Poppa Big rocking the hall crowd like a seasoned performer. Wak wanted to smack himself to make sure he was seeing correctly. Lady Light slid in her sultry vocals once Poppa Big stopped rhyming, causing Wak to think to himself her voice was almost the best he had ever heard. It could have been his loyalty to the Industriland culture that wouldn't give Lady Light her props over the celebrated Nipoly, but the light skinned beauty was blowing her words so hard she had Wak considering his position about who's the best he ever heard.

"Follow me", Evan said with his light grin.

Evan wasn't surprised by the travelers' reactions. He had witnessed other travelers react to seeing Poppa Big for the first time in the same way through his years. He himself had never traveled too far from The Brook, so he didn't know his land was the only place in Muzena with a big black bear as their leader.

Evan took the two guest to an empty table in the back of the hall and they settled in front a bowl of fresh fruit and dried cinnamon bread.

"Is this how your people enjoy each other every day?" Wak asked.

"Sometimes, but tonight is a special night for us", Evan said pouring himself a cup of wine.

"Why?" Mosie asked, speaking his first words since they walked through the front gate. He too was bewildered by the mystifying scene.

"Because we have the Queen of Pakisound and her brother the young Prince visiting us tonight", Evan said.

Wak and Mosie gave each other a quick glance, then scanned the festive crowd to see if they could spot the Queen without her being pointed out to them. One of the table hands appeared and asked what would the three men be eating?

"What was made for the people tonight?" Evan asked, clearly more interested in food than the entertainment bouncing around the hall.

"Over by the high table", Wak said under his breath, as he tapped Mosie and gave him a head nod into the direction.

Nalani danced one-two step- slide with Steven, while a smiling Zahara sat back comfortably clapping her hands to the beat.

"They will bring us some cooked snapper and greens", Evan said once the table hand walked away.

"What is his name?" Wak asked staring at the rhyming bear.

"That is Poppa Big, ruler of the jungle city and leader of the Brook", Evan said proudly.

"He is the ruler?" Mosie asked, even more dumbfounded then when he first walked in on the energetic site in the hall.

"Yes, and singing with him is his wife Lady Light", Evan added.

"And he's married?" Wak said even more confused.

"And she... she is a human?" Mosie said with questionable eyes.

"Of course she is. That's how it happens in the Brook some times. Why, that doesn't happen where you come from?" Evan asked, clearly looking like the confused one now.

"Not exactly", Wak said, not wanting to drag out that part of the conversation. "So how long will the visiting Queen be staying in your land?"

"Hopefully she will be blessing us with her presence for a long time, because word is their land was attacked and destroyed by the Industriarmy", Evan said, and poured himself another cup of drink.

Wak silently agreed, before he took a gulp of his own cup of drink. Once their food arrived, the hall was in full swing. Wak and Mosie watched the royal table as they ate their food, while Evan finished his food and jumped into a dance step with one of the jungle city women.

Poppa Big and Lady Light left the festival, while a dark chocolate woman with long hip length locks kept the celebration going. Her smoky style of sultry wordplay danced over the constant flow of the band, which showed no signs of letting up any time soon.

When Wak saw the Queen and her entourage gather themselves and head for the side door he tapped Mosie and they silently drifted away from the table. Evan was too occupied with the woman he was dancing with to notice he had lost sight of his detail.

Mosie and Wak weaved through the crowd and made it to the side door just in time to see the group turn the corner 100 yards away. They put a pep in their step, and when they turned the same corner they watched the group disappear into a large structure that told Wak it had to be the ruler's castle.

"Hey! Wait up!"

Wak and Mosie turned around and were surprised to see Evan jogging to catch up with them.

"Why'd you leave?" Evan asked as he tried to catch his breath.

"We wanted to find some place to rest, so we can continue on our journey in the morning", Wak said.

"Oh. So why didn't you say something? Follow me, I know just the place", Evan said, leading his two guests away from the castle.

Heading back to the other side of the jungle city, Wak continued to take a mental picture of every part of the city that was in his line of vision. He knew for this important information Tmus would be more than thrilled to give him a promotion in the ranks. The thought of becoming a commander in the Industriarmy was a dream that could soon become a reality, and Wak couldn't wait for his moment.

"Real soon", Wak mumbled to himself as the trio made their way over to a wooden house, and retired for the rest of the night.

$$*****$$

"Sir, they're coming back", one of the sentries called out to the commander. The small hunting group sat idly around the camp waiting on word from Wak and Mosie about the inner walls of The Brook.

"Very good", Commander Vance said in his deep dark drawl. He stood up and pitched away half eaten apple he was peeling with a knife.

Wak and Mosie rode through the high trees and bush until they met up with the rest of the group. Everyone joined the commander as Wak and Mosie hopped off of their horses. They saluted the commander and waited to be spoken to before they made another move.

"So tell me, what did you see?" Commander Vance asked with the seriousness of a human tracker locked into his eyes.

"Well commander, there was a lot of activity buzzing within those walls last night", Wak said, wanting to limit the information he would share with Vance.

"Were there any royal visitors in the city?" Commander Vance snapped, clearly frustrated with the cat and mouse game he had been engaged in.

"Yes sir", Mosie said.

"Good. Will they be staying in the city, or will they be moving on to another city?"Vance asked.

"It definitely appears as if they will be staying here for a while?" Wak quickly answered, not wanting Mosie to speak for the two scouts anymore. "They were celebrating the arrival of the Pakisound royal family, and spoke on how their presence in the city will be a boost to the allegiance between the two powers".

"Oh really? Well, we'll just see about that when the army arrives", Commander Vance said to no one in particular. He looked to be lost in deep thought as he made his way over to his horse, and stopped short of climbing on it. "And you saw the Pakisound children with your own eyes, right?"

"Yes Sir", Wak said.

"Good let's go. Tmus, and the Major will be pleased with this information", Commander Vance said before climbing onto his horse and leading the search party back the way they came.

Chapter IX

The intense flow of energy that flowed through the city of Industriland was motivated by the devoted members of the dark nation. To be part of a world take over was the most exciting highlight of most of their brain washed lives, and they were enjoying the lead up to the actual campaign. On the other hand, the supply carriers, water fetchers, and men who weren't allowed into the army silently rejected the celebrating energy around them as they did the heavy lifting around the preparing city.

Preparation for the long mission took days for the high ranking officials and organizers to coordinate. 10,000 Industriarmy soldiers were put on notice that they would be marching to the Kingdom of Soul, leaving a few hundred soldiers behind to guard the mother city. Hundreds of supply carriers guided horses and mules carrying canvases, food, garments, extra weapons and shields, and the most valued instruments that would keep the flow of industrialized beats and sounds rolling through the ranks.

The women were told to bring their children and if the child was old enough they would be used to help set up the camps and fetch the water from the lake or stream. If needed, they would be forced to pick up a weapon and assist the army in its fight if they found themselves losing the battle.

The travelers who were not a part of the army could not help but whisper amongst themselves about how the Industriarmy must have used the same type of preparation when they came to take over their land. Claims that no one would dare speak about out loud. The fear of what will become of the person that speaks blasphemy toward the ruling power was too great to face.

Within the hundreds of wagons assembled, Tmus rode in the largest one. His wagon was pulled by eight stallions and traveled in the center of the procession.

If Tmus wasn't in a conference with Major Zor and his other commanding officers or being entertained by some of the women from the traveling party, he was left alone to soak in his powerful visions. Whenever he was locked into one of these supernatural experiences, whomever was riding on the side Tmus' wagon could feel the heat coming out of the large transporter, which was as large as a servants house from the slave community in Industriland.

Tmus sat on his throne, which was bolted down to the wagon floor, with his eyes closed. The constant drum beat, rattling maracas, and humming that floated through the air soothed Tmus' subconscious mind, as his conscious mind talked to the Gods of Force for guidance into the unknown.

"I speak to you in my quest to occupy the entire Muzena, making this my duty to Industrialize these people", Tmus chanted. "There shall be no more of the independent rhythm and sounds, words and verbs that seep their way into the minds of the mentally weak".

The sounds of the industrialized beat outside of the wagon continued to pulsate around him, causing his nerves to throb with the rhythm.

"Give me the spells, speak from the dark grail. Let the souls from the home of hell scream to those who have failed." A fire began to build in his cold heart, as his eye lids flickered and his skin tightened.

"Yesss I feel your words of power. Damn those who shall choose to resist the plan you have bestowed upon me. I shall carry it out to my last breath", Tmus said, continuing to let the energy from below rise up and roll through him. Making his body a beacon that transmitted the negative cries from souls Tmus had condemned. The eery wailing excited Tmus as he let out a grotesque wail of his own that floated across the entire procession, making most of the traveler's insides quiver.

Tmus opened his eyes and stared at the wooden wall for a moment, itching to send a powerful blast from his eyes into the wall just for the hell of it. He restrained himself, remembering he wasn't in his dark tower, the usual recipient of his violent outbursts. He stood up, walked over to the draped doorway and stuck his head out, "Bring me fruit and water".

"Yes Sire", one of his female servants said quickly.

The sight of Tmus with sweat running down his bald head and bare white cheeks startled most of his people, but he didn't care. Feeling drained he plopped back down onto his throne and took a couple of deep breaths as two female servants were helped up into the wagon with a bowl of fruit, a fresh pale of water, and a bread basket just in case Tmus wanted more than he asked for

Tmus bit into a juicy cantaloupe, savoring its sweet taste. "Ahhh, Refreshing", he exclaimed with a slight grin, as the nectar from the melon slid down the side of his mouth.

One of the women handed him a cup of water and he gulped the entire cup down in one long swallow, and said, "Send for the Major".

"Yes Sire", the girl holding the water snapped, and headed straight for the door to relay Tmus' message.

Tmus grabbed another piece of fruit and sucked on its juices, as he stared at the woman holding the fruit basket. She was feeling the heat from his prying eyes, but she was too afraid to move out of his line of vision.

"What is your name?" Tmus asked.

"I am Della", the honey color beauty said.

"Ahhh, Della. Do you sing?" Tmus asked in his slow sinister drawl.

Nervous about how she should answer the question, Della shifted her weight from one foot to the other thinking about remaining silent, but everyone from Industriland either witnessed, or heard the scary and hideous stories of how Tmus loved to use his powers to create excruciating pain on people who refused to answer him. Della had no plans of being the day's entertainment.

"I...I only know how to serve Sire", Della said, trying to play it safe.

"That's too bad. You may have been able to move up in status if you did", Tmus said as he stared into her eyes.

Della refused to look him back in his eyes because word around the city was one should avoid looking directly into Tmus' eyes at all cost, because of his ability to read people's soul.

"Thank you Sire", was all Della could manage to say, then the thought hit her to move around a little. "I'll get you more water."

Major Zor and the other woman servant climbed into the wagon as Della poured the water for Tmus. "You requested my presence?"

"Yes. Leave us", Tmus said, causing the two women to stop what they were doing and quickly head out of the wagon.

"Have you heard anything from the scouts?" Tmus asked, as he continued to suck on his fruit.

"Not yet, but we should be hearing something very soon, because we are within two days reach of Dirty Gold", Zor said.

"They should be a minor nuisance. How many men do you think you'll need for that excursion?" Tmus asked uninterested.

"A few hundred, but we believe the people of Dirty Gold will happily agree to our terms of occupation, because the land is unstable in its growth for food", Zor said.

"Fine. Just get it done quickly because I want to continue on to the greater challenge on this side of Muzena", Tmus said, taking a sip of his water.

"The Brook is a greater challenge and the army is up for it", Zor said confidently.

"They better be", Tmus warned.

Not liking Tmus' tone, Major Zor was ready to get back to the front of the convoy. "Is that all Sire?"

"For now. Send the two servants back in here. I need some...entertainment", he said, laughing to himself as if his last statement amused him.

"As you wish", Zor said before he made his way out of the moving wagon.

The two women stepped back up into the wagon and stared at the dark leader. "Della...Come entertain me".

The order sent chills up Della's spine as she quickly looked over to the other woman. Tmus patiently waited as she slowly made her way over to his throne and began to fulfill his order.

✻✻✻✻✻

When Major Zor hopped out of the back of the wagon with Tmus his intention was to ride straight to his position at the front of the slow moving procession, but he was stopped along the way.

"Ah, Major. Can I have a word with you?" Nipoly asked, with her head sticking out of the side of her wagon.

"Okay", Zor rode his horse up on the side of her wagon and lightly tied the horse's reins up to her wagon. Then he climbed inside.

Nipoly's wagon was half the size of Tmus', but hers had a more homey feel to it then the dark leader had in his. In the back of the wagon, on the floor, was a neat pile of hay and blankets where she could rest comfortably. Off to the side was a pitcher of fresh water, a basket of fruit, pieces of jerky, and some fresh bread nicely arranged for the songstress. The sweet smell of incense lingered in the air around a neat stack of colorful gowns and head wraps accompanied by one of the largest traveling collections of perfumes and oils in the entire convoy.

The aroma of the incense danced up into Zor's nose as he looked around the wagon in amazement. "How did you get all of this stuff in here?" he asked.

"A woman's secret. Why don't you come in and sit down", Nipoly said with a welcoming smile on her face.

Major Zor was hesitant.

"I ahh… I have to ride up to the front of the convoy".

"Not at this second. You can sit for a piece of bread and fruit", Nipoly said. Then added, "Can't you?"

"I ahh... I really shouldn't", the Major said. Inside he was cursing himself for stepping into her inner sanctum, because Nipoly had an aura that no man was safe to resist falling into it while in her presence. Especially if he was left alone with her.

Nipoly got up off of her comforter and walked up on Zor. Her perfume hit his nose with a combination of intrigue and lust. A bad combination.

"Come on Major. You've been at the front ever since we've been on this journey. Even you need a break sometimes", Nipoly said. Then she used two fingers to gently caress the side of his face.

"Come taste the fruit with me", Nipoly said. She took his hand and pulled the reluctant Major over to the comforter.

"Okay, but just for a moment", his lips and voice managed to say. But he could feel his body in full disagreement with that statement.

"Only for a moment", Nipoly agreed. "But stop acting like it's a crime to keep a girl company for a little while", she joked.

Major Zor wasn't the humorous type, and it showed in his blank stare, but Nipoly knew she could change that if he gave her the chance.

"Here have some grapes", she said feeding him two green grapes.

Zor was shocked. He never had a woman as beautiful as Nipoly ever feed him fruit before.

"Don't look so uneasy Major. Try to relax a little", she said with a smile.

"I am relaxed...I...I'm just a little..."

"Worried that someone is going to tell Tmus you were in my wagon?" she asked cutting into his thought.

"Well...ah...yeah", Zor said before she fed him another grape.

"Oh, don't worry about Tmus. As long as I come to sing when he calls, he doesn't mind who keeps me company", Nipoly said seductively.

Zor wanted to say 'That's not what I heard!' But instead he asked, "Do you like singing for the Industry?"

Nipoly appeared to think this question over. "I love singing for the people Major, but it's a drag at times when I would like to rest and duty calls."

Zor knew she was talking about Tmus, but he kept his thought to himself. "Do you like leading the Industriarmy on these campaigns?" she asked. Now it was his turn to think about his answer.

"I don't know anything else. I was raised by the Industriarmy when I lost my arms, to one day lead it", Major Zor said realizing he had never told anybody that before.

"Wow... I never knew that", Nipoly said sounding truly interested. "So when will you get your own army and land to lead?" she asked.

Major Zor looked startled. "What? Why would you think that?"

"I don't know...I...I just thought that Tmus and the council would recognize your hard work and dedication to Industriland and maybe reward you with something you could call your own", Nipoly gently said. "That is how it works, right?"

Major Zor thought about this. "I don't know... Maybe...I mean, I've never seen anyone be granted their own land to rule before."

"But surely if anyone could be granted such a great reward for their services, it would be you", Nipoly said, and then gently kissed him on his neck.

Zor was beyond nervous as he jumped up out of his seat like her kiss just burned his neck. "I...I have to go Nipoly... thank you for the fruit", and before Nipoly could react, Zor was out of her wagon and back on his horse trotting away.

Nipoly sat there staring at the cloth doorway for three minutes before she erupted in laughter, then laid back down on her comforter.

"Don't worry Major... you will run now...but sooner, than later, you will be the one..." she said to herself, and basked in her plans of enticement for the straight as an arrow Major Zor.

"You'll see it my way soon enough".

"Major are you alright?"

"Huh?" Zor snapped out of his trance and looked over to his commander as if this was the first time he'd seen him all day.

"I asked you are you alright?"

"Oh…ah... yes commander. I will be in my wagon if you need me", Zor said. Then he rode upon the side of his personal wagon quickly tying his horse reins up to the wagon and climbing on board.

Zor knew that the sweat sliding down his back and chest didn't come from the mid-day sun. Even in the safety of his own wagon, Zor was still a little off balance by the scene that took place in Nipoly's wagon. Zor would have never thought Nipoly would come on to him until he lived through the experience like he just did.

One thing was for sure, Zor thought to himself as he washed his face in a basin of warm water, for the rest of the journey Zor was going to avoid Nipoly as best he could. Because the last thing he wanted was for one of his subordinates to use this as an in to get close to Tmus for a higher position in the army. Zor laid down to collect his thoughts, staring up at the ceiling, the Majors heavy eyes got heavier.

The night was filled with smoke as villagers ran for cover. Screams could be heard deep in the Tru-can valleys as the Roland army attacked the Tru-can people.

A young and frightened Zor tried desperately to get his wounded mother to her feet, but the woman was fading fast. Zor's small size and lack of strength made his weak attempts fruitless, as the elder woman laid there motionless.

"Mama, please get up, before the men come back", Zor pleaded, with a stream of tears rolling down his cheeks.

"NNNooooo!!!" a woman cried out in pain causing Zor to look over to the ajar door.

"Mama please!!!" He pleaded, shaking her and pulling on her arm at the same time.

The dazed woman stirred and gazed up into the eyes of her only child, "Zor I won't make it...Please...go-find-safety", she managed to say before falling into a bad coughing fit.

He ignored her coughing distraction and continued to take his stand, " No Mama!.. I won't leave you...I... I help you", Zor cried, while still trying to pull her to her feet.

"Zor...Remember I love you", his mother said with a slight grin as her eyes slowly closed.

"Come on Mama...I help you..."

Suddenly the door swung open, hitting the thin plywood wall with so much force it cracked the wall. Zor jumped up off of the floor and froze as his mother's limp arm hit the ground.

"You! Come with me!" a big man, with a scruffy sandy brown beard snarled at Zor. His sword was pointed at the young child's face, sending a chill straight down his spine.

""No! I must help my Mama!" a defiant Zor said, standing over his dead mother's body.

The large man did not expect a crying child to put up a show of resistance at this stage of the invasion. His anger quickly took hold of him as he lurched forward snatching Zor by his throat, and kicking the dead woman in her side all in one violent motion.

"Noo! Ch! Ch!", Zor tried to fight the man off, but he was to strong. "PL...Please!!! I... I can't breathe!" he cried.

"Shut up you little rodent! Before I snap your neck!" the man spat as he dragged Zor out the front door.

The streets were filled with smoke and crying death.

"Major! Major!"

Zor snapped out of the horrifying dream that had been haunting him for years and tried to focus. "Yes!?" he called out in a groggy voice.

"The scouts have returned. You would like to speak to them personally, Sir?" the voice said from the other side of the cloth doorway.

Zor shook off the cobwebs and said, "Yeah...yeah. I'll be right out."

Zor got to his feet and poured himself a tall cup of water. Once he finished it he poured another one and poured the water over his face. The dreams had been invading his rest periods ever since his land was assaulted by the Roland army. He wiped his face knowing these memories would never allow him to sleep peacefully again, because they were too painful and graphic.

The Major grabbed a few pieces of dried apple bread and hopped out the back of his wagon. The sun was descending behind the 20,000 foot tall Scabline Mountains, making the entire sky a red-orange hue. The convoy moved like a traveling city on the slow wheels of progression. This was purposely planned to help preserve the traveler's energy for the long distance they will be traveling. Zor walked over to the wagon he used to meet with his commanders and soldiers at arms and met with one of the guards.

"They are on board Sir."

"Okay. Tell the runners to prepare the convoy for the night rest period", Zor ordered one of the guards, before he caught up with the rolling wagon and hopped onto its platform.

"Yes Sir."

Present in the wagon was Zor's most trusted Commander Alhotic, and the chief of the archers, Commander Gossie. Smoke from the rolled up tobacco leaves Alhotic was smoking surrounded the two scouts- Shan and Lee- as they stood nervously in the close confines with their superiors.

"What do you have?" the Major asked getting right to it.

"They say, they left the Dirty Gold people in talks amongst themselves", Alhotic said in his husky drawl. Alhotic was a big man in size- standing at 6 feet, 5 inches tall, and weighing close to 250 pounds. He lived only for the strong dominance of the Industriarmy in Muzena and the integrity of their way of life under the powerful guidance of the Gods of Force. Whenever Major Zor did not feel like addressing the army, Alhotic was the voice that did so. He was the Major's closest friend and he grew up in the army, making this life the only life he knew.

"And what were they speaking on, war or surrender?" Zor asked getting right to it.

"They seemed to be split down the middle", Alhotic said.

"… but my guess is they might put up little resistance, before giving in to a smooth surrender", Shan added. The young scout was skinny in size and quick in movement, making him hard to detect or catch when he went out on his canvassing missions.

"Why do you say that?" Zor asked.

"Because the village elders were in agreement to surrender under the terms. But a few of the younger soldiers in their army were prepared to fight." Shan concluded.

"That means, unless the young soldier's over throw the Dirty Gold leadership before we arrive, we shouldn't have any problems out of them", Alhotic added.

"Good, because Tmus wants this done quickly so we can move on to The Brook", Zor said. "Alhotic, send in a two hundred man force, with fifty archers as a second tier."

"Yes Sir. Anything else Major?"

"And the convoy should be preparing for the overnight rest period. I will be in my wagon if anyone needs me", Zor said, he then saluted his commanders and jumped out of the back of the moving wagon. Zor wanted to be alone tonight and mentally preparing himself for a more worthy opponent in Poppa Big and his land – The Brook.

<u>Chapter X</u>

Surrounded by the thick forest she continued to run, as the loud voices and sounds cried out all around her. Her heartbeat was thumping so hard, she thought her chest was going to burst. Every breath she took made her lungs feel like she was exhaling fire. She grabbed at her chest, but it did no good. With no more options she started to run again through the forest.

But what is she running from?

What is she looking for?

She stopped in mid-stride and looked around the forest that was quickly losing light. The perspiration slid down her deep chocolate back, making her blouse stick to her skin. She ignored the discomfort her body moisture was causing and looked down at her chest. She seemed to notice for the first time the glowing heart that dangled from the solid gold chain around her neck.

She touched the heart and the voices in the forest began to get louder, but she could not understand what they were saying. 'What language is that?' she asked herself, turning her focus back to the heart.

The thumping beat echoed throughout the forest giving her the urge to hum to it. The rhythmic beat flowed in an intoxicating steady sequence.

She released the heart and tried to speak, but no words came out.

Then she tried to scream, but no sound came out.

The beat and the voices got louder. Unable to ask the voices what they were saying or what they wanted was scaring her.

Tears began to mix with the perspiration as they slid down her cheeks.

She tried to scream one more time.

"Zahara, Zahara, Wake up!"

Zahara's eyes snapped open and she found herself staring up into the concerned face of Lady Light. For a moment, Zahara did not know where she was.

"Are you okay?" Lady Light asked.

"Water", Zahara said with a dry mouth.

Lady Light reached over and poured her a cup of water. Zahara sat up on the thick comforter she slept on, drank the cup of water and looked into Lady Light's eyes.

"I'm sorry."
"For what my Queen? You only had a bad dream. There's no wrong in that", Lady Light said with a grin on her face.

"I just...I don't know... I was scared", Zahara said looking down at the ground.

"Don't worry about that...We all get scared sometimes."

"But I can't let my people ever see me scared, right?" Zahara said with her eyes full of questions.

Lady Light sat down next to Zahara and said,"No Zahara. I'm afraid not. We are our people's inspiration. We are the force that drives our people's will to protect us with their lives and build a land for us to govern and rule".

"If our people ever witnessed us having a moment of weakness- for any reason... then our position of power and leadership will be in question. And somewhere down the line a resistance might build", Lady Light told the young Queen.

"So, do you think I will ever have a moment to myself...where I...like I might be having a scary moment...but."

Lady Light saw the young Queen was struggling with what she wanted to say, so she spoke up for her. "Zahara, we all have scary moments and bad dreams, but always remember when you are in the face of the people, always stand firm in your position as their Queen and leader.

Zahara nodded, then asked, "Do you ever get scared Lady Light?"

Lady Light smiled and said, "Sometimes", in a conspiratory tone.

"But what do you do?"

"I say a silent prayer to the Gods of Song and I ask them to give me the strength I'll need to lead the people. Always in a peaceful light."

Zahara subconsciously cradled the heart with her right hand. "Do you think I will ever be able to rebuild Pakisound back to the beautiful city it once was?" she asked with a sadness in her eyes.

"Of course you will Zahara", Lady Light quickly said. "Did you forget what I just told you about being the force that drives your people to do things they never believed they would be able to do on their own?" she asked with a big smile.

Zahara giggled. "No. I didn't forget."

"Alright then. Now, when you get the opportunity to rebuild Pakisound, what are you going to do?" Lady Light asked.

"I'm going to lead my people to build a productive society", Zahara said with authority, then she smiled.

"That's the spirit. Remember, your people will always follow you, if they can believe in you", Lady Light said as she took Zahara's hand. "But a people that can't believe in their leader, will be lost and confused and they will eventually turn against you."

"So always lead with firm laws and words, but maintain your love and heart for your people."

Zahara nodded, "Thank you Lady Light."

"You're welcome. I remember when I was a young Queen with similar questions on my mind. So I know how you feel. Now come with me. I want you to meet someone today", Lady Light said with a lot of enthusiasm in her voice. She pulled Zahara to her feet and they bumped into Nalani as they stepped into the hallway.

"Well hello my Lady", Nalani greeted Zahara with a bright smile. "I was about to come check on you, but I see the Lady of the house has beat me to it."

"I'm sorry Nalani." Lady Light said returning the smile. "But I wanted Zahara to meet someone today."

"Oh, and who might that be?" Nalani asked.

"Why don't you join us and see for yourself", Lady Light said taking Nalani's hand.

The three women chatted amongst themselves as they made their way down the castle halls. Every person they passed greeted the two Queens and Nalani with bright smiles and kind greetings, before turning their attention back to their chores.

Lady Light took the two women to a big door that did not look like it had a lock on it. But she still knocked on the door as if it was locked.

"Who's there?" a voice barked from the other side.

"It's me P.D", Lady Light said, then she looked back to her two guest. "Don't worry, his bark is louder than his bite." The three women giggled, then the door clicked.

A man wearing a pair of wire rimmed spectacles on his chocolate brown face stuck his head out the opening in the door. The first thing Zahara took notice about him was the long part running through the side of his short afro.

"Lady Light you were supposed to stop by and see me week ago. How do you know I'm not busy now?" he asked with a hint of a grin on his lips.

"Number one, it was only two days ago, and two I know my favorite wizard can make time for his favorite student", Lady Light said with a smile big enough to melt the toughest heart in Muzena.

"You used your flattery card on me the last time. Who are these two beautiful ladies with you today?" he asked.

"These two ladies are guest of the house who would love to spend some time with you, because I told them you had the answer to all of their desired questions", Lady Light said, trying to entice the man.

"Oh really? They are seeking answers?" he asked sounding more interested.

"That's right. Now are you going to open the door? Or are you going to continue to be rude."

P.D. smiled, and then opened the door. "Come on in ladies."

Lady Light led the way through the steel door and down the torch lit stairwell. They descended down into the cellar dwelling in silence until they reached the bottom landing.

"Zahara and Nalani, I would like you to meet P.D. The Wizard", Lady Light said. "P.D. this is Zahara, the Queen of Pakisound, and her trusted guardian Nalani."

"Your kind of young to be a Queen", he said looking her up and down. Then his eyes rested on the heart dangling from around her neck.

"Is that a good thing or a bad thing?" Zahara asked as he shook her hand with a gentelness she did not expect to come from him.

"Not too many bad things come through the land of The Brook looking as pretty as you", P.D. said making Zahara blush. "You're just as pretty looking as your young Queen here", he said to Nalani, as he took her hand with the same gentle touch, making her blush just as hard as Zahara just did.

"Thank you", Nalani said.

"No, thank you for bringing some sunshine down here- "

"Alright, that's enough P.D", Lady Light said cutting the wizard off. "He swears he's the smoothest man in The Brook." The three women giggled, as P.D. held a look of enthusiasm. Having the women in his underground abode was stirring a good feeling inside of him.

Zahara looked around and was amazed at the colorful pieces of furniture and other unidentifiable objects in the wizards dwelling. She was sure P.D. had a method to his decorative coordination, but from a distance, it looked more like the perfect place for a mad scientist, than a great wizard.

Books, large and small in length and width were spread across the room on bookcases and two tables. In the center of the room a large oak wood table the size of a five person dining table, held the biggest book in the room. Zahara had never seen a book bigger than the book of Pakisound. If the books in The Brook were almost the size of her little brother , she could only imagine the size of the books in the Kingdom of Soul.

A medium size fire crackled in a make shift chimney, with a black pot suspended in mid air over it. Zahara was about to question what she knew she had to be seeing, but P.D. quickly directed his guests to join him over by another large table. Five glasses the size of pineapples bubbled with white smoke spilling off into the air.

"What is that?" Nalani asked, pointing at one that had blue liquid spilling out, when it touched the ground it disappeared.

"This my love, is my romance potion", P.D. said with a twinkle in his eye. "You want to try it?"

Lady Light slapped him on his shoulder, "NO she doesn't want to try it."

Zahara giggled and P.D. quickly turned to a long wooden staff. "Okay. Well this is what I wanted to show you. I've been working on it for some time now, and I think I finally have it under control."

Lady Light stared at the wooden stick, then moved up to it's gold handle. Engraved in the handle was The Brook insignia. After sizing it up she concluded it is a walking stick.

"That's nice P.D. But do you think it's time for you to be walking around with a walking stick? I thought you had at least another ten years in you before it came to that", Lady Light said with a grin dancing on the corners of her lips.

"Ha,ha,ha very funny", he said sarcastically. "For your information, this staff was made for the Queen of The Brook."

"Oh really?" Lady Light chuckled. "Last time I checked, you were the one around here with the gray and white afro."

Zahara and Nalani chuckled at the funny exchange between the good friends.

"You just reminded me; I have to make a potion for that", the wizard said as he subconsciously patted his three inch high afro. "Anyway, this isn't just any ole staff or walking stick. This, my Lady, is to enhance your powers of touch."

"I didn't know you had powers of touch", Zahara said with a surprised look in her eyes.

"I do. I try to limit its use for encounters with people I don't trust. Then I look into their person", Lady Light briefly explained, and turned back to the wizard. "So what is it supposed to do?"

P.D. handed her the staff and said, "Here, see for yourself."

As soon as she handled the staff, Lady Light could feel its energy flow through her body. "Wow… this feels… it feels like its alive", she said with a slow smile creeping up on her face.

"That it is my dear", P.D. said. Then he shuffled over to the other side of the room. "Here, aim the staff at this. Then focus on what you want to happen."

"You mean, I can make that into whatever I want it to be?" Lady Light asked.

"That's right. If you want it to disappear, then that is what will happen. Go ahead, try it", P.D. said, and he stepped away from the large bookcase he told her to aim at.

"Okay."

Lady Light aimed at the bookcase and a white flash of light shot out of the staff. The bookcase turned into a tan colored cat.

"Meow", the cat purred.

"Wow", Zahara and Nalani said at the same time.

"Can I do it again to the same thing?" Lady Light asked.

"Sure can", P.D. said with a pleased look in his eyes.

Lady Light zapped the cat and turned it into a small snake. Before the snake could slither off, she zapped it and turned the snake into a grape plant.

"Whoa P.D. it has such… a real feel to it. I can't even explain it right now", Lady Light said with a twinkle in her eyes.

"It's supposed to give you that feeling."

"But if someone else got a hold of it, then they could use it on me. Right?" she asked with a concerned look on her face.

Of course not when I said, I made it specifically for you, then that's what I did my dear. It will only respond to your touch. Not anyone else", P.D. said with a proud look on his brown face.

"Really? Well let's see. Here Zahara, you try it," Lady Light said handing her the staff.

"Always one to question the great one", P.D. said shaking his head, as he stood off to the side with a smirk on his face.

"You sure?" Zahara asked with a timid look in her eyes.

"Zahara, what did I say to you earlier when you woke up?" Lady Light asked. The two women's eyes met and the silence between the two was a moment that only they would forever know about.

Zahara shook her head. "Okay." She took the staff and aimed it at the grape plant.

"Do you feel anything?" Lady Light anxiously asked.

"No. It feels like a normal stick", Zahara said unimpressed the staff didn't work for her.

"Now can we move on?" P.D. asked.

"Okay, you win this round Mr. Wizard", Lady Light said with her bright smile lighting up the room. "Thank you."

"No problem Mrs. Light. Now, what brings you two ladies to the land of The Brook?" he asked as he stirred up a yellow colored liquid in one of his bubbling cylinders, the drunk it.

"Our land was attacked. So we are on our way to the Kingdom of Soul", Zahara said, then she giddily asked, "Please don't tell me that was some type of altering potion, that's going to make you blow up?"

The other two women giggled.

"No my love. That was just some good ole orange juice", P.D. said and he walked closer to Zahara.

"And what is that you're wearing around your neck?" he asked intrigued by the glowing gem.

"Well my father said it's the heart of Pakisound."

"I know of Pakisound. That's where you travel from?" P.D. asked.

"Yes. My father said, my mother found it in the woods one day, and ever since then it has been called the heart of Pakisound", Zahara explained.

"Can I touch it?" he asked.

"Yeah. I guess", Zahara said without any reservations.

P.D. gently jigged the gem in his hand and it seemed as if all of the life it suddenly died under his touch. "Huum, Interesting", he mumbled to himself. Then he shuffled over to the big book that laid open on the large desk in the middle of the room.

"What is it P.D.?" Lady Light asked as she strolled over to the table to look over his shoulder.

"I don't know", he mumbled to himself as he flipped through the large pages.

Zahara and Nalani walked over to also take a look at what the wizard was looking for in the book. "What kind of book is this?" Nalani asked.

"This my dear, is one of the most knowledgeable books in Muzena", P.D. said without taking his eyes off of the pages.

After a moment of silence, Nalani continued her inquiry. "You said most of Muzena. Does that mean there are others like it?"

"Yes, there's at least one in the Kingdom of Soul that's just as strong – if not more powerful in some of its scriptures, and there may be a few others scattered throughout the world", P.D. said as he continued to flip through the large pages.

Nalani and the two Queens tried to quickly scan the words and languages P.D. was scanning over, but the wizard had the advantage of knowing what he was looking for, while the three women needed more time to put the sentences together. He stopped flipping the pages for a second, read something to himself, then turned around. "Back up!" P.D. snapped.

The three women jumped back with embarrassing looks on their faces. "Give me some air." P.D. said fanning himself. "I can't breathe with you three breathing down my neck."

They giggled as he stared at the heart again.

"Zahara let me ask you something, what kind of powers does this heart possess?" P.D. asked.

"I don't know. My father said, my mom was the only one who knew about its powers, but she died one day and I guess its secret died with her", she tried to explain the little information she had.

"And you've never tried to channel in with its powers?" he asked.

"No. Why?"

"Because it looks like it's only responsive to your touch. Just like how the staff is to Lady Light's touch. But we know about her powers and what happens once they are married with the staff. But what about you?.. What kind of power do you possess?" P.D. asked with a curious look in his eyes.

Zahara felt a little ashamed. "I don't have any."

"Of course you do. You just haven't channeled them yet", P.D. said nonchalantly.

"Why do you say that?" Nalani asked.

"Because I can feel the friction a person gives off when they come around me, and from the moment you came around me I felt the friction", he said as he stared at the young queen.

"For real?" Zahara said with a surprised look on her face.

"Yes for real. Now, the only problem I have is the book doesn't mention anything about the heart. However, I'm sure if you stuck around here for a little while I would be able to help you cultivate your powers- and get them to blend with the powers within the heart", he said confidently.

The three women were silent, while Zahara milled over the idea of discovering inner powers she never knew she had. Zahara had so many unanswered questions running through her head, now that the wizard bought this news to light, but her journey was more important at this moment in time. "No, sorry P.D., but we have to get back on the road. I wouldn't feel right laying over for a long period of time when my parents are looking for me to get my brother to the Kingdom of Soul safely."

"That's even better. I'm pretty sure the Queen of High-Hop Soul can help you in the same ways I was planning on helping you", P.D. said.

"He's right", Lady Light said. "Queen Mary Jane is very powerful with the Gods of Song."

Suddenly hit with a thought, P.D. asked, "Are you going to be around tomorrow?"

"Yes. We should be back on the road in two more days", Zahara said.

"Great! I want you to come here tomorrow", P.D. said excitedly.

Zahara's face lit up. "Okay."

"Good. Now you three – shoo. I have work to do", P.D. said, as he playfully shooed them toward the stairs.

"You see this?" Lady Light asked as she made her way up the steps. "One minute he's on me for not coming down here. Now he's rushing me up out of here."

The three women chuckled all the way back up the stairs and back out into the castles main hallway. Before stepping over the cellar's threshold, Lady Light quickly spun around on her heels and kissed the wizard on his cheek, causing him to blush.

"Thank you P.D.", Lady Light said, and the three women headed back down the hallway following the strong scent of baking bread.

"The Jungle City Board is in secession", Poppa Big said from his seat at the head of the large circular table. All of the small talk around the room died down as he continued. "We have received word from one of our field scouts. Brendan will fill us in on what is going on outside of our walls."

Brendan was the highest ranking human on the Jungle City Board, and head of the front line brigade. Standing at a stiff 6 feet 3 inches tall and weighing a solid 230 pounds, Brendan was the prominent definition of a jungle city warrior who would be hard to take down in a hand to hand combat encounter.

Brendan stood up to address the board, "Thank you Poppa Big. We have received a full report from one of our scouts in the western sector, and he tells us that the small land, Dirty Gold, was overrun by the Industriarmy a few days ago."

"How many casualties?" D.Tiger asked. The red tiger had his front paws resting on the top of the table, with his hind legs on the ground, giving off the appearance of sitting on a chair like everyone else.

"He said, there were only 20 to 30 casualties", Brendan answered.

"Why so little?" Lil Kay, the Dutchess of the Brook, asked. Being the only female on the Jungle City Board, Lil Kay always made her presence felt in the room when she attended the city meetings.

"I would say, the elders of Dirty Gold were the ones who were in agreement with any peaceful surrender they could negotiate with the Industriarmy", D.Tiger interjected.

"And the young were the ones who put up the resistance", Lil Kay added giving everyone in the room a moment to digest her thought.

"What about the Industriarmy?" Poppa Big asked, breaking the silence in the room. "Now that they are occupying the land of Dirty Gold, are they returning back to Industriland?"

Brendan knew there was no easy way of sharing the tough news he had to deliver to the counsel, so he just let it be known, " No, they are on their way to The Brook."

"How big is their force?" D.Tiger asked, ready for the fight.

"The scout said, the force that attacked Dirty Gold was a very modest squadron."

"Probably because they didn't see Dirty Gold as a major threat", Lil Kay interjected.

"That was also my thought", Brendan said.

"So why would the scout believe the army is on their way here?" D.Tiger asked.

"The Dirty Gold monarchy had some people search the outer limits before they were attacked. They say word was the army is traveling with enough people to fill up The Brook, with a force that is about 10,000 strong", Brendan told the council.

"So the words I've been hearing are true", Lil Kay said in a matter of fact tone.

"That the army is seeking world dominance", Poppa Big shared with the counsel, also hinting that he had light knowledge of the army's intentions.

"Yes. It has been a known fact for some time that Tmus has a thirst to follow in his great uncle Boliy's footsteps to Industrilize the entire Muzena", Lil Kay said. "But, it seems like he has stepped up his campaigns as of late."

"I agree", D.Tiger added. "And he must feel his army is now strong enough to try us. Maybe even The Kingdom of Soul."

"Okay, so now that we know he is on his way here, we must prepare the welcome they will be looking for", Poppa Big said as he stood up.

"This is going to be the biggest battle our land has ever engaged in. I want our plan of defense, as well as our initial offense, with the management of winning every battle against them, and ultimately being successful in war", Poppa Big said with the strong eyes of a leader.

"You said, offense... Do you have an offensive plan in mind?" D.Tiger asked.

"Yes. I know Tmus will send a small reception, to try and send off the impression that they come in peace. What we're going to do is ambush them in the woods before they can make it here", Poppa Big said.

"If we do it deep enough in the woods, the army will think someone else committed the act", Lil Kay added, feeding off of Poppa Big's energy.

"That's right. And they will spend a few days combing the woods looking for the culprits. When they do, we will pick off as many of their soldiers as we can, until they catch on to our game of separate and pick off", Poppa Big said, as he paced back and forth with an animated feel flowing through his body.

Around the jungle city people, Poppa Big was the gentle and understanding big black bear that paid attention to their needs and protected them from all unwanted forces outside of The Brook. His ferocious leadership on the battlefield, and his competitive spirit helped him secure many victories for his land. Now that they were faced with going up against their biggest opponent in a long time, Poppa Big was brewing on the inside.

To defend his land against the Industriarmy, and win the war would put Poppa Big in a storied class of defenders of High-Hop, such as Queen Mary Jane's father, the great Godfather.

"That sounds like a great plan Poppa Big", Brendan agreed.

"This will give us a jump on them", D.Tiger snarled. The thought of leading a sneak attack on the most hated enemies in Muzena made his fangs drip with saliva. "We can also send out some scouts to take a rough count of their forces."

"Do you want me to send in one of mine to scout out their camp?" Lil Kay asked. "A woman might be able to penetrate their inner grounds."

Poppa Big stared at her, taking in the Dutchess' suggestion. "It sounds dangerous. Did you have someone in mind?" he asked, weighing the idea.

"Why not me?" Lil Kay asked, making everyone sitting around the table look at one another with uncertain expressions. A smile slowly crept up into the corners of the cocoa colored baby face Dutchess.

Chapter XI

"What's going on?" Someone asked out loud as people slowly made their way out into the main road.

"I don't know, but it has to be something big if Poppa Big is calling out all warriors of the Brook, to come hear him speak", another man said out loud.

A sense of urgency began to break up the peaceful and festive state that occupied the jungle city when their new guest arrived. Increased security was added around the front wall as big black kettles with cold black tar in them, were rolled out to specially built stations. Once they were locked in place, small fires were lit underneath the kettles.

Brendan walked up and down the top catwalk, barking orders as he checked every soldier's weapon that crossed his path. While the ranks of warriors moved into position to scan the forest and beyond for any approaching threats.

Word quickly spread throughout the jungle city about Poppa Big summoning the people, and humanals of the Brook to come hear their leader speak on the current state of their land. A calling of this importance was taken seriously by everyone in the city, and prejudged as a potential threat to their land's very existence.

The Game Arena quickly began to fill as everyone made their way up to the slow moving lines at its front gates. The gray five story stone structure could seat close to one hundred thousand people and was the biggest building made on the south east end of Muzena.

Conversation bounced around the moving crowds as the thick air of tension that was in the jungle city streets slowly began to hover over the arena.

"I can't remember the last time Poppa Big ever called on everyone to attend a major announcement like this", a man said as he took his seat.

"Me neither, and I've been in this city for decades," an old humanal said as he pulled in his wings so he could sit down.

In the middle of the arena field, a large platform stage held a nice array of beaticians, who steadily worked themselves up into a rhythm, slowly catching the crowd's attention. Tom Tom thumps, echoed through the stone walls of the arena, as a rattling rhythm of maracas began to fill the air. Some could be heard lowly humming to the building rhythm.

Back inside the main castle dining hall, Poppa Big had assembled the jungle city's most respected heads of state. It was important to inform them of what was happening on the outer walls of The Brook, before he set out to the arena to speak to the people and ready them for his course of action.

Lady Light sat beside Poppa Big dressed in a dark blue gown, that flowed down to her ankles, with her hair wrapped in a dark blue cloth crown. The Queen of The Brook had a concerned look in her eyes as she held their 10 month old son. The baby stared up into his mother's worried eyes, sucking on an ice stick, with his own look of uncertainty about his city's future.

Zahara and her small retinue were also in attendance, but only as observers of the meeting, not as speakers. They sat off to the side and listened to every word spoken without disturbing the proceedings.

"I would like to thank everyone for coming out on such short notice. This is a very crucial time in our city's history and I feel we must address this situation head-on, and together as a family", Poppa Big stated. As he stood up, towering over his audience at the rectangular shaped table, with his 8 foot tall frame, he placed his large paws behind his back and continued.

"We have news about an approaching threat to the Brook's sovereignty. I already had a meeting with the heads of our military to prepare our army for what looks to be the Brook's biggest battle."

"Who is it Poppa Big?" Maurice asked. The husky man was in charge of the preservation of the Brook's water supply.

"The Industriarmy", Poppa Big said without blinking an eye. Causing an eery silence to blanket the room.

Suddenly a low rumble of murmurs began to work themselves around the room. Poppa Big let the council members voice their opinions amongst themselves for a few moments before he cut in.

"I know it sounds intimidating, but a challenge of this multitude will only make us stronger", Poppa Big said, clapping his paws together for emphasis.

"He's right. A fight with the free world is biggest enemy will bring us together as a people, and bring us closer to the Gods of

Song", Keenan said, causing a slow round of head nods to circulate around the room. Being the top controller of The Brook trading market, Keenan was used to having people agree with his words of wisdom at decision making times.

"I agree", Diop said from his seat next to Poppa Big. "For years civilizations outside of the Brook have held questions about our true identity, because of our unique integration. They don't trust that we as a people have been blessed by the Gods of Song. Our defiance will show our loyalty to the Gods of Song, and the respect we demand as a strong sovereignty that will forever be here."

"Is it a possibility that we at least talk to them first, before we alert the city of an eminent war with those savages on our front door step?" Lenya asked. Being the schooling center head mistress, Lenya always thought of trying to resolve a problem, before a full scale massacre came to the city. All done for the sake of the city's innocent children. Talking with the big boned, honey colored mother of four, one could immediately feel the natural love she has for her people and culture.

"Lenya, I've thought of that. I also weighed against Tmus' long history of being a snake, and a follower of the Gods of Force", Poppa Big said looking into her eyes from the head of the table.

"Knowing how he has successfully appeared to come in peace, to many other free cities, only to leave and come back unleashing death and destruction upon the people. That is not something I'm willing to put my people through, and I should hope no one in this room feels otherwise", the black bear said, letting his red eyes roam across the room.

"He's right Lenya", Lady Light's gentle voice flowed across the table, catching everyone's attention. "Tmus is not coming all this way to talk in peace. The stories of his quest for world dominance are real."

"He's coming to take what we've worked all of our lives to build", Poppa Big said, causing an exchange of worried looks to work their way around the room, as it began to sink in as to what was really at stake.

"To help everyone here understand the seriousness of this situation, I would like the Queen of Pakisound to please join me", Poppa Big said, holding out his paw. "Zahara"

Zahara did not want to be directly involved in a emergency meeting of this magnitude. Especially sense she wasn't from the jungle city, but who could turn down an invitation from a King as big as Poppa Big?

Poppa Big took her hand, and surveyed the faces in the room. "I did not want to put the young Queen on the spot, but she is the only one in this room that has suffered an attack from the Industriarmy." Low murmurs rolled through the room.

"We did not inform the whole city about the Queen's encounter, and the devastating lost of her father, the King, and his wife... And I am truly sorry we were not there to help our brothers and sisters in Pakisound defend themselves against Tmus and his army", Poppa Big said, as he looked down into Zahara's eyes. She felt his sincerity was genuine, almost causing her to get misty eyed; but she had to hold it together in front of an important audience like this.

Zahara smiled, and said, "Thank you", so low, her words carried through the air like a feather.

"I think I speak for everyone in this land when I say, thank-you for blessing us with your presence, and giving us the strength we will need to defend our land to the end, as your people did", Poppa Big said. Then he bowed down to her, causing everyone in the room to rise up out of their seats and salute Zahara with a strong round of applause. The gesture hit the young Queen right in the core of her soul, and she could no longer hold it in. The tears slowly rolled down her chocolate colored cheeks, as Poppa Big wrapped his large arms around her.

Zahara knew she lived in a world that was full of wonder and sometimes unexplainable surprises. But to receive a loving hug from a big black bear had to finally top her list as her ultimate experience. Poppa Big had a strong emotional vibe Zahara found easy to connect with.

Once everyone calmed, Maurice broke the silence, "So what are we going to do Poppa Big?"

"First, we will go down to the arena and address the people of our land. We have to assure them that we will stand together in the face of this approaching enemy, and we shall accept nothing less than victory", Poppa Big said, igniting a round of head nods and words in agreement.

"As we speak, our brigade divisions are making the preparations necessary to secure our perimeters inside and outside of The Brook. Our leverage over them, is knowing at all times when and how their army is moving", Poppa Big said.

He turned to his wife and put out his paw. Lady Light took it and rose out of her seat. "Now ladies and gentlemen, it is time we go down to the arena, address our people and prepare them. For they will be our last line of defense."

Everyone climbed out of their seats and made their way down the hallway to the front of the castle. Poppa Big turned to Zahara to ask her to join them, and was surprised to see P.D. the wizard step out of the shadows.

"What do you need me to do?" P.D. asked, bringing a smile to Poppa Big's hairy face.

"I need you to put together every spell and mixture you can think of that's going to help us win this battle", Poppa Big said, feeling a sense of relief that he had one of the most powerful and talented wizards in Muzena on his side.

P.D. had always been a free spirit in The Brook and never joined the table at the council meetings. Instead electing to hear about what was said from the gossipers. P.D.'s main activity was to use his power to help cultivate the talent of those who were born in the jungle city with special powers. A gift that could have easily carried the wizard to the throne of The Brook. But P.D. wasn't a fan of the everyday spot light, and the charismatic big black bear with the nasty flow was.

“I already have a slew of words lined up just for this occasion. I also have some weapons for some of our soldiers”, P.D. said.

“Special weapons?” Poppa Big asked.

“Only the best for ours”, P.D. said with a smile growing in the corners of his mouth.

“Good... Come join us in the arena...”, Poppa Big said, as Lady Light and Diop listened in on the entire exchange. “I want you with us until this war is over.”

*****

Zahara stood in the background of the large stage, with her brother and Nalani close to her side. She could not believe how many people and humanals were locked onto Poppa Big's every word, as he smoothly worked them up into a frenzy. The entire building was pulsating with energy, as people cheered and applauded their leader with a sense of admiration Zahara hadn't seen since she last witnessed her father hold his last state assembly.

Looking up into the stands, Zahara was in awe of the sea of faces that rounded the stone bleachers. Whether it was a human face, animal, or a mixture of both, they all seemed to be in attendance. Zahara did not know there was that many people in the land of The Brook, and they all approved of Poppa Big's words of togetherness and defending their land at all cost.

"Can you hold him for me, please?" Lady Light asked with her motherly smile.

"Sure", Zahara answered, taking the little one off of his mother's hands. "Hey little man", Zahara cooed with a big smile. Chris giggled and reached out to touch her face. Zahara moved in closer and found herself wondering will he grow up and take on the features of his father- fur and all. Or will he remain light skinned and furless like his mother.

Poppa Big took in a deep breath and raised his paw to silence the large crowd. "My people, we have been the most peaceful family in the east, always welcoming those from other lands with open arms."

"Now our peace is being threatened by forces that want to shatter our Independence!!!" Poppa Big blasted with a passion that ignited the crowd into a frenzy.

"That's right!" Lady Light snapped, as she stepped forward. "We must not let outside forces feel like we don't count in Muzena. We do count!"

The crowd burst into another round of cheers.

"We must remain firm in our stance, and stand together!" Poppa Big growled. "We will be respected in Muzena by any means necessary!" he said, raising his right paw. The arena boomed into a thunderous applause.

Zahara leaned over to Nalani, "This is beautiful."

"Yes it is", Nalani agreed.

Prince Steven looked over to his sister and asked, "Do you think we will be able to build our land into this again?"

Zahara looked into her brothers young questioning eyes and said, "Of course we will Steven", with a seasoned Queen's confidence.

A steady drum roll began to echo well beyond the arenas walls, as a flow of horns and clarinets worked their way into the rhythm. Lady Light stood center stage with her eyes closed. A low hum slowly rose up deep from within the depths of her soul.

Zahara was immediately struck by the power of Lady Light's voice, as she hummed, then began to sing effortlessly. The Queen's voice carried for an unbelievable length, without the help of a device to help amplify it throughout the arena.

"One force// One love// I hug// My people, we walk with the truth from above// The Gods of Song are with us'til the end// Let's stand together// And fight to win// Let's stand together// And fight to win!!!"

"Poppa// My people of The Brook// Our time has come// To defend our homeland// And represent where we from// Our war drums// Will sound off from here – to west north// To let them all know// You cross our threshold at a cost// I'm the big black boss// Spread love with my people// And my Light is the torch// She's rough on the edges// But her heart is soft// Puff – Excuse my cough// We in this to win – In the land of the lost..."

"Lalaaa la la la// We are that One Force// One Love// I hug// My people, we walk with the truth from above// The Gods of Song// Is with us'til the end// Let's stand together – And fight to win!!!"

The entire arena was rocking to one of the best performances Zahara had ever witnessed. Poppa Big and Lady Light made their flow together look so easy. As if they didn't need to practice with each other, because their rhythm came together naturally. They fed off of each other's vibe, and their audience really believed in their words of love and togetherness.

Feeling overwhelmed with emotions from the beautiful scene, a tear dropped out of the side of Zahara's eye. She quickly caught it before anyone could notice it, but her little friend playing with one of her locks of hair smiling up into her face witnessed the moment.

"I know you saw that, but it can be our little secret", she said, smiling down into Chris' eyes.

The baby giggled, and Zahara could not help but laugh with him as his mother and father continued to rock the crowd into a frenzy.

The more Lady Light sang she began to glow. With her hypnotizing melody and her skin shining brighter than the descending sun behind the valley, Zahara knew she was a part of history in the making that would always be remembered.

✳✳✳✳✳

"What was that?" an Industriarmy guard asked, as he looked over to his partner.

"I don't know." His partner replied. "It sounded like a large crowd cheering."

They eyed each other, then shrugged it off. Being stationed one hundred yards into the woods wasn't very exciting duty for the two army sentries, and so far they had a quiet night on their hands. No need to ruin it.

Back at the Industriarmy camp, the sudden roar that echoed throughout the land snapped Major Zor out of his deep rest. He let his eyes adjust to the darkness, then began to realize he was laying in the back of his wagon. He got up and threw some water on his face before swallowing a large gulp of the cool liquid.

Taking a deep breath, the general tried to mentally prepare himself for the affairs that would need his undivided attention outside the private confines of his wagon. Zor put on his chest armor and head gear, then shouldered his sword.

Stepping out the back of the wagon, the general could feel the cool breeze rolling through the valley, as the sun disappeared behind the mountains. Clouds from smoked wood floated in the air, and the faint scent of meat beginning to cook traveled around the camp.

Zor needed to have a word with Tmus before he began planning his design of attack on the land of The Brook. His only concern at the moment was walking from the front of the camp, past the middle, which is where Nipoly's wagon was, and on to the back of the camp where Tmus' wagon was stationed.

The songstress has been requesting his presence ever since their encounter, but Zor had a war to prepare for. This wasn't the time to be on Tmus' bad side. Which is what will happen when word gets out he has been spending time with Tmus' favorite song bird.

To avoid Nipoly, Zor simply sent a messenger to the back of the camp when a communication was needed. But things changed now that the army has finally met up with Commander Vance and his band of trackers. They returned to camp with some valuable information about the army's next target.

Flanked by two assistants Zor made his way through the bubbling camp uninterrupted, until coming across three women preparing the night's meal of broiled beef, over an open fire. Two guards watched on, savoring to taste the apple spice flat bread the women had cooling in the night air, as they put their touches on the main course.

Everyone saluted the general as he took a close whiff of the simmering food. "Would you like a bite to eat general?" Della asked with a warming smile.

"Yes. Can you bring it in with Tmus'?" the general requested with a slight smile.

"Yes Sir."

General Zor stepped up into the wagon and found his leader in his usual meditated state. Tmus opened his eyes when he felt a presence enter the room."Ahh... Nice of you to join me general. I was beginning to get the impression I would have to enjoy the rest of my dinners on this trip alone."

"No. There are a few things we have to discuss, before we embark on our target", Zor said, taking a seat on top of a stack of pillows.

"Yesss...I know", Tmus said, folding his hands in thought. "I have received vibes of a heavy resistance being prepared in this land."

Zor agreed. "This might be true. The Brook people traditionally have been fierce defenders of their land."

"Your Excellency, your meals are ready!" one of the guards called out from behind the canvas.

"Good. Send them in."

Della and Letty brought in two plates of beef and apple spice bread. The wagon was silent as Della poured two cups of fresh water. Then the two women quickly left.

"So what do you have to say about the state of The Brook?" Tmus asked, before tearing into his beef.

"We have made contact with Commander Vance, who was tracking King Steven's children, and…"

Tmus cut him off, "Steven's children are alive?" he asked with a raised eye brow.

"It appears so. And they are special guests of Poppa Big and Lady Light", Zor said, biting into his bread.

The look of disgust was pasted on Tmus' face for a few moments, before he turned his attention back to his meal. "How did they make it this far from Pakisound?"

"They received some help from forest people. And it looks like they are making their way to the Kingdom of Soul", Zor said. "They are only resting in The Brook."

"Good, we can kill two birds with one stone when we seize The Brook", Tmus said with his chest full of confidence.

"So, how shall we proceed?"

Tmus drifted into thought, then said, "I want you to send in a small delegation. I want to see how the black bear reacts to our demands."

"And once he resists, we begin our attack?" Zor asked, knowing the answer already.

"Yesss... They will move their forces into position for battle once our delegation is on the other side of their walls", Tmus said.

"I agree. I will get right on it."

"Tonight I will summon the Gods of Force to guide our troops to victory", Tmus said, as Zor finished his meal, then stood up to leave.

"Thank you Sire. Our troops will be pleased to know they will have protection from the Gods of Force with them", Zor said, then saluted Tmus. "I'll keep you posted."

The Major stepped out of the wagon, causing everyone to stand at attention."Can I have some flat bread to take with me?"

Della smiled at the Major, "Of course sir. Would you like anything else?"

"No", a preoccupied Zor answered as he looked out across the camp. A tribal beat bounced off of the thick trees, guiding a group of villagers laughing and dancing together under the moon light.

To Industrialize a land of people was a short process that took place the moments after the Industriarmy destroyed their home. Once the people were taken prisoner, everything from the food they eat, to the garments they are to wear is immediately changed. With the main focus of change being their culture and the musical sound of freedom the people grew to love it as their own.

The mission of the Industriarmy is to strip the people of their style of social and artistic expression, bringing about a mental defeat that they will never be able to come back from. By Industrializing their arts, behavioral patterns, and beliefs gives Tmus the ability to control them for generations. Making his campaign of world dominance stronger with each mile of land he conquered.

Major Zor continued to observe the spectacle fifty yards away from where he stood, thinking about those same laws of force he had grown accustom to honoring as a soldier and commander in the army. For those few moments of watching the villagers happy in their song and dance – even though they were surrounded by their captures – made Zor wonder what it would have been like to grow up in his old family culture and traditions. Customs he was robbed of at an early age by the same army he now runs with unconditional love.

"Your bread sir", Della said, handing over a wrapped basket.

"Huh...Oh yes", Zor snapped out of his trance and took the basket.

Della gave the handsome Major an inviting smile, without looking desperate. But Zor was a man with a lot of things on his mind, and it showed as he turned away from her and headed back toward the front of the camp.

Della did not want to reveal her disappointment to Letty and the two guards stationed outside of Tmus' wagon. So she quickly busied herself with straightening out the table that was set up next to the smoking kettles. Della strongly believed the only way she would ever be able to escape from being Tmus' servant, a disgusting detail she would have to be chosen by a man of some status within the Industriarmy. But her advances on the general always came up short. Being one of Tmus' personal servants is a very demanding job.

"Bring me more meat!" Tmus shouted from his wagon.

"Yes Your Excellency!" Della said, with a distaste in her mouth.

"Hopefully the general will soon take notice of me", Della told herself, as she prepared Tmus another plate. "When he gives me a chance to prove myself, I will fulfill my duties like no other woman he has been with, and always with a smile on my face".

Della's private thoughts of the Major saving her one day from this daily depression was what kept her going. Knowing in her heart the general will treat her better than the monster she is forced to serve meant the world to Della. She never witnessed Zor publicly disrespect a woman like the rest of his underlining's in the army, and his leader.

"Ahh, Major! Can I have a word with you?" Nipoly called out from her section of the camp, where they were roasting wild turkeys.

Zor cursed himself for not paying attention to the route he was taking back to the front of the camp. "Yes", he answered, and stepped over to the side.

Nipoly wore a sexily fitting green silk gown, with her brown hair curling down to her shoulders. Zor was glad he had his assistants along side of him tonight. This would put Nipoly on her best behavior.

Nipoly walked over to him and looked at the basket. "I would ask you, if you would like something to eat, but it looks like someone beat me to it."

"Yes, I've eaten already", Zor said, trying to put on an impatient front. "If there is nothing else, I have work to do."

"Yes there is", Nipoly said, tempted to grab the general by his powerful arm. "Please join me in a private chat."

Before Zor could resist the invitation, Nipoly walked away into the direction of her parked wagon. Zor looked over at his assistant and wasn't surprised to come face to face with the typical neutral stare all the soldiers in the army give the Major. The general's private life wasn't any of their business. But Zor could never be too careful in a world where even he could lose his job, or his life to a scandal.

"I'll be right back", Zor mumbled before walking over to her wagon.

Inside three scented candles burned out a sweet smell, shining light on the clean space. Nipoly stood next to her fluffed up pillows toward the rear of the wagon, with her arms crossed against her large breast.

"Why haven't you come by to visit me?"

Zor felt awkward being questioned by a woman like this, and it showed as he shifted his weight from one foot to the next. "I...I haven't had...the time." He answered, sounding as nervous as he looked.

"I don't believe you", Nipoly said, with a pouty expression on her face.

"Nothing I can do about that", he quickly countered. "So, uh...if there's nothing else, I really must be going."

"Why are you so quick to leave?" Nipoly asked, filling the gap between them. "I know you can spare a few moments of your precious time for one of your biggest admirers."

Zor slightly flinched when Nipoly touched the side of his face.

"Come on Major. You have to know I won't hurt you", she said, slowly pushing up on him. His nose soaked in her sweet smelling perfume.

"I know you won't intentionally do any bodily harm to me, but Nipoly, I told you before, I'm not comfortable with having any type of intimate relations with you."

"Why!?" she snapped, "Because of Big Bad Tmus?"

"Exactly."

Nipoly quickly simmered down, and put her arm around his neck. "You give Tmus too much power and credit. He doesn't care about what I do Zor. I told you that. As long as I sing for him and the people of Industriland, when I'm called upon, I can do whatever I want to do on my time."

"I don't know Nipoly", Zor slowly whined.

"You don't have to know Zor. Just trust me", she said, and kissed him softly on his lips.

The couple stood suspended in their embrace for what seemed like an eternity, until Nipoly pulled back and said, "Zor, a woman has a need and a want to be shown some real affection every once in a while."

"But, why would you want that affection from me?"

"Because your powerful presence is irresistible", she growled, stroking his ego.

Zor stared into her brown eyes and couldn't help but return her smile.

"Come on Zor, give me a chance to help you enjoy our last few nights before this war begins", she said. Then she passionately kissed him again, this time pushing the bread basket out of his hand and on to the floor.

Zor pulled his head back, looked into her eyes and asked, "How do you know it's going to be a war?"

"The people of The Brook have always been resisters to the Industry. Their independence is very important to them and their mixed culture", Nipoly said, lightly rubbing her hand down the back of his head.

"So did a lot of other lands we industrialized in the past."

Nipoly smiled, "This is true, but none were as powerful with the Gods of Song in these parts, as the people of The Brook."

Zor let her words sink in, as she poured on her seductive advances to a higher level. Nipoly showered him with strong wet kisses. Slowly pulling him down on top of a stack of sleeping pillows, Zor found himself lost in her powerful grip, as she pushed down and hopped on top of him.

Nipoly slowly undressed herself, then the general before he had the chance to come to his senses. Not this time, she said to herself, as she smothered him with a lovemaking performance Zor would never forget.

When Zor finally emerged from the back of the songstress' wagon, his two assistants maintained their neutral looks, but their eyes were filled with curiosity. Nipoly was one of the most lusted after women in Industriland. But to come out and ask the general about the late night visit could earn them a death sentence.

The villagers ignored the Major's departure, lost in the small feast of wild turkey and drink, dancing well into the night.

Chapter XII

Moving through the camp with the ease of a shadow in the night, Lil Kay wore the hood to her dark blue poplin cloak, low over her eyes. After a night of good food and drink the traveling community had whined down to a few staggering drunks wondering around the sleeping camp. Smoke billowed into the night sky from the dying fires, with a lot of the soldiers and servants wrapped up in blankets stretched out under the cover of the large trees.

Lil Kay maneuvered through the strong presence of body odor and stale wine. Making it half way through the camp without being stopped and questioned by anybody, she finally got a feel of how the camp was set up.

"Hey little lady, why don't you come on over here and have a drink with me?" a slurring voice said from the within the shadows, not to far from where Lil Kay stopped in her tracks.

She tried to adjust her eyes to the moonlight fixing her vision on a hairy faced white man. "No thank you", Lil Kay said, and tried to move on.

"Come on honey, just one drink," he whined.

"Maybe next time. I have..."

Lil Kay stopped short, as the man quickly climbed up from his seat and grabbed her by the arm. "I'm trying to be nice, but I see you like it rough."

Lil Kay was now able to see the man was wearing an Industriarmy uniform, and his breath reeked of wine. "Please don't hurt me", Lil Kay pleaded in a timid tone.

Feeling a minor power surge from his quick dominance over the smaller woman, the army soldier pulled on her arm and said, "So come drink with me."

"Okay...okay", She backed down, not wanting to cause a scene and wake anyone else in the area. Lil Kay let the soldier pull her into the shadows and they sat down on some blankets. Lil Kay's eyes were everywhere, trying to quickly gather herself, as he shoved a bottle of wine into her hand, and began to fondle her chest.

"Awww, They're so soft."

Lil Kay swallowed hard, then smoothly slipped her hand from underneath her cloak. The soldier never saw the dagger flash before his eyes as Lil Kay jabbed it into his throat. His scream froze in mid-air as he grabbed her hand that held the knife.

Lil Kay jumped away from him and watched as he unsuccessfully tried to pull the dagger out of his throat. The soldier gagged and gasped, then fell silent.

Lil Kay looked around to make sure no one witnessed the man's last fighting moments.

All was quiet.

Lil Kay reached down and freed her dagger from his throat. She wiped the blade clean on his trousers, then quickly moved on before someone suddenly woke up and tried to stop her escape.

Lil Kay thought about a good way to keep a low profile, and infiltrate the large camp without being targeted by another Industriarmy soldier. She knew sleeping out in the open, like most of the camp, was not the safest way to rest around these savages, and her best bet was one of the parked wagons.

But which one? There were so many. Not knowing who was in any of them compounded the problem. She suddenly stopped walking and stepped off to the side when she spotted what looked like a camp patrol.

Absorbing the darkness around her, Lil Kay know the only way to knew who was in the wagons was to pick one, and waltz right in. Choosing the closest one to her left, Lil Kay sniffed the air around the wagon to get a feel of what was inside. Then she took a deep breath and disappeared behind the canvas.

A candle burned in the far corner giving off a shadowy light in the cabin. A sleeping figure snored lightly, bundled up on top of a hay comforter.

Lil Kay contemplated her introductory move, as she sat down on the floor Indian style. She put her face in her hands, then began a low audible whimper that slowly turned into light crying.

The sleeping figure stirred and quickly sat up. He rubbed his eyes then stared at the crying woman, not sure of what to do.

"Are you okay?" the young boy asked in a low tone.

Lil Kay pretended to be startled, "OH.. I'm sorry...I didn't mean to wake you", she was surprised to be face to face with the cocoa complexioned adolescent, with a scruffy five inch thick Afro. He was sleeping in a pair of high water moleskins and an old cotton shirt.

"What are you doing here?" he asked.

"I have no place else to go", Lil Kay said in a low tone.

"But they don't like for people to be around me. So is it okay? Did they say you can stay with me?" he asked looking for the company.

Lil Kay stared into his brown eyes and it quickly became clear to her that this was something he really wanted. "No they didn't, but they mustn't know that I am here either."

"Why not? Are you running away?" he asked in a conspiratorial whisper.

"Yes, But you mustn't tell anyone", Lil Kay said with a frightened look in her eyes.

"I won't. I promise", he said, moving in closer to her. "But do you think you can take me with you?"

She stared at him and asked, "What is your name?"

"Cory."

"Where is your mom and pop at Cory?"

Cory looked down at his hands. "They died in the war."

Lil Kay wiped her face, pulled off her hood, then moved in closer to Cory. "I'm sorry to hear that, but why won't they let you be with the other children in the camp?"

"Because of my ability to put words together and help people see the light within the darkness. Sometimes I wish I didn't have no stupid powers", Cory spat.

"Why? If your words are really that special, then you should them as your strength", she said. "If your words can energize the people, then they can also help you in your time of need."

Cory was quiet for a moment, as he continued to stare at his hands. He looked at her and asked, "What is your name?"

"I am Lil Kay."

"That's a nice name. But you still didn't say if you were going to take me with you", Cory said with the seriousness of an adult.

Lil Kay only knew the young prodigy for 20 minutes and she was already convinced there was no way she was going to leave him in this camp to suffer anymore like this. If Lil Kay made her way back to the safety of The Brook without Cory with her, she knew she would be sick to her stomach.

"Yes Cory...I will take you with me."

His face lit up as he suddenly embraced her. "Thank you Lil Kay, and I promise I won't slow you down."

She chuckled, "Okay. Now tell me what you know about the camp."

The early risers within the camp began to appear once dawn broke. A few people lit up new fires, as others made the morning trek down to the creek for fresh water. Once the young - that were allowed to make the journey – woke, then the rest of the camp seemed to come to life.

The morning patrols were out and about making sure order was maintained within the camp. The small groups of two and three man details roamed through the sections making sure all was normal at the wake of a new day.

"Hey, what's that?" one of the patrolling guards asked his partner.

"Looks like one of ours got drunk and passed out."

To come across a drunken soldier in the early morning was nothing new to the patrols. The closer they got to the sleeping figure, the more they began to realize the laying figure was not sleeping off a wild night out. The man's eyes were frozen open with his mouth locked into a scream that never came out.

"Do you know him?"

"Not by name, but I've seen him on the battle field", the patrol told his partner. They bent down to examine the cold body and the condition it was in. To find a dead body or two around the settlement was nothing to sound any alarms over. The oppressed environment bred a hazardous atmosphere filled with heavy drinking, fights, rapes, and even murders. The patrolling guards were used to finding heinous scenes in the morning, especially ones involving women.

Once they finished inspecting the body, the two patrolmen rolled the body up in the blanket it was resting on, and carried it over to the gravedigger wagon.

Chapter XIII

Poppa Big and Lady Light sent for Zahara to join them for a private breakfast. Zahara draped herself in a red and orange full length gown, and wrapped her hair with a matching scarf.

The thought of her having to leave soon lingered heavily in the back of Zahara's mind. A reality she was not ready to embrace just yet. Especially since she was beginning to get used to being dressed up in elegant gowns, and being treated like royalty again. The Brook possessed a spiritual culture that was very welcoming and easy to fall in love with- if they were able to stay.

Zahara was escorted by Santoya and an armed guard to a smaller dining room in the principle wing of the castle, where the royal family and their most trusted aid's lived.

The room held a more intimate feel to it than the bigger dining room they had eaten in. Paintings of different landscapes with bears and people mingling in them, lined the walls of the room. After close examination Zahara was convinced the figures in the pictures where family members of the royal couple.

A large fifteen seat table took up most of the room from its center. It was decorated with two bouquets of fresh flowers, and two bowls of fruit rested on top of a red table cloth. It wasn't hard to tell who the big chair at the head of the table belonged to. The hard part was trying to figure out where was the proper place for her to sit.

Not wanting to be out of place Zahara remained standing, and admired the art work on the walls. Suddenly the side doors popped open and Poppa Big strolled into the room wearing his grizzly grin.

"Good Morning Zahara...Thank you for joining us."

"You know I'm not going to turn down a breakfast with you and Lady Light", Zahara said, as she hugged him. "Where is she anyway?"

"She will be down in a moment", he said, pulling out the chair for her on the left side of his big chair. "The little one was real fussy this morning. So it's taking her a little longer than usual."

Zahara chuckled, "Oh really. He is so adorable. He doesn't look like the trouble maker you're making him out to be."

Poppa Big let out a hardy laugh as he sat down at the head of the table. "Don't worry you'll get to see him in action. That's when I want to see if you still have that easy going attitude with him."

One of the housewives entered the room carrying a tray with some freshly squeezed orange juice, and a plate of sweet smelling almond nut rolls. Lady Light entered the room two seconds later with their energetic son jumping up and down in her arms. She looked beautiful as usual in a light blue gown, lined with gold trim, and her hair was draped down her shoulders in a curly style.

"I'm sorry it took me so long, but this one wanted everything done his way this morning", Lady Light explained with a smile.

Zahara chuckled, "Well, here let me hold him, so you can take a break."

"You don't have to ask me twice", Lady Light said as she shuffled over to the other side of the table, and handed him over. Chris looked as happy to see Zahara, as she was to be holding him.

Lady Light took her seat on the other side of the table, and they enjoyed their almond nut rolls and fruit, while Little Chris sucked on a piece of orange, getting most of the juices on Zahara and himself. Zahara couldn't believe how cute he looked making a mess on them.

"So Zahara, we asked you to join us for breakfast this morning, because it's almost time for you to continue on your journey", Poppa Big said.

"And we wanted to spend a little time with you before you departed", Lady Light said, picking up where her husband left off at.

"I want to thank you two for showing me and my people so much love." Zahara said, "I would have never imagined receiving a welcome with such solidarity, after what we went through. Thank you so much."

"That's the life of our land. We take pleasure in showing our friends up with a soulful reception", Poppa Big boasted in his deep baritone. "Just like, I'm sure you and your people would have done for us."

Zahara smiled, "I hope in the future I will be able to return the gesture".

Zahara got quiet, and Lady Light could sense what was running through the young queen's mind. "Don't worry Zahara, you will rebuild your home land one day. You have a genuine love that the people will always come to. That will take you a long way in your time of rule."

"Thank you Lady Light, that means a lot to me", Zahara said, as she quickly weaved Chris' attempt to put his soiled hand on her face.

"Zahara, I see our son really likes you. That puts our decision at a comforting level", Poppa said.

Zahara shot the couple a questioning glare. "What decision?"

Lady Light looked over to Poppa Big, then back at Zahara, "We would like for you to take our son with you to the Kingdom of Soul."

Zahara was speechless.

"We know this is a lot to ask for", Poppa Big said slightly bowing his head. "But, we didn't know who we could turn to on such notice."

"We hope we're not out of order for asking you this", Lady Light said, her voice full of worry to Zahara's slow reaction.

"Oh no... I mean...no, I would be delighted and honored to fulfill your request", Zahara said with a big smile brightening up her face. "But are you sure? I mean, I'm pretty sure there are plenty of people here, that are closer to you then I am."

"You may be right, but there isn't one person from The Brook, who will feel comfortable leaving us at this time. Even if it's at our request", Poppa Big said.

"And we love that about our people. This is an important time in our existence, and everyone has to be a part of it", Lady Light said. "No one from here will leave and I'm not leaving my husband. But I trust you are the one that can take our son to safety and care for him like I would in my absence."

"I don't know what to say", Zahara exclaimed with a bright grin.

"Say yes", Lady Light said ready to cry and laugh at the same time.

"Of course I will take him with me."

Lady Light stood up and went over to the other side of the table. "Thank you Zahara. I knew from the moment I laid eyes on you the Gods of Song had sent you our way for a reason", she kissed Zahara on her forehead and took her son out of the Queens hands. "Let me get Mr.Messy here cleaned up."

"Preparations are being made for your trip. But, I would like for you to visit P.D. the wizard before you leave", Poppa Big said as he rose from his seat.

"Okay...But why?" Zahara asked.

"Because our son has an inner voice that is still being developed as he grows, and P.D. has been studying it", Poppa Big said, leading her out of the dining room. "And he will be able to explain it to you better then we can."

"I can feel it. Every time I hold him, its a vibe I get from him."

"Just like we felt that special vibe when we met you", Poppa Big said, as he lead her down the hall so she could go change, and go meet with the wizard.

✳✳✳✳✳

Zahara changed into a dark blue gown and let her hair down, before she was escorted down to P.D. the wizard's lair. Her personal guard remained out in the hallway, while Zahara was down the stairs with the wizard.

"I'm so glad you could come visit me, before you left for your journey", P.D. said, as he moved with ease around his large, but crowded dwelling.

"Why? Did you find out something about the heart of Pakisound?" Zahara asked.

"Not a lot, but enough", he said, moving from his table of bubbling potions, to his big book.

P.D.'s place looked more active today, then it did the last time she was down here. There were three rows of swords that had a sparkling powder substance on them and at least four stacks of body armor that looked unusually shiny.

"P.D. what's I in these jars?" Zahara asked as she eyed three trays of jars no bigger than an apple.

P.D. looked up from his book. "Hey...Don't touch that!"

Zahara giggled. "Okay...But what is it?"

"That is one of my special crowd controls. Now come over here, so we can get started please."

P.D. looked so cute to Zahara, with his thick spectacles and short afro. Making the rest of his colorful outfit of brown trousers, with an yellow and green shirt a desperate cry for a makeover. Zahara could see why Lady Light loved to spend time with the wizard. He was extremely light hearted, and his snappy style mirrored one from a funny uncle you visit when you need your spirits lifted.

"Now, according to the words, the heart of Pakisound is at least 10,000 years old, and it was made by one of our very spiritual ancestors named Acorn. Have you ever heard of him?" P.D. asked, looking over the rim of his spectacles.

She thought for a moment. "No. Not that I can remember."

"Well he wrote a lot of our spoken words from the spirit world, because he understood the language better than the other ancestors of the times.

"The book says, he made a few power gems with the scriptures, and after the great war, some of the pieces were stolen or misplaced." P.D. said, flipping through the pages.

"So what happened to Acorn?" Zahara asked, clearly intrigued by the wizard's tale.

"Well, as we all know the great city was destroyed and a lot of the survivors established new civilizations all over Muzena. Some of these nations adapted their own cultures and traditions, and most are still going, till this day. But apparently Acorn disappeared in the midst of that large exodus."

"What does the heart do?" Zahara asked, trying to read over his shoulder.

"Well, it says it has a very deep history of opening up doors, to very spiritual dimensions. That only the chosen can touch...."

"What does that mean?"

"It means, anyone can possess the heart, but if you're not spiritually rooted to open the heart, will be unresponsive to you. Making it useless to its possessor", P.D. explained.

"But, if you are one of the special walkers of Muzena, chosen by the Gods of Song at birth, then you will be able to open up doors to a world that only a selective few can", P.D. said.

"How do you know if you were chosen by the Gods of Song with this birth right, to be a speaker of the word?" Zahara asked.

"That is something the child's birth parents would know, and hopefully develop with the child when they're old enough to understand. From that moment the most powerful parent spiritually will begin to teach the child everything from the basics of the spirit world, to the more advanced dimensions of the heart", P.D. explained.

Zahara thought for a moment, then said, "My Mom was the more spiritual one out of my parents. But she passed before I was able to know her let alone have her tell me about myself. So do you think I can be one of the chosen ones the book speaks about?"

"Yes, I believe so", he turned to face her. "Zahara, I told you I felt a very strong energy from you when we first met. And the way the heart responds to your touch – and not anyone else's – is a clear sign you two have some type of spiritual connection between the heart and your spirit."

"But how do I... like really connect with it?" Zahara asked.

"That was a task for your mom to show you. Because somewhere down the road she was taught about how to pass on your bloodline powers. I'm just the messenger of the word." P.D. said.

"So, I'll never be able to learn how I can connect with it. Or even if I'm supposed to be in possession of the heart in the first place", Zahara said, with defeat in her voice.

"Of course you will."

Zahara's eyes rose, "How?"

"At the Kingdom of Soul", P.D. said with a smile. "Your father knew you would be taught by the powers within the jam tower, and of course Queen Mary Jane herself. That is why I believe he sent you on this journey."

"NO. He sent us because our land was being invaded by the Industriarmy."

"This is true. But I believe your father has always had this journey planned for you. This is a part of your life he couldn't raise you in, and the only place you can get clarity in it is at the Kingdom of Soul", P.D. explained as best he could. "It just so happens to be the time in your life when you're being sent away. And I'm sure he didn't want to run the risk of you being captured, or killed in the battle. So the best answer was to send you off on what's turning out to be your studies."

Zahara slowly nodded her head, then asked, "So what about little Chris? Is he chosen too?"

"Yes. He is a very special child, with very special powers", P.D. said. "He has a very exceptional mixture of bloodlines within him from his Poppa Big and Lady Light.

"Lady Light has two strong powers from the spirit world she can use as a gift of love, or a tool for war. Not counting the other abilities she has within her, which she hasn't learned how to control yet. And I don't have to tell you about how special Poppa Big is", he said with a ton of admiration for his two leaders.

"So when the little one gets bigger, what do you think is going to happen with his inner spirit?" Zahara asked.

"If I'm right about this, Little Big's defense mechanism will be one of two things: Either he will transform into a bear like his dad, or some other kind of animal or he will grow into a very destructive light of fire like his mom", P.D. said.

"But I won't be able to explain his powers to him. Shoot, I can't even explain my own powers", Zahara said with some distaste.

"That's why we felt it'll be a good idea if he goes with you to the Kingdom of Soul. You both can grow there. And the jam tower will be able to supply you both with any answers you shall seek as you both get older. This is the place where all of the spiritual leaders of Muzena matured into their spiritual selves", he said, grinning from ear to ear.

Zahara returned the smile, "Thank you P.D. for helping me. Now I want to get to the Kingdom of Soul more than ever."

"I know you do my Queen. And for the rest of your journey I want you to take this", he said, handing her a red, black, and green scarf.

"Wow...This is beautiful", Zahara said, handling the silk garment as if it was going to break under her touch.

"This will shield you and the little one whenever you need that extra support", he said with a twinkle in his eye. "Make sure you wear it at all times, until you get within the safety of the Kingdoms walls."

"I will. Thank you. And P.D..."

"Yes my dear?"

"Everyone knows you're the true chosen one", Zahara said.

P.D. laughed and led her back up the stairs. "Flattery will get you nowhere in my shop." He gave her a hug and said, "Now have a safe trip, and remember the Gods of Song are always watching over you".

Zahara nodded, then stepped into the main hallway. She was met by Santoya who was standing next to Zahara's personal guard. When P.D. closed the door behind her, Zahara was left wondering if this was the last time she would ever see the great wizard again.

"Zahara are you okay? You look like a taste of sadness has come over you once you stepped in the hallway", Santoya asked as they walked toward the guest wing of the castle.

Zahara looked over to her and said, "Only time will tell if that flash of sadness will be a lasting impression, or just a moment of reflection".

Chapter XIV

The sound of five horses trotting through the forest could be heard twenty yards away. The sun began to break through the fifty foot trees, giving the riders the light they needed to reach their destination.

The five man group had been peppered by Major Zor and his board of commanders with Tmus' non-negotiable arrangement. Their orders were to lay down Tmus' agenda to Poppa Big. Once Poppa Big refused Tmus' offer of coming under their umbrella, ending The Brooks long history of being an independent nation, they were to leave the city immediately, rejoin the rest of the army and prepare for the inevitable invasion.

Captain Andrew was placed in charge of the five man group. Standing at six feet, with a husky frame, his size complemented his salt and pepper beard as a man with rank within the army. He was designated as the primary speaker once they entered The Brook. The Major and his committee of Commanders knew they could count on Captain Andrew to deliver Tmus' message down to the letter.

"Hey Captain, what kind of women do you think they have in The Brook?" Toby asked from Andrew's side. Toby was a young soldier on the come up within the army.

The Captain shot him a side glance, took his chew stick out of his mouth and said, "Probably a bunch of humanals".

"Humanals? Really? Have you ever seen one?" Toby asked with a hint of fascination in his voice.

"No, but Dell has", Andrew answered.

"Really. What do they look like Dell?" Toby asked over his shoulder.

Dell was a very reserved soldier, who kept to himself. His dark eyes made him seem unapproachable. But Toby did not care about the serious personalities he was surrounded by. As long as he was able to soak up the knowledge the older men possessed.

"Some have a human body, with an animal head. And others are all animal, living and speaking like a human", Dell said, his voice as dark as his demeanor.

"Do real humans live and love these...humanals?" Todd asked. He was older then Toby, but still a youngster in the Industriarmy.

"Ha ha ha" Captain Andrew laughed, "Wait until you see Poppa Big."

"What does he look like?" Toby asked, trying to keep pace with the Captain.

"I'm not sure, but I hear he's some type of bear", Andrew told his captive audience.

"A bear? And he talks like a human?" Todd asked, looking over to Dell for the older man's input.

Dell did not want to participate in this line of conversation. All he wanted to do was go into The Brook and make Poppa Big surrender to his leader's demands.

"Yes he talks like a human. He's even married to a human woman", Dell said.

"He's Married?" Toby asked clearly amazed by these valuable pieces of information.

Captain Andrew let out another hardy laugh that was abruptly cut short by an arrow. The lethal shot pierced through the air and slammed Toby in his chest.

"What the..." Todd blurted out, as he watched in horror as Toby's body flipped backwards off of his horse and landed on his face without a sound.

The remaining four quickly stopped their horses and got into defensive positions.

Three more arrows shot through the air and attacked Todd in his back, his screams echoing through the thick forest, "Aaawww!"

"Show your selves!" Captain Andrew barked, gripping his sword, as eyes scanned the area. Dell and the captain took up position behind their horses, as the third soldier attempted to ride off.

"Ron where are you?" Dell's words were cut short by an arrow blowing through Ron's cheek sending him into a 360 degree spin off his fleeing horse.

"Damn-it! Come out you cowards, and face us!"

"Do you see anything?" Dell asked the captain.

Still holding his horse reins to keep him in position, "No, but it has to be coming from that area." Andrew said, pointing his sword toward the northeast section.

Dell quickly agreed. "Yeah. What should we do?" His nervousness was all over his dark face.

"We wait. Eventually they will show themselves", the captain said with beads of sweat running down his white forehead. In his mind he found himself wondering how long could he really stay in that open position without being picked off too.

High up in the thick oak tree Dell saw a few leaves ruffle. He knew it wasn't because of a sudden breeze. "I think I see something."

Andrew followed Dell's line of vision and stared into he same area. "It's hard to tell."

They were so focused on the area in the trees that they didn't feel the men approaching them from behind.

Crack!

Someone stepped on a twig causing the captain to swing into action, with Dell backing up his blindside. The two remaining horses cried out in fear and scrambled out of the way, as Dell and Andrew faced off with two men with swords and a 450 pound red tiger.

"Who sent you?" D.Tiger asked with a malign tone.

"We come on behalf of the mighty Tmus. We wish to speak with Poppa Big", Captain Andrew said, while maintaining his defensive stance.

"Well, Poppa Big doesn't want to speak with you", D.Tiger informed them, taking two steps forward.

Andrew and Dell tensed up when they felt the presence of more behind them. Dell turned his head and was quickly hit with the reality of being surrounded. Andrew stared down D.Tiger, then decided they would not be leaving the forest alive unless they struck first.

"You misfit!" Andrew spat. "I'll see you in hell!!!" then charged at D.Tiger.

RRROOAAR!!!

D.Tiger leaped with a monstrous roar as Andrew swung his sword in a east to west motion. D.Tiger's mid-air motion made everyone freeze in awe as his body spread flat, causing the captain's sword to cut nothing but air under the airborne tiger.

Suddenly the tiger's paw swung out and smacked Andrew cross his right cheek. Blood sprayed into the air from the four large claw cuts the vicious hit produced.

"AAAWWW!" the captain cried out in pain.

Dell reacted with the look of death in his eyes, side stepping a charging Brook soldier. Dell aimed at his head and swung, connecting with the side of the soldier's face with enough force to freeze his body from the shock of losing half of his face.

"Rrrrooaarr!"

D.Tiger went straight for the captains legs, as a Brook soldier swung his sword at Andrew's upper body. But Andrew weaved D.Tigers attack, causing him to miss. Swinging his sword in a counter motion to block what appeared to be an oncoming death blow.

Ching! Ching!Ching! Swords banging up against each other echoed through the dense forest, sounding off the last fighting cries of the two remaining Industriarmy soldiers.

Dell took a swing at another approaching Brook soldier, but his sword was met in mid-air by his attacker's blade. The connection sent a vibration through Dell's body and into the forest floor. Dell's brain told him to block the swing that was coming from his blind side, but his actions weren't as fast.

"AAAWWW!" Dell cried out as he watched his left arm leave his body. Another blade swung through the air with enough force to decapitate Dell before he could gather himself from his first wound. His head rolled in the grass, leaving his body to crumble to the ground.

Captain Andrew continued to battle one of The Brook swordsman, as D.Tiger roared again then jumped on his back.

"Aww..Aww..Get off!!" Andrew cried, trying to shake the big tiger off of his back. D.Tiger held on as Andrew spun around in a circle two times before D.Tiger bit into the man's thick neck.

A scream stopped short of the captain's lips, as he lost his footing and dropped down to his knees. D.Tiger locked on his neck, then ragged him for a few seconds before he let him go to fall face first in a pool of his blood.

With blood still dripping off of his facial fur, D.Tiger began to laugh at his opponents final attempt of fighting against him and his troops. "Who's the misfit now?"

*****

"Cory, come out and get your food."

Lil Kay snapped to attention, then leaned over to Cory and asked, "Who is that?"

"It's okay. That's Ms.Linda. She won't come in here." Cory said with a slight grin. "I'll go get enough for the both of us."

Lil Kay returned his grin and said, "Okay, be careful".

Cory hopped out the back of the wagon, then jogged over to a makeshift fire place. Ms.Linda had to work her magic everyday with the little bit of scraps the Industriland food ration division gives her. With her portion of rice, wheat, breads, and meat, Ms.Linda was ordered to prepare daily meals for Cory and ten other people in her campsite section.

Cory was the only child in the area and the adults were ordered to make sure Cory did not interact with any other adolescents in the camp. He was only allowed out of his wagon to relieve himself and get his food. The Industriarmy did everything short of assigning Cory a personal guard to keep him on a short leash. His direct value to the army would come in the future, but for now they felt his limited contact with the more seasoned captives should be enough to convince Cory he would never know anything else in his life but the laws and culture of Industriland. Once that is imbedded in him his submission to the Gods of Force should be an easier one.

Ms.Linda did not have any children or siblings of her own, so she looked at Cory as a little brother. She knew who Cory's mother was, but she didn't know her personally. When Small Land was invaded by the army and the survivor's were taken hostage, Ms.Linda made it her business to somehow get access to the special one. She was in the area when Cory's mom was killed by two Industriarmy soldiers; causing her heart to go out to the young boy, who was having a real hard time being isolated from the rest of the camp and losing his mom all in the same breath.

Lil Kay was with Cory for only a few hours, but the impression she got from him was a very good one so far. She never had a highly intelligent conversation with a child Cory's age before. Until she met him.

The more they spoke the more she began to see how dangerous he could be if he had the right audience to deliver his strong wordplay to. Cory spoke like a natural born leader, and when she asked him to speak in Song, he blew her mind.

Somehow, Cory's words made Lil Kay have an outer body experience, which got her to thinking about how special he would be standing next to Poppa Big and addressing the youth of The Brook.

Lil Kay peeked through an opening in the canvas of the wagon to see what was moving around the camp in the daylight hours. Smoke floated through the air from the bubbling fires, as small groups of three and four people congregated all over the sectioned off camp. Most were eating their late afternoon meals or conversing about the coming invasion of The Brook.

From her position, Lil Kay focused on any strange facial expressions, or anyone that might look like they were speaking about the dead drunk that was found at sun break. But after thinking about it and realizing where she was, Lil Kay realized there's not going to be an uproar about one dead body in an uncontrolled environment such as the Industriarmy camp. At least from where she was sitting, the camp looked like it was used to brutal incident's taking place every day.

From her little talk with Cory, Lil Kay found out a lot about the Industriarmy and its movements for the last couple of months. But she needed more.

Lil Kay needed to find out what Tmus and his higher ups were planning. The only way she was going to be able to gather better information is if she blended in with the camps night life, and mingle with its inhabitants.

Cory stood by the bubbling pot of stew and inhaled its strong aroma. Ms. Linda was always able to find some good herbs that mixed well with whatever meal she was preparing. Ms. Linda's cooking is all Cory had to look forward to most days, and she always made sure she didn't disappoint her favorite customer.

"Where have you been all day? Are you feeling okay?" Ms. Linda asked him, putting her hand on his forehead to see if he had a fever.

"I'm okay. I was tired, that's all", Cory said, while holding out his bowl.

"Let me find out you didn't want to go down and help me with getting the water this morning", she joked, then poured some stew into his bowl.

"Naw, you know I like that daily feel of water on me. It's so refreshing", Cory said, then sat down on the ground Indian style and turned his attention to his meal.

"Well, we'll be able to go down there tomorrow. The patrols won't allow us down by the water now," Ms. Linda said, sitting down next him.

Cory's eyes remained focused on his bowl as he stopped eating and asked, "Ms. Linda, do you ever think of walking away?"

Ms. Linda put down the piece of bread she was nibbling on, then looked around to make sure no one was in ear shot of their conversation.

"Of course I do Cory", she said in a hushed tone. "Why do you ask?"

"I don't know. It's just something I was thinking about. I'm seeing that during the months we've been captive in Industriland, you seem to be getting more comfortable in your roll", Cory said, as he continued to stare down at his bowl.

Ms. Linda always loved talking to Cory, because he spoke with feeling and love as if he was a full grown adult. But when you watched him talk you could see his timid adolescent ways come to surface. Like his lack of looking at her as he delivered his powerful words to his caretaker.

"It's not that I'm getting comfortable Cory", Ms. Linda looked down at the piece of bread she was picking off of and continued, "It's just, most days I wake up in this land, and the feeling of being surrounded by these people wears me down. It's like this is going to be our reality for a very long time, and there's nothing we can do about it."

Ms. Linda sounded so sad, Cory wanted to reach out and hug her. But any type of unwarranted affection was totally forbidden when it came to Cory. If any patrols rolled by their section of the campsite and saw any body hanging around Cory's wagon for too long, they would cause a ruckus about it. They would chase Cory back into his mobile dungeon.

"Ms. Linda, don't give up on our freedom", Cory said, looking up over into her face.

She let his words sink in. "I won't Cory...It's...It's just so hard to hold on to hope, when we're surrounded by so much despair."

"I know...But trust me, the Gods of Song are on our side. They will not leave us to suffer forever", Cory said with a preacher confidence.

Ms. Linda nodded in agreement, then finished off her bread. Cory finished his bowl of stew and asked could he have more. "Wow...You woke up with a big appetite, huh?" she asked, taking his bowl and filling it up with more stew.

"You can say that. I'm going to eat the rest of it in my wagon...If that's okay with you of course?" Cory said with a bright smile growing on his face. He grabbed two pieces of roman bread and slapped them on top of his stew.

"Sure...If that's what you want. But don't leave that dirty bowl in your wagon over night", she said handing him a canteen of water.

"I won't. I don't want any unexpected guest to smell your good cooking, and wander in for a sample", Cory said, giving Ms. Linda the laugh she needed to pick her head back up and move on with her day in captivity.

Lil Kay watched Cory gather up the food and drink, then stroll on over to the wagon. No one in the area gave him a second look.

"I brought you some of Ms. Linda's stew and roman bread. It's delicious", Cory said with a convincing smile.

"She wasn't suspicious about the food?" Lil Kay asked, taking the food and taking her seat on the floor.

"No. Trust me, it's okay."

"Who is she?" Lil Kay asked.

Cory sat down next to his new secret friend and said, "She's like my big sister. When they was looking for someone to watch over me, they picked Ms. Linda. I think its cause she's from Small Land too."

"Does she report to them? Does she tell them if your eating or not? Or anything you might tell her about running away?" Lil Kay asked, feeling a slight nervousness about the honey complexioned caretaker, who from a distance appeared to have a warm motherly feel to herself. Lil Kay couldn't be sure until she spoke with the woman herself.

"No...Ms. Linda is a slave to the rhythm of the army just like everyone else in this camp", Cory said. His voice was low, with his face showing the toll this life was taking on the young boy.

"Ms. Linda is the only friend I've had, since we were taken by the army. And she takes good care of me. Even though the rations of food they give her to feed all of us is very little. Ms. Linda always sacrifices to make sure I'm full by night fall", Cory said as he smiled at the burning candle, as if he could see a clear picture of the moves Ms. Linda was making for him ever since they were paired together.

"That's why I'll do anything for Ms. Linda. Because I know she'll do anything for me."

"That was delicious", Lil Kay said once she finished the stew.

"I told you. Ms. Linda can make anything taste like a delicacy. So what do you want to do next?" Cory asked.

"I'm going out tonight to see what I can find out about what the Industriarmy preparations are for my homeland."

"Can I sneak out with you?" Cory asked.

Lil Kay looked into his eyes and could see the intellectual facade that surrounded his young person, slowly began to melt with his question. No matter how mature his words were, Cory was still a lonely boy that thought a little mischief at the expense of the brutal army was no big deal.

But as she continued to stare into his questioning eyes, Lil Kay got the feeling Cory believed when his new friend stepped out into the night, she would not come back. Lil Kay took his hand so he could feel her energy.

"Cory you don't have to worry. I won't leave you in this camp."

Cory bit on his bottom lip, then nodded his head, "You promise?"

Lil Kay smiled, "I'm coming back for you. So be ready."

Cory returned the smile, "I'll be ready, you don't have to worry about that."

The two conspirators chatted until the night sky took over the light, allowing small groups of gatherer's to pop up in different sections of the camp under the light of small fires. Drums, maracas and a few mandolins could be heard playing in unison, causing a rhythm to brew around the camp.

Slipping out of the wagon, Lil Kay hugged the shadows and headed deep into enemy territory. As she passed scenes of late night festivities Lil Kay noticed the camp seemed to be free of children. Which was another indication of how dangerous the camp must be at night once the drink is in the soldier's systems, and their wandering around looking for action.

Lil Kay made her way to a section of the camp that housed a large wagon in the center of the settlement, with a few smaller wagons parked around it. Lil Kay felt this was a sign that the person riding in the larger wagon was someone of importance.

Lil Kay decided to try her luck in this section of the camp first, and if she didn't get anywhere then just move on to the next one. From how it looked, patrols were much lighter in the night, and the people were free to move around at their own risk.

A nice sized fire roared under a big black pot, and from her position in the shadows Lil Kay could smell the sweet aroma of cooking venison, brewing with some type of herbs. A few feet from the fire a curious group of people sat around on the ground as one man beat on a drum, and a woman sitting next to him rattled a pair of maracas.

Standing in the center of the group was a woman dressed in a low, red flowing dress, with yellow and orange patterns riding down the sides of her gown. Everyone seemed to be completely enchanted by the woman's presence, as her words flowed over the drum beat vibration from her two piece band, like they were married to a rhythm.

It began to work its way into Lil Kay. Her urge to move in closer got her body easing closer to the gathering. With every step she took, the harmonious melody began to sound clearer. No one paid Lil Kay any attention as she slid up on the small crowd and pretended to be a part of the group.

The only one who looked like they noticed Lil Kay make her way from the shadows, then coolly sit amongst the people, was the singer. Their eyes seemed to lock for a few seconds, then the singer suddenly closed her eyes and let out a line of notes, that made Lil Kay think otherwise.

"Fill my lonelyyy – heart// With the love I need to let be// We lost eveythinggg// It doesn't show on the outside// Just on the inside of meee// Surrounded by depression// But our souls must remain prettyyy// One day we all will enjoy our old city's// Mmmmuuum – Mmmuuumm."

Lil Kay only absorbed one verse and was already convinced the woman was a different type of royalty. Her words spoke of the pain she was feeling, even though her appearance would have you believe she was a person of high status. Most of the people in her small audience had a rip or two in their gowns or trousers, while the songbird with the beautiful voice's garment looked clean and free of any wear and tear.

Her words spoke for everyone in the camp that was being held against their will. Forced to live the life of an Industriland slave.

Stripped of their culture and the original sound they grew up with in their home lands.

Late night patrol enforcement of the Industriland doctrine must have been a minor focus after hours, Lil Kay thought to herself. Because another gathering she side stepped before stopping at the one she was attending wasn't vibing and flowing.

Lil Kay faded back into the shadows and moved on to the next settlement. The gathering in the next community resembled the same set of activities, as the last one she attended. The only major difference she could see was this gathering seemed to be filled with a lot of soldiers; which quickly made her remember her last experience with a drunk Industriarmy soldier in the late hours of the night. Knowing how much of a bad idea it would be to stop in an area with a strong Industriarmy presence, helped Lil Kay move on and try her luck in another section of the camp.

Seeking past two more settlements, Lil Kay finally came across a settlement that housed what appeared to be one of the biggest wagons in the entire procession. It sat under the watchful eye of four armed knights-men, and there wasn't a late night gathering around the fire like in the other communities. She knew someone with a very prominent position within the army lived in that wagon.

"Probably Tmus", Lil Kay mumbled to herself, then slowly worked her way around the perimeter of the settlement.

The Knights men seemed to be on point, and relaxed at the same time. A fire blazed on the far right side of the large wagon. As she got closer, Lil Kay could see two women having some words with each other by the fire. They suddenly gave each other a quick embrace, then one of them veered off to one of the much smaller wagons parked off to the side.

Lil Kay held her position and watched the security around the large wagon. Every once in awhile the guards would converse with each other for a few moments, then go back to their positions. The other woman stepped up into the large wagon for a few moments, then she suddenly emerged looking shaken as she clutched her arms across her chest. She shuffled down to the same smaller wagon the other woman had stepped into earlier and closed the canvas behind herself.

The guards seemed to share a joke at the fleeing woman's expense. Then they fell back into their duty of protecting the wagon. Lil Kay made her way around and down to the wagon the two women disappeared into. She eased up on the much darker side of the wagon and listened to the voices inside.

"Della I can't take it anymore. His touch make my skin crawl", a voice protested in between sniffles.

"Mine too. But what can we do", Della said, sounding just as helpless.

"There has to be something we can do..." The crying woman said, sounding like she was about to have a full breakdown.

"Shhh Letty, before someone hears you."

"Della, I don't care anymore. I just want to die already", Letty cried. "It will be more satisfying to be taken into the welcoming arms of the Gods of Song, then to be violated by that monster."

"Stop It Letty! Don't talk like that", Della snapped. Her voice was at a suppressed tone, but Lil Kay could tell from its force that the other woman was serious about stopping Letty from her negative thoughts.

"Letty we will get through this. You hear me? And not alone either. We will get through this together."

"But how Della?" Letty cried. This time her voice was toned down a lot more than her last outburst.

"They are planning their attack on The Brook. Once the small delegation returns, they will move forward with their invasion. When they move out to do that it will be our chance to steal some horses and food, then run away."

"But where will we go?"

"First we will return to Industriland and free Queen Taila. I promised her I would not leave her to die in that dungeon. And I plan on keeping my promise."

"But even if we do make it back, and free the Queen, where will we go after that?" Letty asked.

"Queen Taila will want to rejoin Princess Zahara and Prince Steven in the Kingdom of Soul."

The two names sent bells going off in Lil Kay's mind. So Zahara's mother was still alive, and being held in Industriland. Poppa Big will definitely want to know about this, Lil Kay told herself as she continued to listen to the two women plan their escape.

"Will the others leave with us?" Letty asked.

"Some of them will. But many are too scared of what Tmus will do to them if they're caught."

"I don't care Della. It can't be worse then what he is already doing to us."

"I know Letty...But, don't worry. Our moment is coming. And when it does, we will take it...You understand."

"Yes...I'm with you...You my sister girl."

"Now, come and let's get some rest."

Lil Kay applauded the two women for keeping each other strong in their time of need. She eased back into the shadows and headed back to the front of the large camp with a better understanding of the captives in the camp.

Lil Kay never witnessed firsthand the pain Tmus had been inflicting on the people he tried to Industrialize. He was slowly killing people with his powers, probably for his own viewing pleasure. And they couldn't defend themselves without their own energy helping them stand up against him and his forces.

As she hustled by through the camp, Lil Kay made a promise to the Gods of Song. If you give me the strength I will need to destroy Tmus, I will use it to the best of my abilities to take him down. Somebody had to stop Tmus. Lil Kay knew she might not be the one who could take him down. But she definitely would try if given the chance.

The broken souls that wondered around the traveling death camp depended on it.

Chapter XV

Night fall blanketed the city with a cool air breeze. Preparations had been worked out days in advance, and only a few elitist and high ranking members of the brigade knew of the details. The move was too important to be broad casted in the city. With the agreed upon routes of travel being very sensitive, having the traditional royal sending off in The Brook was not possible this time around. Tonight things were designed to be different as a small group gathered in the royal barn for their final good bye's.

"I'm going to miss you, my little cub", Lady Light said. Sharing her last private moment with her son was heart wrenching, but the Queen maintained her composure pretty well in front of the onlookers. She would have her moment to cry in private once she retired back to her chambers.

Lady Light rubbed noses with her little one and chuckled right on cue. "Always remember that's for me and you", she cooed with a strong smile.

Poppa Big eased up on his wife and son. "You ready?" he asked Lady Light, putting a paw around her shoulder.

She inhaled a deep breath, then let it roll out slowly. "Yes...I guess. You want to say good-bye?"

Poppa Big nodded, then took his son off of his wife's hands. Chris squealed in his dad's big paws, which brought a smile to the sad bear's face.

"Well Chris...This is it. Your first trip out of The Brook", Poppa Big said as the onlookers stepped away to give the King a moment with his only son. "Always remember you are royalty. Nobody will ever be able to deny you your right's to this land, and if for some reason I was to lose it, I know will return one day to reclaim it.

"What's that? How do I know that? Because The Brook is in your heart. This will always be with you. So embrace it, because this will always be your home", Poppa big said staring into his son's eyes.

"I love you Lil Big", Poppa Big told his son, then kissed him on his forehead. When he turned around Poppa Big was surprised to see everyone was waiting on him.

"Oh, I'm sorry. It's time right?" Poppa Big said putting on a brave face.

"Don't worry Poppa Big. We can still make good timing", Santoya said.

"Come on and give me my kisses", Lady Light said, taking her son out of his father's hands. She flooded his face with kisses, causing Chris to giggle with delight. "You be good...And I love you." She kissed him again, then took him over to Zahara.

Lady Light put on a strong grin as she handed him over. "He's all yours."

"Don't worry Lady Light. I will do as you asked", Zahara said with a comforting look in her eyes.

"I know you will", Lady Light said. Then she hugged Zahara and Chris sending a surge of energy flowing through the three of them.

When Lady Light stepped back Zahara saw a tear in the corner of the Queen's eye, but it would not fall. "Zahara thank you. And may the Gods of Song bless you."

Zahara nodded, then handed Chris over to Nalani.

"Come on little one", Nalani slipped the toddler into the carrier Zahara wore on her back. Then they helped the young Queen onto her horse.

Horses were provided for everyone in the traveling procession, except Prince Steven, who was to ride with Gond. Zahara felt more at ease knowing her brother had an experienced rider guiding him to the Kingdom of Soul, than Steven being out on his own.

They wanted to keep the group small, so only a few more travelers were added to the procession at Poppa Big's request. Santoya was labeled Chris' aunt, and if anything was to happen to Zahara, Santoya would step up in her absence. Santoya served the King and Queen of The Brook long enough to know any history Chris would need to know as he gets older. Santoya had her own personal love for the baby she helped deliver into this world, making Lady Light and Poppa Big's request to join the traveler's a welcoming one.

The three Golona warriors were good security, but Poppa Big needed to add two of his trusted men to the journey, to put his mind more at ease. Poppa Big was a nervous wreck about his son leaving the nest for the first time without him and his mother. So no one was going protest about being sent out on a mission of such importance.

Poppa Big selected one of The Brook's best swordsmen by named Grant. His skin was as dark as the night and he wore a thick head full of long lox. Standing at 6 feet 4 inches tall Grant was an intimidating looking man when you also weighed in his 210 pound frame. Grant was a man who mixed his size and gift with a blade well on the battlefield, and was always rewarded for his achievements defending his homeland.

Red Ryan was also selected by Poppa Big to travel to the Kingdom of Soul. A skilled archer who lacked the big size of his partner Grant. Red Ryan only weighed 175 pounds and stood at 5 feet 9 inches tall, but made up for it on the battlefield with his accurate shooting and cunning movements through the forest. Many believed the brown skinned man was given the name Red because of his red hair. That was until seeing him in the annual shootout held in The Brook. That is when Red Ryan really showcases his skills and shoots a red apple off of the head of someone standing 2000 feet away.

Poppa Big hugged Lady Light and they watched as the group of ten were escorted out of the barn and headed for the front gate. The portcullis was raised, giving the group a clear pathway. Grant and Tusi lead the way, with Gond and Steven right behind them. Zahara, Nalani, and Santoya were the middle core of the group, with Red Ryan and DanDan bringing up the rear.

The full moon provided a nice silhouette for the beginning of their journey, but Grant knew once they reached the eastern part of the forest and its tall trees, the only line of light that was going to be helpful to the group was the torch light he carried guiding them. The front portcullis lowered as the tower guard watched the red light float into the trees and disappear.

Chapter XVI

Lil Kay hid out in Cory's wagon for another long day, then she stepped out into the night to comb the camp for more information. It seemed like every night, by night fall, the young children were put to bed, and the camp's squatters would set up in little groups to converse amongst each other. They played a little of their homeland music, share some drink, then turn in for the night.

Lil Kay mingled with a few groups, but never stuck around long enough to come under question as to who she was. She probed the ones she felt were open enough off of the drink, giving some of them the ear they needed. Talking about the everyday feel of despair that ran rampant in the camp gave Lil Kay a strong sense of everyone being tired of the current circumstances.

The thing that stopped people from speaking their mind about their harsh treatment and horrible living conditions was the thick cloud of fear that floated over their heads.

But she could feel it. If the right person emerged from within these troubled souls, Lil Kay felt that could be the right piece of motivation these people would need to form a coup against the Industriarmy from within. She just hadn't run into that person yet.

The one person Lil Kay felt was a good candidate for the job was Cory. His words of strength and freedom, and why it would be important for them to stand up together against the force that was trying to Industrialize them, would move any group of oppressed people to stand up against their oppressor. But Cory was too young and only a hand full of the elders would take him seriously.

Moving through the camp, Lil Kay decided to focus on finding the right person who had small influence with the women and men who weren't fully Industrialize yet. This person would be a big help to her people and The Brook brigades. Especially if they could build up a minor campaign from within the camp. While the army is out attacking The Brook, Lil Kay could get the people to destroy the camp. Then possibly leave, or help us by attacking the army from behind.

As the nights wore on, Lil Kay continued to move around the camp with a strong sense of freedom, which saddened her because she knew the good people she was mixing and mingling with lost their sense of freedom, and desperately wanted it back. Lil Kay maintained her composure every night, and tried to stay focus. The future of the captured souls by the Industriarmy depended on her strength.

Going through the faces in her mind of the people she had come across since she has been in the camp, Lil Kay found herself thinking about the honey complexioned singer who voice was hypnotizing. The woman seemed to draw people to her, but she didn't leave an impression on Lil Kay strong enough that told the Dutchess of The Brook she possessed that killer instinct needed to start a coup.

Before Lil Kay totally disqualified the woman as a potential alley, she wanted to have a few private words with the singer. The shadows shielded Lil Kay well enough for her to make it to the singer's wagon undetected.

The deep night had befallen upon the camp, with a lot of the small gatherings breaking down. Two Industriarmy soldier's sat around a fire outside of the singer wagon with a few women. Lil Kay took note of having seen the women sitting outside with the singer under the light of the fire every night she canvassed the camp. They seemed to be having a good time, but the wrong step could alert the guards to her presence. So Lil Kay moved lightly around the group.

Lil Kay got as close as she could, without sticking her face in the wagon. Then she put her ear to the canvas to listen in on what was going on inside.

"So do you think he will give you the next land you invade for him?" The woman's voice was clear enough for Lil Kay to determine it was the singer speaking.

"Nipoly, I told you before I don't know about something like that happening, because there is no one that could lead the army in my absence."

"Come on Zor, every man has to be recognized for his accomplishments."

"This is true, but I don't see Tmus granting me a position like that."

"How do you know, if you don't ask?" Nipoly asked in a low tone. "A closed mouth don't get fed Zor."

They were quiet for a few moments, then Zor said, "Your right Nipoly. I'm going to ask Tmus about me obtaining my own land. I can start my own piece of history in the name of the Gods of Force. But I know he's not going to honor my request until after we capture The Kingdom of Soul."

"As long as you say something to him now, because you will feel passed over, if you accomplish all of these for the army, and the land is given to someone like Solomon to govern", Nipoly said.

Zor sucked his teeth. "That swine can't govern a stream of water. That incompetent fool is probably ruining Industriland right now as we speak."

Nipoly giggled, "You might be right, but Tmus still trusts him enough to govern the land in his absence".

"I don't want to talk about him anymore", Zor said.

"Okay, so what do you want to talk about?" Nipoly asked. Then her voice dropped down into a seductive tone, "You want to talk about this?"

Lil Kay could hear kissing sounds, then Nipoly asked, "What's wrong – you still uncomfortable?"

"Nipoly, if Tmus finds out about this, I don't know how he's going to react."

"Zor, I told you before. Tmus doesn't care about me. He's only interested in my voice."

"And that's enough to make any man fall in love with you."

Nipoly giggled, "Come on Zor, you know Tmus doesn't love me."

"You'd be surprised by who loves you in this land", he said with a chuckle.

Lil Kat thought Nipoly was going to take the baited question. But she dismissed Zor and said, "Are you going to come see me before the invasion?"

"I will try, but I don't know when it will be. We still haven't received word from the committee we sent with Tmus' demands."

"Well, I'll be here waiting for you", Nipoly told him. More kissing sounds could be heard through the thin canvas walls; then the wagon rocked a little, followed by a set of footsteps heading toward the rear of the wagon.

Lil Kay dipped underneath the wagon and watched the strong legs of Major Zor jump down out of the wagon. "Let's go!" she heard him say. Then Zor and his two guards hopped onto their horses and galloped toward the front of the camp.

Lil Kay waited for a little while before she got up the nerve to move from under the wagon, and slip inside of it.

Nipoly was laying on her thick comforter, basking in the after incandescence of spending some private time with Zor. A few candles set the tone with a warm glow. As a heavy scent of sweat lingered in the air, Lil Kay could tell the couple had shared an intimate moment together before she arrived.

Sensing someone was watching her, Nipoly opened her eyes, then sat up. "What are you doing here?" she asked in a soft voice.

"I don't mean you any harm. I would like to talk to you", Lil Kay said, pulling off her black hood to reveal her coca colored baby face.

Nipoly wrapped a silk top across her bare top. "You have watched me sing a few times", she said nonchalantly.

"Yes." Lil Kay confessed. "You have a very beautiful voice.

"Thank you .What is your name?"

"I am The Dutchess Lil Kay from The Brook."

Nipoly's eyes shifted. "That is why I've never seen you in Industriland. So why are you here?"

Without wasting any time, Lil Kay went right to the point of her sudden appearance. "I was hoping to free the people from within. With your help of course."

"My help? Ha, I'm no rebel my dear Dutchess. I'm a songstress. So I don't see what kind of help I can be to you", Nipoly said, standing up and wrapping the rest of the silk garment around her exposed body.

"Your songs tell me otherwise."

"That's because my songs are about our freedom, and my voice is for the people. They depend on me to carry them on to the next day", Nipoly said moving over to a pitcher of water. "Would you like something to drink?"

"Yes. Thank you."

Nipoly poured them each a cup, then said, "Come sit with me."

Lil Kay accepted the invitation and sat down next to the songstress. "Lil Kay, I love my deprived people of Industriland. Mainly because some of them are from my homeland. But I'm no leader of them", Nipoly said in soft voice.

"Nipoly, a lot of leaders are not conscious of their powers and strength to move the people out of their state of depression", Lil Kay said, matching the softness in her voice as her hostess.

"Nipoly, I've seen you sing, and I can tell from your ability to hold your audience captive that the power is in you. You can move people with your words to stand up and they will follow."

Nipoly stared at her cup for a long time in silence. Lil Kay could tell the woman was weighing the situation in her mind, and she did not want to interrupt her. Lil Kay remained quiet, as a steady thumping sound could be heard traveling through the sleeping camp.

"I don't even know how I would start what you are asking of me", Nipoly said finally breaking the silence.

Lil Kay looked over into her eyes and said, "I can help you."

"But why do you want to help us?" Nipoly asked. She was pretty sure she already knew the answer. But she wanted to hear it from the little woman's mouth.

"Because an uprising by the captives of this camp – while the army is attacking my land, will give the Industriarmy two battles to fight at the same time. And my leader believes that will be to much for them to handle."

Nipoly slowly nodded in agreement. "I see what your vision is. But I want you to remember, this camp may have a lot of people that will fight for their freedom, but there are also many who will not."

"Because of Tmus", Lil Kay said.

Nipoly nodded. "Yes, he has imbued a state of fear amongst the people that is the culture around here. And many will not go against the power he has over us."

"This I know", Lil Kay said. "But if we motivate enough of them, I think the rest will follow."

Nipoly stared into her eyes and knew the woman was serious about the words she was speaking. Lil Kay gave her the impression of a person who was willing to go all the way for her beliefs.

"Lil Kay, I have dreamed of separating myself from the grips of Tmus for a very long time. And many days I'm left realizing it's an impossible feat." Nipoly said. "But, tonight you brought in an air of possibility that I haven't felt in a long time. I know if I can trust you, then the people will trust you...So...I will do it."

Lil Kay smiled. "Thank you Nipoly. I promise you, together we can make a difference in the living conditions of the people in this camp."

Nipoly looked into her eyes. "Lil Kay, for all of our sakes, I hope you're right. Because if you're wrong, we all just signed our death sentences."

Chapter XVII

The next morning Major Zor woke up with a sense of worry flowing through his system. Something was wrong. He could feel it. They hadn't received word from the negotiating party they sent to The Brook with Tmus' demands. Which was very unusual, because Captain Andrew was one of the most thorough soldiers in the Industriarmy. A mission of this importance would not be carried out to the tee, and he would stick around there behind enemy lines for too long.

Major Zor emerged from the back of his wagon sporting the look of a man who was ready to take care of business. His two armed guards snapped to attention, then hopped right in step with the general. They headed straight for the Commander's wagon without saying a word.

"Major", Commander Alhotic greeted Zor with a firm salute. Alhotic was usually the first one in the Commander's quarters for their meetings.

"Alhotic, have we heard anything from Captain Andrew and his party?" Zor asked, as he strolled over to a small table that held a pitcher of fresh water and some dry apple bread.

"No sir. I was thinking we might hear something from the captain and his party today", Alhotic said, clouding up the wagon with his first leaf roll up for the day.

"Something is not right", Zor said as he sat down and nibbled on a slice of apple bread.

"You think those humanals will try to hold the captain and his party prisoner?" Alhotic asked.

"I don't know. I've never dealt with these type of people before. A lot of them are part beast, and that beast blood might be doing the thinking for them", Zor said, feeling unsure about the entire situation.

"Do you want to send in another group?" Alhotic asked the general. "We can send in a bigger one this time."

"That sounds like a good idea", Zor agreed. "And we send out a scout with strict orders to travel in the shadows of the group. He is not to enter The Brook with the group, and if things don't look right he is to return to the camp immediately."

Commander Alhotic nodded in agreement, "I will put that together immediately."

The first knight, Fungi, stepped up into the wagon and saluted both men. "How are things looking with our next venture?" Fungi asked, grabbing himself a slice of apple bread.

"Excuse me", Alhotic excused himself, then exited the wagon to put together the group for the next operation.

"We are in the midst of putting together another party to send to The Brook", Zor answered.

"Why? What happened to the first one?" Fungi asked with a surprised look on his bearded face.

"That's what we want to find out", Zor said. "Fungi, what do you know about Poppa Big and the humanals?"

Fungi was born into the Industriarmy. Hence the right for him to become a first knights man within the army. He sat down across from the general and said, "Not much. I think when it comes to information about The Brook we've been in the dark about a lot of things, because this is a part of Muzena we haven't traveled to since the days of Great Uncle Boliy."

"Our focus has been on the western parts of Muzena", Zor added.

"From what I've heard through the years, the people of The Brook are fierce fighters", Fungi said. "But I don't think they've been tested by an army as large as ours."

"I don't believe so either, but that doesn't mean we underestimate these humanals", Zor said with a taste of disgust in his mouth.

"Of course not sir. Is there anything you need me to do today?" Fungi asked, as he stood.

"I want you to make sure the army is ready to move out on a moment's notice", Zor answered." Med and Alhotic will get to the bottom of what happened to Captain Andrew and his party. If something did happen."

"Yes sir", Fungi saluted the general, then left him to his thought's.

Nipoly's words had been running through Zor's mind all night long. He did not know why Nipoly was so interested in Zor having his own piece of Muzena all of a sudden. But her words did run true.

One had to tread lightly when dealing with Tmus. Zor did not have an approach for a delicate meeting like this, and he needed to have his words together before he went to his leader. Tmus' photographic mind allowed him to remember everything, then enter your mind if you don't live up to the words you spoke to him.

Zor needed some air, and a nice ride around the large camp would give him a sense of independence and duty at the same time. Stepping out of the commander's wagon, Zor took a look around. A lot of the Industriarmy soldiers and commanders were working out or running through a few drills of hand to hand combat preparation. Zor took in a deep breath of the clear fresh air, and let his thoughts flow with the energetic scene before him.

A troop of soldiers came jogging through and Zor watched with admiration. The Industriarmy had come a long way since he has been at the helm. Major Zor's firm position on every soldier being physically prepared for the journey toward world dominance had been a welcoming one by Tmus and the governing body of Industriland. Giving him free reign to build the army into the powerhouse everyone in Industriland could be proud of.

"Aim! Fire!"

Zor looked over to his left and watched as three rows of archer's took target practice on makeshift targets posted on some trees.

"Aim!- Fire!"

As the first row of archers released their shot, they would step back and let the next row of archers unload on the same target. Major Zor made his way over to the Commander's post, with his two guards close on his heels.

Commander Gossie saw the Major approaching the post and decided to meet him halfway. "Sam take over for me."

"Yes sir."

"Morning Major", he greeted Zor with a salute.

"Morning Commander. How are they looking?"

"They're looking more ready than they were a year ago", Gossie proudly said.

"That's good. Make sure they're ready to roll out in a few days", Zor said.

"Yes sir. Did word come back about The Brook's status?"

"No. We are sending in another committee, to see what happened to Captain Andrew and his party", Zor said. The two leaders strolled away from ear shot of the other soldiers, with the general's two personal guards stepping over to give them some space.

"You think something went wrong with the first committee?" Gossie asked, as he played with his chew stick.

"In my gut – yeah. But we don't know for sure yet. How are things within the camp?" Zor asked.

Gossie was head of the Industriarmy's massive battalion of archers. Even at the top of the ranking's Gossie was still well in-tune with the lower rankings of the army. Word had it that Gossie had spies within the army that kept him abreast of everything that occurred in and outside of the army.

"Everything is rolling along, but the need for more food might come up in a few weeks. I figure we should be within the walls of The Brook by then", Gossie said nonchalantly.

"I don't want to underestimate The Brook."

"Neither do I, because we don't know their army's capabilities yet. But the strong belief of survival should be preached to our troops in more ways than one to give them the sense of urgency they'll need to go in there and hammer them", Gossie explained with his view of wisdom.

"Procrastination will be costly this time around", Zor added in a matter of fact tone.

"I agree."

"What about the regular ones?" Zor asked. He never referred to the Industriarmy captives as such, or slaves. Always the regular ones.

The two men stopped strolling and Zor could feel the sun's rays beaming down on him through the tall trees. He told himself it was going to be another hot day in the tropical forest.

"They're holding up pretty well with keeping the camp going."

"What about the sounds of their native music I've been hearing during the nights?" Zor asked. The question made him sound more concerned, than he actually felt. Since he was promoted to the Commanding Major of the Industriarmy, there never was a worry of their captives reverting back to the cultures and traditions they were stripped of.

"Do you want it to stop? I can put together a patrol that will put an end to any late night activities", Gossie said. Zor always liked Gossie's loyalty to Industriland. Any lawlessness within the walls of Industriland would be dealt with an iron fist. And the commander took great pride in making sure every order was carried out with bloodshed if need be.

"Yeah..I do", Zor said. "We can't have these people believing they can serve the Industry when the sun is up, then return to their independent roots by night. That will create camaraderie amongst them."

Gossie nodded. "I agree. I will put some men on it tonight."

They stood there quiet for a moment and Zor could tell his commander had something else on his mind. "What's wrong Gossie?"

"Well...Not to be in your business or anything like that, but what about when the patrols go to the Songstress' section of the camp?"

"What do you mean?"

"Well, she does have the biggest following at these night get togethers. And I hear most of the songs she sings are native songs", Gossie said.

"And that's what we are trying to stop here, right commander? No one gets favorable treatment. Not even her", Zor snapped. The thought of what he and Nipoly did under the shadows of the night, made Zor feel vulnerable.

Gossie stared at the general, giving him the look of not being a fool. He knew about Zor and Nipoly having meetings together, but he couldn't come right out with it, because even though Gossie was a well respected commander within the Industriarmy he could still find himself in a bind if he speaks the wrong words.

In Industriland everyone was expendable to the Major and Tmus.

"Understood. I just thought that Tmus might have an objection with us going to disrupt the songstress", Gossie said.

"Nipoly and her section receives the same treatment as the rest of the camp", Zor said. "And don't worry about Tmus. I'm on my way to speak with him now. I will explain the crackdown, and he will agree", he added confidently.

"Yes sir."

"You may carry on with the exercises commander", Zor said, indicating the end to their private meeting.

"Get the horses."

On his ride through the camp Zor replayed his conversation with Gossie in his mind. If the commanding officer was talking about his relationship with Nipoly, then it was safe to say Tmus was also in on his late night escapes with the songstress.

Zor knew Gossie was smarter then he appeared to be in their talk. His felt was Gossie might have saw through Zor's reaction when the discussion turned to Nipoly.

He couldn't display his true feelings for Nipoly. The bottom line was, no matter what Nipoly did on her leisure time, she still belonged to Tmus.

True feelings.

What are my true feelings for Nipoly? Zor asked himself. But he was too scared to answer himself, because then he would bite his tongue about the call he made to clean up the gatherings at her section of the camp. Blocking all thoughts of her, Zor and his two guards rode up into Tmus' section with his focus back on the army and their task at hand.

A fire was already going with two women servants working on the day's batch of fresh bread. Down the hill from the settlement a lot of activity was moving to and from Tmus' wagon, to a stream of clean water. A hand full of Tmus' knights men were engaged in a mid-day workout session, while a few others sharpened their weapons under the hot sun. The general's presence brought a succession of salutes from the troops, as the captain of security stepped up to greet Zor.

"Major is it time?"

Zor hopped off of his horse, "Not yet captain. However, I still want you and the rest of the knights-men to be prepared to move out on a moment's notice", the general ordered. "I look forward to knocking down there in the next few moons."

The anticipation of a battle brought a smile to the captains rotten tooth mouth. "Yes sir. We are ready when you need us."

"How's his Excellency?" Zor asked.

"He's maintaining his spirit's. I can tell, he can't wait until the battle is underway."

"Has he had any visitors?" Zor asked.

"No one out of the ordinary. Just the usual board members and he ordered Nipoly to come sing for him last night. Other than that its been nothing but preparation up here."

Her name raised his eyebrow, but that was the most emotion the general was going to show at the mere mention of her name. Nipoly must have been summoned by Tmus after Zor left her last night.

"His Excellency is being washed right now. Would you like for me to announce your presence?" the captain asked.

The aroma coming from the cooking pots caught Zor's attention. "You may captain. I will wait until they're finished."

"Yes sir." The captain saluted Zor, then made his way over to the wagon, as Zor wondered over to the tables where the two women were preparing the day meals.

"Good day Major", Della said with a bright smile on her face.

"It smells good over here", Zor commented, as his eyes surveyed the tasty layout he couldn't see from a distance.

"Are you hungry? I have some smoked trout that's ready", Della said. She didn't wait for his response, as she quickly hustled over to the pot and put a tray together for the general.

"Yes, that would be nice."

Della was always amazed at how respectful Major Zor presented himself when he interacted with the women servants of Industriland. Della figured a man of his stature would be as mean and verbally abusive as the army he leads. But that wasn't the case, making this manly quality highly attractive to Della.

Everyday Della played scenarios in her mind on how she can escape the creepy clutches of Tmus. Her most personal scenario was being chosen by Zor, or a man of rank and stature in Industriland. Della knew her days would go by much easier if she was chosen by the Major to work in his sector. But instead of him seeing her value, Zor always seemed to look right through her, and this frustrated Della to the point of anger.

Della made Zor a healthy tray of fresh fruit, smoked fish, and the morning bread. "Would you like some water or drink?" she asked handing him his food.

Zor took the tray as if she wasn't there. "Water", is all he said, as he dug right into the fish.

Della shuffled off and the Major found himself watching the slender brown-skin beauty. "How does your food supply look in this sector?" Zor asked.

This wasn't the kind of question Della was looking for to spark a conversation with Zor, but she would take it. As long as he recognized her for something more than her good tasting breads.

"It looks like it can last us about two weeks. Do you think we will get a food stimulus before then?" Della asked, feeling a little comfort from making herself look busy.

"Hopefully, if everything goes as planned", Zor said, turning his attention back to his meal.

"How's your trout?" Della asked trying to fill the silence.

Zor swallowed a mouth full. "This is delicious. Ah, what is your name again?"

"Della how could you forget that?" she asked with a playful smile.

Zor cracked a rare smile. "I'm sorry. It's just, every time I turn around Tmus has a different set of attendants. So it's hard to keep up."

"I understand", Della said. Then she waited for what seemed like an eternity for Zor to say something else to her, but his interest turned back to his food.

"Would you like some more?"

"Ah…Yes, but I have to go inside", Zor said rising up from his seat.

"That's alright. I will have it wrapped and ready to go when you're done", Della said, putting on the best smile she had to offer in years.

"Okay", Zor said, walking off to Tmus' wagon.

"He is ready for you Major."

Zor nodded, then climbed into the wagon. The air inside was warm, with a steamy coat floating around. Incense burned an aromatic fragrance that gave Zor's senses a relaxing feeling as soon as he inhaled it.

Tmus sat in his chair bare chested, looking refreshed. His porcelain skin glistened, as one of his servant's rubbed oil on his back and bald head. Tmus raised his hand, "That's good enough. Leave us."

The woman nodded and quickly grabbed a few items, before climbing out the back of the wagon.

"How is everything looking up front?" Tmus asked. He dug into a bowl of fresh fruit and picked out an orange.

"Everything is ready; we're just awaiting word from the committee", Zor reported.

Tmus raised his eyebrow. "We still have not received word from the committee?"

"No. I put together another one this morning. I also sent out a scout to trail them", Zor said.

"And they left already?" Tmus asked.

"Yes Your Excellency."

"Good. Mobilize the first wave of attack", Tmus said without any hesitation.

"Without receiving word from the committee?"

"Poppa Big knows we're here. He'll never comply. He will depend on the Gods of Song for guidance", Tmus said. "And they will tell him we will apply our force to make him and his people submit to our life of Industrialization."

Zor nodded. "I will put together a seven thousand man wave when I return to the command post."

"Good. Tell Fungi to have my escort ready", Tmus said, sounding like he was ready to step out onto the battlefield at a moment's notice.

"Yes sir", Zor said, then he stood in silence, staring down at the ground. Tmus could see his general had other issues on his mind. So Tmus continued to suck on his orange until Zor got his thoughts together. He tossed aside the dry orange, then grabbed a fresh one, and continued to patiently wait.

"Your Excellency, I've been thinking. I've been with the army all my life."

"And we are grateful for your presence", Tmus said when Zor paused.

"Thank you. I was thinking...after we Industrialize The Brook, do you think I can finally have a piece of land I can govern?" Zor asked. Feeling the awkward air thicken in the wagon.

Tmus was silent for a long time. He continued sucking on his orange until it was dry, then he tossed it to the side. He stared at his general, then asked, "You no longer have the desire to lead the army?"

"Of course I do...But, I've been thinking about what a great asset I would be to the Gods of Force, if I was able to build a piece of history within the Industry", Zor said looking up into his leader's haunting eyes.

"It will be with your blessings, under the traditions of Industriland that I will be able do something new and prosperous for our culture."

"I knew this day would come when you would grow into a new chapter in your life. This is why you were chosen to lead the army Zor", Tmus said. "Your ambition for growth."

"I would like the opportunity to begin the development process to build another land. One Industriland can depend on as a sister territory."

"Zor there is no one more deserving than you when it comes to the discussion of having their own territory to develop", Tmus said with a glimpse of sincerity in his eyes.

"But the march to the Kingdom of Soul has been the road layed out to us since the beginning of time. That is history", he declared with conviction in his voice.

"This is true, and I've been blessed by the Gods of Force to be a part of the reviving of this historic campaign", Zor said with pride. "I would just like the opportunity to show my abilities in another form."

"You sure this sudden change of interest doesn't have anything to do with Nipoly?" Tmus asked without a hint of emotion in his dark voice.

The air was so still it seemed like the smoke floating up from the incense froze right before Zor's eyes. He did not know how to respond, and Tmus didn't give the Major any indication on his true feelings. Tmus' blank stare remained unchanged as he waited for a response.

"Why would it have something to do with Nipoly?" Zor asked, trying to feel his leader out.

"Ha,ha,ha", Tmus let out a sinister laugh, without the extra theatrics of a smile and said, "Zor, I am the ruler of this land because I don't let anything or anyone get in the way of my vision. Not even some sweet words from soft skin and beauty."

Zor just nodded and said, "I understand."

"Do you? or have you fallen victim to the flesh?" Tmus asked. His eyes seemed to be on the verge of turning red, but his anger seemed to be still under control.

No matter how much he prepared himself for this discussion, Zor still was not ready for the direction the conversation was headed into. No one was worth getting into a skirmish with the leader of Industriland. So the Major remained silent.

After a brief silence Tmus said, "I will have to share your desire to move on, with the Gods of Force, but, that won't be until after we take over The Brook".

Feeling like he should accept that answer and be satisfied, Zor nodded and said, "Understood sir".

"Zor remember, the flesh can be destroyed at anytime, but the pleasure is in capturing the soul."

Zor understood too well what Tmus meant by his last resolution. Zor had witnessed Tmus exert his powers too many times on people who had crossed him and Industriland. Capturing their souls and feeding it to the Gods of Force was ministered daily in Industriland.

Without having anything else to say, Zor quietly nodded his head again. Then he slowly backed up and climbed out of the wagon. Leaving the wagon the Major found himself having more baggage on his mind, than when he first went inside.

Seeing the Major exit the wagon, Della grabbed the package she wrapped for him and tried to make her way across the open area to hand it to him personally. Not liking her aim of direction, the captain cut her off.

"Where do you think your going?" he asked her stepping into her path.

"I...I have this package of food for the Major, like he requested", Della said with a slight nervousness in her voice.

The captain looked down at the package. "Oh yeah.. Well I'll take that", he said snatching the package from her. "You go back to your duties over the fire."

"Yes sir", Della said in a defeated tone.

The captain put an end to any hope Della had to interact with the Major one last time before he left. Zor didn't look her way as he and his two guards hopped onto their horses.

"Let's go", Zor ordered without acknowledging anyone in the area. Not even the captain.

"I guess he didn't want the food after all", the captain said chuckling. Then he ripped it open and helped himself to the goodies, as Zor and his guard's road off to the front of the camp.

Chapter XVIII

Commander Alhotic put one of the up and coming captains in charge of the second committee. His strict orders were to pull out if things did not look right, and the scout was trailing them to be the second line of communication back to the camp, just in case the group did not make it back.

"What do you think happened to Captain Andrew and his group?" Boyd asked Captain Samuel as they lead the way through the forest.

"I don't know. I would hate to see what's going to happen to them if we find the captain and his group feasting, and drinking wine with those humanals", Samuel said.

Boyd laughed, "The commander and major definitely won't take those actions lightly".

Commander Alhotic wanted the second group back at the camp by the next day's noon moon. Motivating the group to ride through the forest with a purpose. Grass and dirt kicked up under the steady pounding of the ten man team that rode in a two man formation.

The scout stayed far behind the group, trotting at a leisure pace. He wanted to give himself ample space where he wouldn't lose them, and he wouldn't be too close to be seen with them.

Captain Samuel's mind was focused on the carnage the Industriarmy was going to bring to the people of The Brook for disobeying his leader's demands. Then he was on the road he was leading his small battalion down. Samuel's horse kicked up a wire, setting off a small barrage of arrows. Six of the horses squealed in pain, as bodies flung from the crumbling animals.

AAAWWW!!!

The agonizing cries of the men and animals hit by the onslaught rocked the entire forest, causing the scout to stop in his tracks. The eerie cries sent a chill up his spine; making him continue forward with more caution.

Captain Samuel and his horse took a nose dive forward, giving him no time to break his fall. His face hit the ground as dirt and dust exploded into the air. Clearly shaken and disoriented, Samuel tried to crawl out from under his fallen horse.

"What's happening?" Samuel said out load, as his vision began to clear up in the dust cloud. The captain saw five of his men disembark from their horses, and jump right into sword to sword combat with a group of soldiers.

Samuel tried to free himself from under his dead horse, but the task seemed to be easier to accomplish in his mind than in real life.

RRRRROOOAAAR!!

A loud roar blasted the captain on the side of his face causing him to close his eyes. The fear he felt flowing through his body had never been present in Captain Samuel's life before that moment. He slowly opened his eyes and found himself face to face with a red faced tiger.

"What the..." Captain Samuel mumbled in pure shock.

D.Tiger lashed out with his paw, cutting open three straight lines on Samuel's cheek. With another swift swipe of his paw, D.Tiger snapped the captain's neck, killing him instantly. Satisfied with his work the red tiger moved on to his next victim.

The ambush proved to be too much for the Industriarmy soldiers, forcing the survivors to attempt a surrender.

"Okay! Okay! We surrender!" one of them cried out as he raised his hands into the air.

"RRRRROOAARR!" D.Tiger barked, as he jumped on the soldier from his blind side.

"Ahhh!! NNOOOO!" the soldier cried out, before D.Tiger silenced him with a swift bite to his neck.

The rest of The Brook fighters fed off of their leader's aggression, and finished off the last Industriarmy soldier with a barrage of cuts and chops from their bloody swords.

All was still by the time the scout reached the horrific scene. He hopped off of his horse and tried to hold it steady, as D.Tiger sniffed around the fallen to make sure everyone was really dead, as his men searched the bodies and their carry pouches.

"D.Tiger, someone is watching!" one of The Brook men cried out from his position high up in the tress.

D.Tiger quickly followed the man's line of vision and spotted the motionless scout. The red tiger broke out into a sprint, with two of his men hot on his heels.

The scout quickly scrambled back onto his horse and made a mad dash back into the direction he came. "Yaw! Yaw!"

D.Tiger picked up his speed, diving forward over a fallen tree bark, missing the scout by a hair. The fleeing scout did not realize how close he was to being swept out of the air, as beads of sweat suddenly appeared on his forehead.

"Yaw! Yaw!"

D.Tiger continued to give chase until he realized the horse's head start was too much for him to catch up to. He stopped running, giving some of his men time to catch up to him.

"Who do you think he was?" one of his men asked out loud.

D.Tiger continued to watch the fleeing horse until they were out of sight. "Probably back up to the team we just took down."

"So what do we do now?"

"We return to The Brook and prepare for the invasion", D.Tiger answered, before walking off.

The war was on.

✶✶✶✶✶
___

"So how much longer are we going to stay here?" Cory asked Lil Kay.

"I have to make one more trip, then we can leave", she answered, as the pair sat under the candlelight in the back of his wagon.

"I think Ms.Linda knows someone is staying with me in this wagon", Cory said staring down at the empty bowl of food they just shared.

"Why do you say that?" Lil Kay asked.

"Because...It's just the little things...Like lately she hasn't asked me to go down to pick up the water with her. And I didn't ask her for a second helping yesterday, she made the bowl and said just bring it back when I'm finished."

"But did she ask you about someone being in here with you?" Lil Kay asked, looking uninterested. Lil Kay was more worried about getting Nipoly to start a revolt from within the camp, than she was of Cory's caretaker knowing about her presence. Lil Kay saw the sadness in Ms.Linda's eyes and knew if she walked up into the wagon and found Lil Kay there, she would go along with the plan once she found out Lil Kay was going to sneak her and Cory out of there.

"No...Not exactly", Cory said after some hesitation.

"So don't worry about it", Lil Kay said. Then she stood up and peeked out of the canvas. The elders were out gathering around a fire, as the night's activities seemed to be winding down.

"I have to go", Lil Kay said, pulling on her black hood. "I'll be back." She winked at him and slipped out of the wagon. She was glad to see Cory finally sporting a smile. When she first met the young boy he looked like he was ready to give up hope on a moment's notice.

Cory sat there in silence marveling at his luck to meet a woman like Lil Kay, who was willing to help him get out of captivity. Just a week ago Cory thought he was going to die from loneliness in that small wagon. Now his future was looking a little more promising.

Cory had witnessed firsthand what the Industriarmy will do to people when they come in to Industrialize the city. This led Cory to question Lil Kay on why she would help him escape, only to bring him to her land which was next in line to be invaded.

Lil Kay simply told him to trust her. "The Brook is the safest place on this side of The Kingdom of Soul", she told him. The genuine look in her eyes won his heart to do so.

Cory didn't know what Lil Kay had planned for the rest of the camp, but whatever it was she seemed more satisfied with her findings every time she returned from her late night excursions. Whenever Cory would ask her about her plan, Lil Kay would smile and say, "Freedom".

That would spark a long conversation between them about freedom and the people living under the beautiful culture and traditions of High-Hop, and how the Industriarmy has watered down the cultures of others in the past.

"Cory? Cory?" Ms.Linda called out from the other side of the canvas.

"Yes?"

"Can I come in?"

"Sure Ms.Linda", Cory said, as he remained sitting down Indian style.

Ms.Linda climbed up into the wagon, then let her eyes roam. "Are you okay?"

"Yeah...I was just sitting here thinking that's all. You're not going to sit around the fire tonight?" Cory asked.

"Nah...I wanted to hang out with you for a while tonight, before I turned in", Ms.Linda said, sitting down on the floor across from him. "I see you ate all of your food."

Cory looked down at his empty bowl, then suddenly remembered he had to get rid of Ms.Linda before his guest returned. "Oh yeah, it was delicious."

Ms.Linda was quiet for a moment, then she said, "I saw her leave Cory."

Cory did not respond. He stared into her caramel colored face and wondered what she was going to do now.

"You don't have to worry though. I think I'm the only one who has seen your friend come and go", she said with a smile.

"You're not mad at me?"

"Of course not Cory", she said scooting next to him. "I'm glad you have someone to talk to in here. I just want you to be more careful that's all. Because if one of the others find out, they will report it to the soldiers."

"I want you to meet her, but she said its not time yet", Cory said.

"What do you mean she said its not time yet?" Ms.Linda asked looking confused.

"I don't know, but I do know she's going to help us get out of here", Cory said confidently.

"Oh yeah? And how is she going to do that?" she asked unimpressed. "How many have we seen try to leave here and end up in the dungeons of Industriland...or worst – killed."

"I know Ms.Linda. I've thought of the same things. But its something about Lil Kay that tells me she's sincere about helping us, and think we should trust her", Cory said.

"Lil Kay, huh? And what's her plan?" Ms.Linda asked.

"I don't really know everything there is to know about it. But I do know she is taking us with her when she returns to her homeland", Cory said.

Ms.Linda chuckled. "Boy, she must've really touched your soul, because I haven't seen you this animated in a long time."

Cory smiled, "That's why I want you to meet her. So you can feel the energy and hope I feel when I'm with her."

She ruffled her three inch afro and said, "As long as I have you to look after, I will always have hope." She stood up and took his empty bowl. "Now get some rest. I have a feeling the army is ready to attack the next city.

"Good night Ms.Linda."

She smiled as she stood in the doorway. Ms.Linda hadn't heard the departing gesture in a long time. It made her feel some type of normalcy, even if it was for ten seconds.

"Good night baby."

Cory laid down and stared up at the roof of the wagon feeling like his current circumstances were about to change, and he couldn't wait until it did.

Lil Kay stood outside of Nipoly's wagon in the dark shadows of the night, listening for signs of movement inside. She knew Nipoly was waiting for her, but Lil Kay still had to be cautious not to walk into a trap.

Inside Nipoly began to hum a rhythm to herself. Lil Kay listened for a few moments, before checking to see if the coast was clear. Once she was satisfied, Lil Kay climbed up into the wagon.

"I didn't think you would come", Nipoly said in a low mellow tone.

"It's hard to move around this camp sometimes. May I sit?" Lil Kay asked.

"Sure, would you like some bread and berries?" Nipoly offered, as she got up and moved around her mobile home with ease.

"Yes. Thank you."

"Did you know the army has implemented a crack down on our late night gatherings?" Nipoly asked, handing Lil Kay a small basket with two honey rolls and some berries in it and a cup of water.

"I've heard something about that. Why?"

"A tactic to stop us from keeping our culture alive", Nipoly said, then took her seat on a thick stack of hay laced comforters. "You know, their whole body of work is to Industrialize us. Strip us of our music, our cultures, and our traditions under the soulful testaments of High-Hop", Nipoly tried to put on a brave smile, but Lil Kay could still see the songstress's pain in her eyes.

"Nipoly, how long have you been in Industriland?"

Nipoly looked off into space as if she could see her memories appear on the canvas wall, then said, "I've been here since I was a teenager. My land was invaded, like so many others I've watched the army conquer. That was about eight years ago."

A cold shiver washed over Nipoly's body. She wrapped her arms around herself, then rubbed the chill. "Why do you ask?"

"Because you don't strike me as a voice that has been fully Industrialized yet", Lil Kay said.

"That's because my talent has grown strong, and I know how to control it even under the watchful eyes of Tmus and his council. See, Tmus and the council's mission is to make everyone in Muzena live, think, and sound the way they feel is prosperous in Tmus' superior takeover", Nipoly explained. "Hence forth the birth of an Industrial life of traditions.

"Now when it comes to me, Tmus fell in love with my voice so much, that the rules became a little lenient over time."

"This may be true, but I'm pretty sure there have been other women who had voices just as beautiful as yours", Lil Kay said.

"Yes, there has, but they haven't been around as long as I have, because I was captured at a young age. And most of the other women were way older", Nipoly said. "It's easier to Industrialize the young, than the old."

"I see."

"Once Tmus gave praise about how the Gods of Force will grant him extra blessings for the possession of my voice within Industriland, the council immediately signed on", Nipoly said.

"But ultimately Tmus makes the final decision in Industriland, right?" Lil Kay asked.

"Yes. The council are just members, who are the face of the government in Industriland. They hold positions that have been in that land for generations", Nipoly said. "They have, some say, because Tmus doesn't like dealing with the everyday dictation. He likes to be in control of the death and destruction part of the people."

"Which are the takeover campaigns", Lil Kay said in a matter of fact tone.

"Exactly."

"I guess the question now is – Are you ready to change history?" Lil Kay asked with the serious look of a teacher in her eyes.

"I have to be ready", Nipoly said with a little bit of confidence in her voice. "If I'm not, then who will be?"

Lil Kay smiled. "That's the attitude you have to have Nipoly. Because if your followers don't believe you're in it 100% and you will lead them to a better place...then they will not follow."

"I know", Nipoly said looking down at her hands. "Like I told you before, I'm no rebel...But I do understand the power of my influence."

She looked up into Lil Kay's hazel colored eyes and continued, "I know they believe in me Lil Kay. So I have to work for them to help both of us get out of this bad state we've been living in for too long now."

"I've been hearing the army is gearing up for their attack. So we have to move with some urgency", Lil Kay said.

"What do you need me to do?" Nipoly asked, finally ready to stand up to her captors.

"Tonight, I want you to start with the people you know, who will fight with all their heart. They will be your chamber of support. And they will help you work on the others."

Nipoly nodded, "Okay".

"You will wait until the army is engaged in battle with my people in The Brook. Then you will make the call to overpower the remaining guards in the camp." Lil Kay said, feeling the power of her plan coming together as she laid it out to the songstress.

Nipoly nodded in agreement then said, "I've been thinking...If we are successful with freeing ourselves, then where will we go?" Every place in south Muzena has been destroyed and Industrialized."

"The Kingdom of Soul", Lil Kay said, bringing a smile to Nipoly's cocoa colored cheeks.

"I've heard nothing but good things about the Kingdom of Soul for as long as I can remember, but I've never been there."

"It's a little journey from here to the Kingdom. But, when you and your people reach it, I know you will be welcomed with open arms", Lil Kay said. "There, you will be given the chance to rebuild your lives – independently."

The two women strategized their plan of attack on the group of soldiers the army would leave behind to maintain order in the camp. Then they snuck out into the night to go visit one of Nipoly's first recruits. They made their way to a wagon one hundred yards from where Nipoly's wagon was stationed, and climbed inside.

"Who's there?" A man's voice called out in the dimly lit wagon, as he sat up.

"It's me Pham", She said in a low tone.

"Nipoly? What's happening?" Pham asked as he wiped the cold out of his eyes. "And who is this?"

"This is Lil Kay. She's going to help us get free."

Pham hadn't heard those words spoken out loud in a long time. His freedom was something Pham had been dreaming about for a long time, and to finally hear it come out of the woman's mouth that he idolized immediately grabbed his attention.

"I'm listening. How are we going to do this ?"

✷✷✷✷✷

By the time Lil Kay made it back to Cory's wagon it was almost sunrise, and she was so tired she just wanted to lay down and rest. But her mind wanted to keep going. Lil Kay knew she was running out of time if she was going to make it back to The Brook before the Industriarmy arrived. Once the front portcullis was closed to seal the city in, the only way it would reopen was by force. And she did not want to be caught on the wrong side of the gate.

As soon as Lil Kay climbed into the back of the wagon, Cory woke right up. "I didn't think you were coming back."

"I told you Cory, I would not leave you here", Lil Kay said with sincerity in her eyes. "Are you ready?"

"Right now?" Cory asked, hopping up from his hay comforter.

"Yes, right now", she said, not wanting to smile too much, because their escape was a serious matter. But Cory looked too happy for Lil Kay not to share a smile with him in this great moment.

"We have to take Ms.Linda", Cory said standing up to face her.

"We are. But we have to hurry, before the camp begins to wake up."

Cory suddenly hugged Lil Kay. "Thank you Lil Kay. I will never forget this...I am indebted to you for the rest of my life."

Lil Kay found herself blushing when he let her go. "We'll worry about that later. Right now we have to go."

They sneaked out of the wagon, and quickly made their way over to Ms.Linda's wagon. Cory climbed in first, then Lil Kay followed once she felt the coast was clear.

"Ms.Linda", his voice and movement around her made Ms.Linda snap out of her heavy sleep.

"Cory? What's wrong?" she asked looking around her dimly lit wagon. Her eyes suddenly focused on the short woman she saw sneaking in and out of Cory's wagon.

"We have to leave", Cory said.

"To go where?" Ms.Linda asked, grabbing her cotton top to cover up her bare breast.

"To The Brook", Lil Kay said.

"Who are you?"

"I'm sorry for this little intrusion. I am Lil Kay, The Dutchess of The Brook, and I will have to make it up to you when we reach our destination."

Ms.Linda stood up still feeling a little hazy. "Okay, I'll go. As long as you know Cory is my first priority", Ms.Linda said as she quickly began to get herself together. "His safety is my prime concern. So can you guarantee us a safe journey?"

Lil Kay liked the woman already. She was glad Cory had someone to look out for him in this dangerous environment. "Ms.Linda, if I said I could guarantee we will make it out of this camp and off to a happy ending, then I would be lying to you. And I don't want to start off our relationship on that kind of note."

"What I can tell you is...this is your chance to take your freedom back. And that is something you have to be willing to take and die for", Lil Kay said.

Cory watched the two women go back and forth, and he was beginning to feel a new form of energy he hadn't felt in a long time. Ms.Linda looked down at him, and Cory grinned, then nodded his approval.

Ms.Linda didn't have to trust the woman she just met, but she did trust the young boy she had been looking after. "Lil Kay thank you for being honest with us. If Cory believes in it, then I have to go with it."

Lil Kay smiled, then Cory finally spoke up. "So can we leave, before the patrols start making their rounds."

"Okay...okay", Ms.Linda said wrapping her hair up in a bun. "I'm ready."

The birds were out chirping with the rising sun, as the threesome climbed out of the wagon and made their way through the sleeping camp, to the densest part of the forest.

The War   .

We shall stand together and fight as one.   .

Chapter XIX

Poppa Big sat in the jungle city boardroom alone, under a low fire. Watching the orange and red flames relaxed the black bear, giving his mind a sense of calm before the storm.

Being the leader of one of the most beautiful cities in Muzena came with many gifts along with days where Poppa Big felt like he was going to lose control. This was one of the latter.

Knowing Tmus and his army were camped out in the forest a few miles from his homeland, made Poppa Big very uneasy. The Industriarmy tried to Industrialize The Brook when the Great Uncle Boliy was the leader of the army. Back then The Brook withstood the assault, and rose up to become a stronger nation.

Now they were back, and this time they had a much larger army of followers then the days of Boliy's rule. Not only were they stronger now, but their tactics had changed. This caused Poppa Big to change his tactics, by sending D.Tiger and some men out into the forest to intercept any unwelcome guests.

So far he hadn't received word from D.Tiger, which didn't worry Poppa Big. The big red tiger was one of the most dangerous creatures in Muzena. With the speed of a cheetah and the cunningness of a deadly hunter, D.Tiger could handle himself really well against any group Tmus sent to present his demands to the people of The Brook.

Poppa Big did find himself worrying about Lil Kay and the mission she was sent on. The Dutchess is one of the smoothest female humans Poppa Big knew. She is a skilled fighter, who rose through the ranks of The Brook brigade, and became the first female member of the Jungle City council. Making her a loved asset to Poppa Big and the people of The Brook. Lil Kay brought a different insight to the humanal and male dominated council she was well respected and recognized as the Dutchess of the city.

Lil Kay being able to take care of herself behind enemy lines was not a problem. The problem was not knowing about her safety, and Poppa Big found himself wishing he had received word from the Dutchess by now. Staring at the flames he silently said a prayer to the Gods of Song for Lil Kay's safe return.

A knock on the door interrupted Poppa Big's moment of peace. "Yes."

One of the hall guards pushed open the door and D.Tiger walked into the room.

"It's about to begin – isn't it?" Poppa Big asked as he slowly rose out of his seat to greet his long time partner at arms.

"Tmus should have received our reply by now", D.Tiger growled, without sharing the bloody details.

"I will inform the city. Has Lil Kay returned?"

"No, but she will make it back in time", D.Tiger said confidently.

The two humanals stared at the flames in silence, each lost in his own thoughts of what was to come to their beloved nation.

"I never thought a threat of this magnitude would surface on this side of Muzena in my lifetime", Poppa Big said after the long silence. "I always thought my son Chris would have to lead this land against a foe like Tmus."

"It's not his time. It's your time", D.Tiger growled.

"Yes...Which means we have to destroy him and his entire following in order to secure a better future for the people of this land", Poppa Big said, with his voice full of passion. "And my son", he added in a more subdued tone.

"Poppa Big, the people are with you in this", D.Tiger reminded his troubled leader.

"I Know. But the only way we will be able give them the freedom that they had all of their lives, is one of us has to kill Tmus", Poppa Big said looking over to his friend.

In that moment Poppa Big flashed back in time to when the two humanals were cubs playing in the wooded forest of the jungle city. No threats of war on their horizon, no brigades to command, just two kids growing together in a new world.

"Understood", D.Tiger said breaking Poppa Big's trance.

"Good. Now we pray", Poppa Big said, rising out of his seat. He closed his eyes and let the heat from the fire soak into his black fur. Poppa Big's side of the large room absorbed his energy and took on a black shade, as the orange flames rose in the chimney.

D.Tiger closed his eyes and the rich redness of his coat sent off a bright red hue on his side of the room. The heat between the two humanal's and the rising flames made the room too hot for any human to join them in what could be their last prayer together.

"Gods of Song...I ask you to take us into your soulful embrace, in our fight for freedom", Poppa Big began. "Our freedom is the most sacrificial life you could have ever given us. It allowed us to grow into a nation no one on this side of Muzena thought they would ever see.

"A walking – talking – power in our own right", he said, then paused to inhale the heat.

"With your guidance we have come long way. You put us into a position of prosperity, and given us a way of life that has lived in this land for centuries...Please give us the strength to stand firm against the enemy who wishes to deprive the people of their sovereignty.

"I stand before you on their behalf...And if this is our last stand, please give us the confidence to feel secure within our hearts, that you will accept us into your waiting gates.

"Our last stand...Peace."

They slowly opened their eyes and flames from the fire grew brighter. A warrior's cry rose up from within the fire. Then it calmed back down to normal height.

"Let's go", Poppa Big said, leading the way out of the room and off to their destiny.

*****

The brisk trek through the forest weighed down on the three runners, as they tried to cover as much ground as they could while the sun was still up. With the shining sun came the raising temperatures, and smoke screen fog that turned the forest into a tropical sauna.

Lil Kay lead the way, with Cory hot on her heels, and Ms.Linda bringing up the rear. Lost in her own thoughts, Ms.Linda always had thoughts of running away from Industriland and its army, but where would she go? And having Cory to care for always made her rethink her plans.

Following Lil Kay through the forest felt surreal to Ms.Linda. She never thought her prayers would be answered. But they were, and she silently vowed to the Gods of Song she would never let the Industriarmy take her and Cory back to their land. Running away made Ms. Linda realize death would be more welcoming, than being recaptured by the army and hauled back to the unknown in Industriland.

Lil Kay could feel they weren't being followed by any of the patrols from the camp, mainly because she would have heard them by now. This put her mind at ease, while she thought about all the valuable information she gained from infiltrating the camp. Once she meets with the jungle city council, they should be at an advantage against their approaching foe.

They covered a lot of ground, coming close to what Lil Kay remembered is a clearing in the forest. The loud buzzing sound of flies seemed to be getting louder the closer they got to the clearing.

"What is that?" Cory asked, pointing to a brown lump laying in the bushes.

Lil Kay stopped walking and followed Cory's line of vision. She knew immediately what they had stumbled across. Dead bodies.

"Hold on", Lil Kay said, sticking out her hand to stop Cory and Ms. Linda. They took in the scene around them and Lil Kay knew it had to take place no more than a day earlier.

"Who could have done this?" Ms. Linda asked staring at the dead men's attire. "They're from the Industriarmy."

"It smells bad over here", Cory said, turning up his nose, and putting a hand over his mouth.

Lil Kay analyzed one of the bodies closely and found a deep bite mark on his neck. "One of The Brook brigades. It will begin soon."

"What the invasion?" Cory asked looking over her shoulder.

She stood up, then turned to him. "Yes...come, let's go", Lil Kay said, subconsciously grabbing his hand and guiding the way through the sight of corpses. Not one of them felt any remorse for the fallen.

"We are close", Lil Kay said over her shoulder once they were two miles from the bloody scene in the forest.

Feeling eyes on them, Lil Kay slowed down her pace. "State your business", a voice called out from the tall trees. From the accent in his voice Lil Kay knew the man questioning them had to be a part of The Brook's defensive line brigade.

Lil Kay stopped her two followers and said, "It is the Dutchess of The Brook." Then she pulled back her hood.

"Sorry Dutchess. Are you being followed?" The voice said, without revealing his position.

"Yes. The Industriarmy will be coming", she said looking up. She found herself wondering how many brigade soldiers were up in the trees watching them.

"Okay. We will return to the city when they are one hundred yards out", the voice reported.

"Travel in peace", Lil Kay said, then grabbed Cory's hand and led the way on to the jungle city.

When they made it to the edge of the forest, the beauty of their destination came into full view. Torch lights could be seen being lit up in the distance under the now darkening sky.

The grass under their feet felt much softer as they made their way up the long hill, and up to the fifty foot high fortified wall that surrounded the colorful city. The closer they got, the more Cory silently prayed they would be able to enjoy the fruits of The Brook before his captures set upon the city with their doctrine of death and destruction. Like they did to his last home.

Chapter XX

Nipoly was summoned by Tmus, putting a stop to her day of recruiting followers for the underground campaign. Two guards escorted the songstress through the trail of settlements within the camp, as the approaching night sky brought on a different life to the array of settlers camped out in groups. Heavy smoke floated into the air, lifting mixed aromas of wild boar, wart hog, and captured bass cooking over open fires. Talk and laughter took on a louder tone once the wine began to flow.

Nipoly being escorted to Tmus chambers was never a reason for alarm ever since her song and flawless beauty silently captured the leader's cold heart. With Tmus' approval, Nipoly became Industriland ever powerful songstress, singing anthems for the army before every battle. Using her words as motivation to get the converted troops to dance to his tune had been a big part of Tmus' strategy with applying his Industrialized doctrine.

Tmus knew he could make anybody in the world do what he wanted them to do, with the simple flash of his hand. His powers were too strong for an average human to contest his will against them. But threatening them would not get the people to bow down before the Gods of Force with the love in their hearts, like what they had for the Gods of Song. Tmus grew up envying the way people outside of the walls of Industriland looked to the Gods of Song for their strength and guidance.

Making a move to finally Industrialize the eastern board of Muzena, would give Tmus the power over the people he would need to take the ultimate goal.

Taking the Kingdom of Soul.

Now that he had reached a critical point in his campaign, Tmus was getting vibes that some pieces in his circle were losing their focus. His conversation with Major Zor was an example of these vibes.

Nipoly entered Tmus' wagon without announcing herself, and stood before her leader with an attitude.

"Nice of you to join me", Tmus said, with a hint of sarcasm in his voice.

"You requested my presence", Nipoly said, crossing her arms across her chest. Her foot lightly tapped on the hay covered floor, displaying her impatient side. A side Tmus never cared to see from the lead voice of his culture.

Tmus leaned back in his custom stone chair, and let a dark smirk ride up in the corners of his mouth. His black robe dwarfed his skinny body, only revealing his pale white face and hands. He slowly began to rub his hands together, forming a red ball of light.

"I hope your voice is well rested. I want you to incite the army with an anthem that will help the beast rise from within tomorrow, when we march to The Brook", Tmus said, as he continued to hold the shinning ball.

Nipoly stared at the ball, trying to avoid the haunting eyes of the only man in the world who has ever read her soul. "Yes Your

Excellency. Don't I always supply the army with the words of victory over our foes?"

"That you do", Tmus said, letting the shining light do its job.

Nipoly began to rock back and forth on her heels, as her eyes locked onto the light. In her mind Nipoly flashed through the many faces of Industriland. Her words gave these people the strength they needed to live through the horror of being Industrialized. Now that strength was being used against her as Tmus invaded her thoughts.

The images changed, as if Tmus was turning the channels of Nipoly's mind. He paused the images, landing on a scene of heavy passion between Nipoly and Zor.

Tmus could feel his anger begin to rise as he watched the Major caress Nipoly's body with his golden arms. Sending shivers up her spine in way's she never experienced with anyone else in Industriland. Not even Tmus.

Turning from that image, Tmus came across the image of Nipoly and Zor having an intimate conversation in the back of her wagon. Tmus knew Zor could not have come up with the idea of governing his own land on his own. Someone had to plant it in the Major's psyche, because Zor's loyalty to Industriland and the Gods of Force was undeniable. He knew nothing else but the culture he was forced into at an early age, and Tmus never believed for one second Zor woke up and decided he deserved a piece of Muzena for himself to rule. His ball of light told him who really was behind the Majors sudden change of direction.

Tmus violently clapped his hands together causing the light to abruptly disappear. Nipoly blinked a few times, then wiped her eyes. "What did you say?" She asked like they were still engaged in a conversation.

"I said, I never thought it would be you", Tmus said with a sadden frown on his face.

"I don't understand. To do what?" Nipoly asked clearly confused by his sudden mood change.

"That's unimportant. Why don't you sing me something before you go", Tmus ordered, folding his hands back into his robe.

Nipoly could not remember what they were talking about, but whatever it was, it was saving the songstress from having to endure a night with Tmus placing his cold hands all over her butter skin. Sleeping with the Major gave Nipoly a new outlook on how a woman should be treated by a man. Being trapped in Tmus' chambers always sent uncomfortable vibes through her body. And if all she had to do to avoid having to go through an encounter with Tmus was to sing and leave, then Nipoly would gladly sing with all of the enthusiasm of a devoted follower of the Industry.

"Okay", she said, then started out with a rhythmic hum, easing into a verse of lost love.

"I saw// I'm told// Its old before// Never// No one// Told me its cold// They figured I lost on this road// That blisters my toes

"Left me// Feenin for what's missing// I spoke// To them with pure affection// Moving their ears to listen// Could I// Lost it// Why am I in this position?// To speak for those confused about the vision// Our future has been written// Our father// Good luck on your mission."

Tmus' eyes were closed as he soaked up the vibes from the best songstress he had ever taken into his grasp. Many believed Tmus was a cold hearted ruler, who felt nothing. What they did not know is he did feel for something. It was Nipoly and her soothing words.

Keeping his eyes closed allowed Tmus the privacy he needed to hide the hurt he felt from Nipoly's deceptiveness. For a long time Tmus believed if he gave Nipoly a better life than the rest of the women in Industriland, she would have undying loyalty to him.

Looking into her conscious he saw otherwise. To want to be with Zor was a minor offense that Tmus could over look. As long as his people that had a position of power within the city stayed on track with his mission, Tmus was at ease. But Nipoly took it a step further by harboring feelings of wanting to leave Industriland under the Major's golden arms. That type of disloyalty Tmus could not tolerate.

✳✳✳✳✳

Nipoly sat in the comfortable confines of her wagon, wrecking her brain about what just took place in Tmus' wagon. She remembered going there, and she remembered the first exchange they had. But after that Nipoly's mind was blank until she began singing. She asked herself over and over again what happened until horse steps approaching her wagon invaded her thoughts.

Nipoly shuffled over to the canvas door and pulled it open. A surprise look covered her face when she saw Major Zor dismounting his horse. And he was alone.

"Come in", Nipoly ordered in a low voice.

Zor climbed up into her dimly lit wagon and faced a surprise of his own, "Are you going somewhere? I thought you would be resting."

Nipoly looked down at her black night dress and realized she still had not changed out of her formal wear. "No, I was just thinking about some things", Nipoly said as she sat down on her comforter. "What brings you out this late Major?"

Zor look down at the ground, then began to fidget with a piece of cloth that hung from his top garment. "I had to see you before tomorrow."

When it came to coordinating his troops through a war, Major Zor was a master at his craft. But when it came to the beatings of the heart for a woman he was still young and inexperienced.

Nipoly could sense his awkwardness. She stood back up and moved in close to him. "I'm glad you came."

Zor put his golden arms around her and they embraced into a kiss, as if this would be the last time they would share a moment like this again.

Before things got too heated between them, Zor pulled back and asked, "Will you be around for me when I return?"

Nipoly's whole body went rigid. "What do you mean Zor? Of course I will be around when you return", she lightly caressed his face, loving the smooth feel of his chocolate colored skin.

Zor seemed to struggle with his words, "Nipoly, I've had a lot of success in Industriland...Because...I'm in tune with a lot of things."

He paused as if he didn't know how to finish his thoughts. "Baby, what are you saying?" Nipoly asked. No other woman, beside his birth mother, had ever called Zor baby before. The softness in her voice sent a chill down the Major's spine.

"Just tell me you will stand with me when its time to build my own city", Zor said. Not sure of what he was saying, but sure of what he was feeling.

Nipoly's face lit up, "Zor, you want me by your side...As in your Queen?"

"Yes.

"Zor I will always be there for you...As long as you want me too", Nipoly said. Her voice hit places in Zor's body that he didn't think anyone could touch.

Nipoly was known throughout the land for her hypnotic voice, but what many did not know about was the prowess in her touch. She worked Zor into a state of climaxing submission, and marveled at her work. Even though Zor was a guarded man, he still was a man that had the potential to be an all giving soul. Nipoly knew Zor grew up in the army and he was programmed to ignore his inner feelings. But in order for the people to be successful in securing a new future outside of Industriland Nipoly would have to bring those feelings out of the Major. Then make them work in her favor.

They layed under the candlelight, enlaced in each other's moisture, which ran down their bodies onto the thick comforters. Nipoly looked down into Zor's eyes and uttered a soft, "I love you." Before kissing him passionately.

The Major was locked into the songstress' embrace, lost in the effects of her words. It was at that moment he knew his life would never be the same once he stepped outside of that wagon. Nipoly made him feel like he could do anything, and if he was able to keep her by his side, then the sky's the limit.

"I..I love you too...", Zor uttered. Speaking word's he only ever said to the Gods of Force.

Chapter XXI

"Ms. Linda! Ms. Linda!"

"What's wrong Thomas?" a short and stumpy woman asked the disgruntled looking man. "Its too early for you to be out here fussing."

"Its time to eat, and Ms. Linda ain't even got the fire going yet", Thomas complained. He stood outside of Ms. Linda's wagon with full intentions of going in there and tousling her out of bed if he had to.

"Maybe she went down to the stream for the morning", Rose reasoned.

"No. We were down there already."

Rose bit down on her bottom lip, and looked around at the hungry faces before her. Rose was more than capable of getting the fire started and preparing the table for Ms. Linda, but a queasy feeling told her to go and look for Ms. Linda first.

"Let me go and see if everything is alright with her", Rose said and climbed up into the wagon. "Ms. Linda?"

Thomas patiently waited all of two seconds before he said, "What's going on in there Rose?"

"Ahh, she's not here", Rose timidly said through the canvas.

"What do you mean she's not in there?" Thomas barked as he climbed up into the wagon to take a look for himself.

"See", Rose said, with her arms spread. "It's empty."

"Well, where the hell is she?" Thomas asked.

"How am I supposed to know", Rose snapped, then pushed past him to climb back out of the wagon.

"Ah Tom, Ms. Linda coming out to cook today?"

"She's not here Rusty", Thomas spat, as the small group of on lookers began to stir.

"What do you mean, she's not here?" Tara asked from the side of the small group.

"I mean she's gone...Nobody's seen her...And it looks like we won't be eating today either", Thomas said, clearly agitated.

"I'll cook. Please, come help me Tara", Rose said, taking the other woman's hand. They made their way down to the supply wagon to gather fresh wood and flour.

Two patrol men were making their rounds and saw the small gathering out front of Ms. Linda's wagon. "Let's see what that is."

"Uh-oh... here comes the patrol", Rusty said, catching the groups attention.

"Everybody, just stay cool", someone said, as a nervous silence hovered over them.

"What's going on here?"

"Nothing. Just a normal morning around here", Thomas said, cracking his missing tooth smile.

"Oh yeah", the patrol soldier said, scanning the faces before him. "And where's Ms. Linda?" he asked looking up at the wagon.

"We don't know", Rusty said staring down at a small rock he felt needed his attention more than the soldier's eyes.

"What do you mean, you don't know!" He snapped, then snatched the canvas door open. The small group gathered behind the soldier, to take a look over his shoulder. The wagon was empty.

"Where is she!?" the patrolman partner snapped, pulling out his sword.

"We don't know", Rusty blurted out, clearly as scared as the rest of the group that the soldier might start swinging his weapon.

"Alright...Brake this crowd up!" the patrolman ordered, as his partner inspected Ms. Linda's wagon. "Go on! You people spread out!"

"You see anything Dru?" he asked over his shoulder, as he watched the small group of onlookers scatter.

"No, the place is empty", Dru said, climbing back out of the wagon. His partner scanned the rest of the area, using the distance to help him see if anything else was out of order.

"Samson, what's wrong?" Dru asked, following his partner's line of vision.

"Something else is missing from this section", Samson said, as he stared at Rose and Tara, who were building a fire.

"You know what, where's the boy?" Dru said, causing both men to make their way over to Cory's wagon.

Rose watched from the corner of her eye, as she busied herself preparing the food. She knew if Cory was also missing then that would definitely sound alarms around the camp.

Dru climbed up into Cory's wagon. "It's empty."

"Damn it! We have to inform the commander of the child's disappearance", Samson said.

"I think Ms. Linda ran off with Cory", Rose whispered over to Tara.

"Good for her", the defiant Tara said, as she continued to work on the fire.

"Huh?" Rose blurted out as if Tara cursed her.

"The thing I don't get is why did they run away on their own? Where would they go?" Tara asked out loud. She stopped what she was doing to watch the two patrolmen walk off in search of their commanding officer.

"I don't know...And don't discuss this with anyone else. Just keep your thoughts to yourself", Rose said with a worried look in her eyes.

Tara put down the piece of wood she was using to build the fire, and walked over to Rose. "Rose in case you haven't heard things are moving in a new direction around here", Tara said facing down the older woman.

"So you better get wit it, and stop focusing on your fear of the Industriarmy."

Rose stared at Tara as if she had just lost her mind. "Tara, what are you saying?"

"I'm saying, there will be an uprising when the army moves out to battle those people in The Brook. And we are going to take back our independence when they do."

"What? Girl are you crazy?" Rose asked in shock. "First Ms. Linda runs away, and now you talking about a takeover. You know these people will kill you for even thinking about something like that – let alone act it out."

"Listen Rose. When it begins, just stay close to me... And remember this is for our freedom", Tara said looking into her eyes. "You remember how it used to feel, right?"

Rose sucked her teeth. "Of course I do Tara. But that doesn't mean we can achieve something like that against these people."

"Why not?"

"Because..I..I guess the main reason is Tmus has so much power", Rose nervously said. "You saw what he did to the resisters in our city Tara...I don't know if I'm ready to die in such a horrific manner. If they want me to play by the rules, and be Industrialized, then what can I do?"

Tara looked into the pleading woman's eyes and said, "We fight. We fight for all those who fought for us. Believe me Rose, I'm not ready to die like that neither. But I don't want to live like this anymore", Tara said taking Rose's hand. "Please Rose, walk with me through this. Just image if we win. We won't have to live like this anymore."

A tear slid out the side of Tara's eye, causing Rose to embrace her. Tara was one of the strongest women Rose knew from her home land. To see a tear come out of Tara's eye, after all of the traumatizing things they witnessed since being captured by the Industriarmy, made Rose realize it may be time for a change in their lives.

"Hey! What's going on with the food?" Thomas barked from twenty yards away. He slowly made his way out of the wagon once the coast was clear of patrolmen.

Rose jumped, and Tara giggled as she whipped her eyes. "It's coming!" Tara barked over her shoulder. She stared into Rose's eyes and asked, "Are you with us?"

Rose closed her eyes, then nodded her head. "I won't let you go alone."

Tara squeezed her hand and said, "Thank you Rose. You'll see when we get our independence back, and you won't have to cook for ungrateful bastards like him anymore."

Rose chuckled, as she wiped her eyes. "Come on and let's finish these meals."

✷✷✷✷✷

"Men of the army!" Major Zor called out from a makeshift podium before his troops. The crowd roared back in approval.

"We are gathered here today, to continue on our quest to bring a more Industrialized way of living to these barbarous cities of Muzena!" the crowd booed and howled. Zor waited until his audience calmed down before he continued.

"Yes! It is our duty – by the will of the Gods of Force to Industrialize those who believe they can live amongst us, and call out to a power that despises our beautiful way of living!"

"Industry!!! Industry!!! Industry!!!" the crowd chanted.

Major Zor let the chanting carry on for a few moments, as he stood stone faced, soaking in the electric energy from his legion of soldiers. This was Zor at his best. Tmus and Nipoly watched the Major from the side of podium, as he worked his leadership impression on an army he helped build into a powerhouse.

Zor raised his hand and the crowd simmered down. "This is nothing new for us...We are the vanguard for the Gods of Force. And we will carry out their words and blessings to the walls of The Brook...To make them Industrialize or die!"

A murderous roar rose up from the crowd, causing the birds in the trees to burst into the air.

"Stomp with me!.. And we will be victorious!.. This is our destiny!.. This is our war to win!.. We are the Industriarmy!"

The crowd was so high off of the Major's speech, it felt like a cloud full of hostility had engulfed them. Zor turned around and extended his hand to help Nipoly up to the podium. They roared into a frenzy at the sight of the songstress. They all knew this would be the highlight of the rally.

Nipoly beamed as she soaked in the scene standing center stage before the sea of faces. When she was standing off to the side, Nipoly was only able to see a few hundred men. But now that she was the center of their attention she could see well over a thousand.

Zor raised his hand to quiet the crowd, then he stepped out of the way to allow the songstress to put the finishing touch on inspiring the army to victory.

"Mmmmuumm// The fire of the sword// Victory is our reward// Army of one// Is our strength in this war// Industry ooh Industry// I know you will always be there for me// Fight to the end// And I'll bear the seeds// Pull up the weeds// Plant the flag for meee!// Industry ooh Industry// Shower us with the vanityyy!// Being the best is a gift// The Gods of Force// Will give you the lift// Wear your armor with pride// And never submit!// Because the fire of the sword// Will win this war// I said, the power of the sword// Will bring us the rewards!//

Nipoly was in a deep trance, as her words blanketed her audience with a strong sense of patriotism. She swayed back and forth causing the crowd to roar like a fire.

Zor returned to center stage with Nipoly. He raised his golden arms and said, "Our march is hard!..And our will is strong!..Follow me! And together let's claim another victory! For the Industry!"

"Industry!..Industry!..Industry!" The loud chant echoed through the forest, warning all those who were in ear shot of what was about to emerge from the vast green land.

Chapter XXII

The heavy clouds of smoke rising up from unknown fires burned up into Ms. Linda's nostrils, as she ran in a desperate search for safety. Cries and screams for mercy could be heard behind her, but she couldn't turn around.

The Industriarmy was invading her land, and the only course of action she could think of was to run, and escape before she was captured like the others. Ms. Linda ran down the halls of the city's main castle, and she could not think of where she was suppose to be going.

"Ms. Linda!..Ms. Linda!..Please don't leave me!"

Ms. Linda stopped running and turned in every direction to see where the voice was coming from. But all she could see was stone walls and small fires cutting off the pathways.

"Cory is that you?!" she called out, reaching out as if he was within her reach. "Answer me Cory!"

There was no answer. Only the same scarey cries from the others she had already left behind. Ms. Linda began to run again, but was stopped short by the boy's voice again.

"Ms. Linda please don't leave me!"

"Cory where are you!?" she yelled over the noise. Tears began to slide down her cheeks as frustration began to set in. "Just tell me where you are, and I'll come for you!"

A loud crashing sound erupted behind her, causing Ms. Linda to jump. She turned around and came face to face with a wall of fire.

"Seize her!" a soldier ordered from her blindside.

Just as a hand reached out to grab her Ms. Linda woke up out of her dream in a panic. Water splashed up into the air from the large bathtub she had fallen asleep in.

"Oh my...I am so sorry... I didn't mean to shake you out of your nap."

Ms. Linda calmed down to focus on the peanut colored woman that was standing before her. She was dressed in a blue and yellow poplin dress that stretched down to her ankles.

"Are you okay?"

"Ahh..Yes Yoki...I'm sorry, was I dreaming?" Ms. Linda asked still a little confused.

"I think so...Those relaxing baths tend to do that to people", Yoki said. Being an aid in the royal castle Yoki was used to seeing people being overtaken by the relaxing scents and calm of heated water from a good bath.

"Can I get out now?" Ms. Linda asked, looking around for something to dry her body with.

"Sure, you've been in there for a pretty long time", Yoki chuckled.

"I did?" Ms. Linda asked with an embarrassed look on her face. She stood up and let Yoki pure clean water over her filmy body.

"Yes you did. So where did you come from?" Yoki asked as she handed Ms. Linda something to dry off with.

When Lil Kay arrived back in her homeland with her new guest, they were immediately showered with food, and beverages. Then ushered into the castle so they could be cleaned and dressed in some new garments. So no one, beside Lil Kay, had a moment with Ms. Linda and Cory to question who they were, and where they were from.

"I'm from South B.Ville. Our land was invaded by the Industriarmy, and we were being held captive in their traveling camp", Ms. Linda said. She dried herself off, then put on a dark green full length rayon garment.

"I've never been to South B.Ville", Yoki said as she scooped up Ms. Linda's old clothes. "The only other city I've been to outside of The Brook was the Kingdom of Soul."

Ms. Linda looked up at Yoki with astonishment. "Wow...you've been to the Kingdom before? How was it?"

Yoki smiled, "It was a fulfilling experience. They say everyone in Muzena who lives with the culture of High Hop in their hearts should make a pilgrimage to the Kingdom."

Ms. Linda continued to fix her outfit when she said, "Yoki, be honest with me...When the Industriarmy comes to The Brook, will your people be able hold them off?"

Yoki smiled, "By the good graces of the Gods of Song, we believe we will".

Ms. Linda bit on her bottom lip, and nodded, "Thank you Yoki".

"For what?" she asked confused.

"For you and your people taking me and Cory in. I never thought we would be able to leave that horrible place. And if we did, where would we go?" Ms. Linda said with a relieved look in her eyes.

"My sister, you are very welcome. Now let's go get you some real food in your system", Yoki said leading the way out of the room.

<u>Chapter XXIII</u>

Lil Kay stood before the jungle city council room feeling refreshed and ready to meet with the rest of the council. One of the guards cracked open the door and announced Lil Kay's presence.

"The Dutchess has arrived."

"Good", Poppa Big said, rising out of his seat, then walking around the table to greet her.

Lil Kay strolled into the room wearing her usual girlish smile. She took some time out to take a bath and change into a new garment, before she made her appearance to the council meeting. Lil

Kay and Poppa Big embraced as the rest of the council rose out of their seats.

"I was beginning to think we were going to have to send in the troops for you", Poppa Big said sporting a wide grin.

"You know you can't rush a woman when she's doing her work", Lil Kay said.

"I know that's right", Lady Light said as she stepped up to greet the Dutchess. "How are you feeling?"

"Better, now that I'm back home."

"Good. So come tell us", Lady Light said motioning Lil Kay to take her seat next to D.Tiger. Before sitting down Lil Kay greeted Brendan and Sekou, the leader of the archer brigade.

"So how was the trip?"Brendan asked as they all took their seats.

"Tiring...But I see yours was eventful", Lil Kay said looking over to D.Tiger.

"We cut off two committees", the red tiger growled.

"Good", Poppa Big said. "So what was the temperature of the camp after that?"

"On edge. They are ready to move out any day now. But, the good thing is I think I was able to find a voice within the camp", Lil Kay said with a slight grin. "There is a songstress in the camp with one of the strongest voices I've heard in a long time."

"So you feel if she speaks, then the people will follow?" Brendan asked.

"I think so. The army has such a strong hold on the people though, that it can go either way. They live under constant fear for their lives. I say we focus on us defeating the army on our own more so, than with the inside help."

"Do you think we should attack the army before they can set up their positions?" Sekou asked looking at Poppa Big.

"Yes", he said after a silent thought. "First we position our archers at the battlement's. Then we send out a thousand man brigade to meet the front line of the army ten feet into the forest."

Poppa Big stood up and used his pointer stick to direct everyone's attention to the map that was engraved on the large table. "Here, here, and here will be vital paths for them to use. We can disrupt their footing right here if we send out a group to soften up the soil."

"To cause a mud slide", D.Tiger interjected.

"Exactly", Poppa Big answered. A smile crept up in the sides of his mouth.

The Jungle City Council continued planning their offensive attack against the approaching army for the next two hours. Once everyone was clear with their assignments for the battle, Poppa Big wanted to say a few words to his close knit family before the meeting ended.

"Now this may be the last time we all as a unit will be able to sit here and enjoy each other's presence. This will be the biggest fight of our lives, and the only way we will make it through it...is together.

"You are my brothers and sister", he said looking over to Lil Kay. She blushed and Poppa Big continued. "And if anyone of us does not make it...I want all of you to know that I love you."

"We already knew that", D.Tiger growled, prompting a chuckle around the tension filled room.

Poppa Big smiled and said, "Please join me in a prayer."

Everyone around the table rose out of their seat, then joined hands. "Gods of Song, we come to you with hearts full of good and a soul full of song...Our harmony has been the strength of a people for many generations. And now that peace is in jeopardy.

"We know with your all powerful guidance, we will be lead onto a path of blessings. Many of us will not make it...So please welcome those souls with open arms.

"We will defend this great land you have given us with the perseverance of warriors...True song warriors...So blanket the jungle city with your holy cover...And walk with us to the end."

A chill rolled over everyone in the room as they soaked in the silence.

"In harmony we pray", Lady Light said ending the prayer. They all opened their eyes and the universal feel around the room was this might be the last time they would share a moment in prayer together again.

"This is for The Brook!" Poppa Big barked, raising is sword high into the air.

"For The Brook!" was echoed around the room in word, and in feeling.

✳✳✳✳✳

Knock! - Knock!

"Yes."

"It's Sekou, may I come in?"

"Yes."

Sekou stepped into the large room and quickly surveyed the colorful living quarters. He smiled, and closed the door behind himself.

"You go out on secret missions without letting me know now, huh."

"You make that sound like you missed me", Lil Kay said with a chuckle. She was laying down on a stack of feather stuffed pillows, smiling from ear to ear.

"Who wouldn't miss all of this beauty?" Sekou said admiring Lil Kay's comfortable set up.

Lil Kay chuckled, "Now that just won you a seat", she said motioning for him to sit next to her.

The Dutchess and the brigade leader silently found an interest in each other, and preferred to keep their late night relationship as such. Private.

In public, they helped govern the city under Poppa Big's leadership. But in private Lil Kay and Sekou shared many nights together, within the last year growing closer, than just two common leaders on the Jungle City Council.

Lil Kay stared into Sekou's green eyes, feeling like a little girl again with a crush on an up and coming brigade soldier.

"Sekou, do you think we're going to make it out of this?" Lil Kay asked. She loved to hear Sekou's insight on things, because even though he kept her blushing and laughing whenever they were together, Sekou possessed a realness that was rare to her. There were no mystery answers with him. Everything was out on the stove.

"I found myself asking the same question some time ago", he said.

"Did this have anything to do with that?" Lil Kay asked, feeling a strong sense of loss was upon them.

"Yes. I've never felt this way for another woman before. And now it feels like all of it is being threatened."

Lil Kay leaned in and kissed him passionately, then said, "One side of me wants to tell you not to say that. But I know what we're up against...I'm just glad you're here with me tonight."

"I wouldn't want to be anywhere else", the smooth talking Sekou said as he moved in to caress her chocolate colored skin.

She chuckled, "You are too smooth for your own good."

"You wouldn't be chilling with me if I wasn't."

"Oh, I'm chilling with you huh? Last I checked that was my room", Lil Kay said.

He ran two fingers through her hair, and said, "Last I checked...this was our room."

Sekou's words made Lil Kay melt as she closed the gap between them and flooded his mouth with more kisses.

Every night together brought laughs, intimate pillow talk, and reminiscent love making. Tonight's meeting was no different. Whenever their minds and bodies met they would share an energy that would make both of them stronger. Taking their attraction for one another to a level, only the two of them could understand.

Once Lil Kay was fast asleep Sekou eased out of the bed, and slipped back on his uniform. He kissed her softly on her forehead, then made his way down to the front line of The Brook, ready to lead his troops to victory.

Chapter XXIV

The first tier of Industriarmy soldiers marched on foot through the wooded forest, as the sun beamed down on them through the thick fifty foot tall oak trees. The group of one thousand men kept their spirit's high and the tension to a minimum as they shared old stories and jokes to pass the time.

Once the first fifty men got within thirty yards of the mouth of the forest a barrage of arrows rained down on them from within the tall trees.

"AAWWW!!! Look Out !!"

A mass scramble broke out as soldiers that weren't hit ducked for cover. Bodies crashed down to the ground with arrows lodged in their head, shoulders and chest. Screams of agony and pain filled the air causing an unexpected chaotic scene.

"What's going on down there?" the front line captain asked, as he watched his surge stop, then push backwards instead of forwards.

"Captain we're under attack!" a discouraged soldier bawled as he tried to get out of the way of the stampede.

"Stand Down! Stand Down!" the captain barked. He pulled out his sword as a group of twenty soldiers surrounded him for his protection.

"Take cover!" the captain ordered, feeling the need to regroup.

The arrows stopped flying, but no one could tell from the mangled disorder where the initial attack had come from. The dead were layed out with bewildered expressions on their faces. While the wounded cried out for help and tried fleeing to safety.

"Attack!!!" brigade leader Elliot called out from his position in the shadows.

The Brook warriors dropped down out of the trees and appeared from behind five foot bushels with their swords drawn and a fire in their eyes.

A massive sword fight broke out with many of the Industriarmy soldiers holding their ground.

"Aww...You Bastards!!"

"Prepare to Die!!"

"You filthy pigs will die for coming to our land!" Elliot beamed with a fire in his eyes his troops fed off of.

"Chief, the south end is beginning to advance on us!"

Elliot looked over, then said, "Tell them to break the ground!"

The messenger ran off and Elliot stepped back into the heated battle. Swords swung and blood sprayed up into the air as The Brook warriors fought like the desperate defenders they were.

The Brook archers who were hiding in the trees slid down on vines and fell back, like they were instructed to do. As the ground crew took out as many Industirarmy soldiers as they could in the heated battle.

The Industriarmy captain was mortified at the sight of some of his soldier's running from the minor onslaught.

"Kill all those who attempt to retreat!" he ordered. Then he turned to one of his men and said, "Tell the men to push through their resistance on the north and south sides."

"Yes sir!"

The protective barrier that surrounded the captain made a fearless push forward. First killing any man that tried to flee the scene, then they moved on to the head to head battle with The Brook warriors.

The screams and cries from the injured drowned out the roars and grunts of the assaulter. Blood soaked the grass and the smell of the dead began to rise as the reinforcements began to arrive.

On the south side of the forest the army was held down by a hail storm of arrows from The Brook archers. While a team of twenty five men with water, shovels, and large pickaxes loosened the land until it began to give way.

"Step Back! The Ground Is Caving!" someone cried.

"More Water! We Need More Water!" The Brook men continued to work feverishly on turning the dirt to mud.

"The captain said to forage ahead!" Someone barked in the mist of the confusion.

"Even under the archer attack?" one soldier asked pointing up to the trees.

"Yes! And those who refuse or retreat will be killed", the messenger barked with his sword out and ready to carry out the order.

"Yes sir...The surge will be pushed", a senior soldier said. Then he turned to the rest of the men and said, "You heard the captain! Charge!"

"RRROOAARR!"

"Fire!" echoed from the tree tops as a rain of arrows flooded the surging army.

✶✶✶✶✶
_____

The war drums rumbled as the rest of the Industriarmy marched on to The Brook. All of the pre-battle jitters were put on hold until they reached their destination. A one thousand man battalion lead the way as the first line of attack, followed closely by Commander Gossie and his fifteen hundred man unit of archers.

In the middle tier of the march was the strongest group of soldiers accompanied by Major Zor. The small but deadly body of knights men was lead by the top knight Fungi. In the middle of knights men formation, Tmus sat high on his black stallion, lost in his own thoughts as he rode on the side of Fungi.

Zor tried to keep his mind off of Nipoly and the last taste of beauty she left in his memory. But it was turning out to be a fruitless battle against himself, because the only words he could hear in his mind were the words from Niploy's send off song to the army.

The steady thumping of the war drums helped the Major escape his thoughts of the songstress and her powerful words. Lightly nodding his head like a man falling into a trance.

Commander Alhotic rode on the side of the Major focusing on the task at hand, until Zor interrupted his thoughts. "Did the scout make contact with the front line?"

Alhotic chewed on the butt of his tobacco leaf roll up, as the tip burned slowly. "No. But we are almost at the clearing end of the forest."

Feeling like he could get a little personal with the commander, Zor asked, "Alhotic, how many of these have we done together?"

This wasn't a question the commander was expecting from the Major. Especially since his mind was on the pain and destruction he was ready to administer to their next target. But the Major had been doing a lot of strange things lately Alhotic had reasoned with himself as he steadied his horse to keep going straight.

"Major...Honestly, I've lost count. Why, does this one feel like the biggest one we've done together or something?" Alhotic asked blowing smoke out of his nostrils.

"Commander, this will definitely be one of our biggest battle's together." Zor said. "But, I think the question I should be asking is if I'm not around for the next campaign, will you be able to carry the torch in my absence?"

Alhotic let the question marinate for a moment before he answered. "Major, being older than you has never come in the way of me being able to learn a lot from you...And even though it was a blessing from the Gods of Force to be able to witness the leadership of the best Major I ever seen lead the army; I feel confident enough to say yes, I can lead the army in your absence if it came down to it."

Pleased with the commander's response, Zor nodded his head and rode on in silence. Zor let his thought's travel back to the days when he was promoted to overseeing Major of the Industriarmy. Zor knew it was a position that should have been given to a more seasoned soldier like Alhotic, but Tmus liked Zor's brutality on the battlefield and the promoted him to Major of the army.

"I know you don't plan on retiring on me", Alhotic joked.

Zor broke a rare smile and said, "Only if I can go out on top."

"That's the only way to go", Alhotic said. "But you sound like this may be your last stand."

"Some days I feel like it will be."

"Zor, you have a lot of years ahead of you. At 35 you have a lot of energy, and there's more than enough room for you to build on your impressive legacy", Alhotic said.

"Thanks old friend", Zor said

"The scout is coming sir", someone called out, as the young soldier galloped through the formation.

"What is it Shan?" Alhotic asked without breaking his stride.

Shan turned his horse around and got in step with the Commander and Major. "Sir the front line was attacked", Shan quickly reported.

The Commander remained silent, seeming unfazed by the news. Major Zor looked over to Alhotic and said, "Well if its a fight they want, then that's what they shall have."

Blowing smoke out of his nostrils, Alhotic looked over to Zor with a sinister grin and said, "Now we're talking my language", as they forged on with their campaign.

Chapter XXV

"The last of the soldiers just left the camp", Letty said as she climbed up into the wagon.

"Did you hear about what they're planning on doing today in the camp?" Della asked. She sat Indian style on the wagon floor twirling a piece cloth between her fingers.

Letty knew Della only did this when she was nervous about something. "Oh no Della, don't tell me you thinking about joining that uprising", Letty asked with a worried look in her eyes.

Della looked down at her hands, then back at her friend and said, "Why not? I mean, we can help our brothers and sisters in the camp, then go back to Industriland to free our Queen. It works out for all of us."

"Yeah, but what if something goes wrong?" Letty asked staring down at the floor.

"Like what?"

"I don't know", Letty said out of frustration. "I mean some of the soldiers could come back to the camp, then how will we defend ourselves?"

"Come on Letty, I'm sure they have some type of weapons if they're going to take over the camp. We just have to stick together and I know we can make it."

There was an unexpected knock on the door.

Both women almost jumped out of their skin.

"Who is it?" Della asked in a nervous tone.

"It's Nipoly. May I please come in?"

Della and Letty looked at each other with questionable eyes, until Della said, "Ahh...Yes..."

Nipoly climbed up into the wagon, giving the two ladies inside a sneak peek of her two lookouts waiting outside. "Hello ladies. I'm sorry to show up here unannounced, but we have pressing matters that need everyone in this camp's attention."

"What do you mean?" Della asked with a skeptic look in her eyes.

"We need your help."

"Our help, for what?" Letty asked nervously.

"Tonight, we will overpower the remaining guards in this camp, and take back our freedom", Nipoly said.

Della looked up at Letty, "She's serious Letty", then turned back to Nipoly, "You want us to help you tonight? But what if something goes wrong? Like if Tmus comes back?" Della asked.

Letty got a warm feeling in her body when she heard Della flood Nipoly with the same questions she just hit Della with.

"That's why we have to act fast, and be on our way. But I'm pretty sure Tmus and the army will be too busy fighting the people in The Brook, than worrying about a camp full of servants and the elderly."

"She's right Letty. If they do come back, we will be long gone", Della said.

Letty nodded and said, "Whatever you want to do Della, you know I'm with you."

"You ladies sound like you have your own plans", Nipoly said.

"We do", Della said standing up to meet Nipoly's stare. "We're going back to Industriland to free our Queen from the dungeon."

"Are you serious?" Nipoly asked shocked.

"Yes. We took an oath to protect and defend our Queen, and we have to honor that", Letty said.

"I understand that, but Industriland is a very dangerous place...Even with the thin security they have left in the city", Nipoly said.

"Its a chance we have to take", Della said.

"Then leave her there to die", Letty added.

Nipoly could see the two women had their minds made up and she wasn't there to try and change it. She was there to recruit them for her plan. If these women had a plan for after the takeover then so be it.

"Okay. You won't get any arguments out from me. So I can count you two in for tonight?" Nipoly asked knowing the answer to her question already.

Della and Letty looked at each other, then back to the songstress, "We'll be there", Della said with a convincing look in her eye.

"Thank you", Nipoly said, embracing both women, then moving on to her next target of recruit's.

✳✳✳✳✳
_____

The wind had always been his friend. Whenever he rode its waves, he always felt free as a bird.

It had been a long time since Airman had taken a late night flight. He really had no reason to. Once he left The Brook brigade, Airman had fallen into a more grounded life in the jungle city. Which was hard to do standing at six feet tall, and having six feet wide wings on his back. His gift made him and his kind some of the most attractive humanals in the city.

Airman was one of the best weapons The Brook had against any approaching enemies. His specialty was flying behind enemy lines and gaining intelligence for the brigade, or eliminating the enemy leader right in their own back yard.

As the years grew on and the threats to The Brook became few to none, Airman's services to the brigade became useless, to say the least. Causing the decorated humanal to retire and focus on his clan of bird-men.

All of this changed when Brendan, the front line brigade leader showed up at his doorstep with a mission; and a big one too. Putting Airman right back in the skies he loved. Doing the work that made him feel like he had a purpose. Going behind enemy lines.

Gliding over the trees, Airman swooped in the camp and landed on one of the sturdiest branches he could find. The camp looked relatively empty, except for a small group that was gathered around a camp fire. Not wanting to waste any more time, Airman decided to fly in for a closer look.

"What the hell is that?" Rusty asked, catching everyone in the groups attention.

"I don't know", Rose answered.

"Looks like a man", Thomas said as they all stood in silence.

Airman smoothly landed eight feet from them, then put his hands up in a defensive stance. "Please, don't be afraid. I was sent here to help you."

"Who sent 'cha?" Rusty asked in his country twang.

"To help us do what?" Rose snapped. Fear rising in her chest about the black and gray stranger. Most of them had heard about humanals in Muzena who had human and bird jeans mixed in their blood. But none of them had ever been face to face with one.

"My council members in the jungle city sent me to assist you and the songstress tonight in your uprising", Airman said trying his best not to spook the group.

They all stood in silence, not sure of what to think of the sudden appearance of the humanal, until Thomas broke the silence. "I've never seen you or your kind before, so how do we know you wasn't sent by Tmus and his sorcerer's?"

"Hey what's going on over there?" a deep voice barked, causing everyone in the group to freeze.

"I said what's going on over there?" the guard repeated, as he and his partner made their way over to the camp fire.

"What is that?" The guard asked, pointing at Airman.

"I am a messenger", Airman said, as he took two steps into the guards' direction. They seemed more amazed at his presence than alarmed by it.

"A messenger from where, bird land?" The guard asked as he grabbed the handle of his sword.

"No sir...The jungle city." Then Airman suddenly leaped high into the air and disappeared into the dark sky.

The two guards pulled out their swords and stared up into the sky. "Nobody move!" one of the guards ordered as they scanned the area for the stranger.

Airman landed behind the two guards, and using one foot on each of them, donkey kicked them in their backs. Both men tumbled forward and landed on their faces.

"I'll kill you!" one of the guards cried as he scrambled to his feet.

"Let's see you try that up here then", Airman commented, gliding in the air and snatching the guard by his thick chest cover.

"Ahhh...Put me down!"

"No problem", Airman said taking the man high into the air, then tossing his body like a rag doll. The guard flew into the fifty foot tall trees and felt every inch of his fall, as he went crashing down into a thick bush.

The guard's partner stood frozen in shock, "What the?"

Tara wasted no time pulling out the billy club she had stashed in her dress, and clobbered the guard on the side of his head.

"Ahhh" the guard fell to his knees in a daze.

Thomas quickly swung into action, taking a five step run then kicking the wounded guard in his face shattering his jaw. Blood and teeth few across the air and disappeared into the night as he blacked out.

Rusty pulled out his billy club and went to work on the unconscious guard. "You bastard!" Rusty cried, releasing all of his years of captivity on the man's bloody face.

"Stop it Rusty! He's dead!" Rose shouted. In that instant Rose wanted to bow out of the small rebellion before it even got started.

Rusty stopped beating him and stepped back to calm down. Airman landed by the group as the stared at the dead guard, all of them realizing there was no turning back now.

"Now what?" Kemela asked.

"Now we go meet with the others", Tara said taking over as the spokesperson of the group.

"Hey! Where are you two going?" a patrol guard asked.

Della and Letty froze in their tracks as the deep voice startled them. When they turned around the two women came face to face with a single patrol guard, under the moonlight. He looked to be on a late night stroll, and just happened to come across the two servants.

"We...we are in search of berries", Della blurted out.

"At this time of night?" the guard asked, with a skeptical look in his eyes. He moved in close enough for Letty to smell the wine reeking off of his breath.

"I don't believe you", he said. "I think you're out looking for some action."

The guard's words sent a chill up Letty's spine. It was common for an Industriarmy guard to stop women in the night, and force her to do what he asked, or face a devastating fate.

"We don't want any trouble sir. We were just out for some berries", Della tried to reason with him.

"Ahh...Don't worry, just come on over here and show me you don't want any trouble", the guard said, suddenly reaching for Letty's neck.

"Get your hands off of me!" Letty screamed as she pulled out a knife Della had given her for protection, and went at the guard in a blind fiery.

"Hey!" the guard jumped backwards and tripped on a broken tree branch.

"Oh no", Della cried, as she watched Letty's momentum carry her into the fallen guard and jammed the knife into his chest.

"Ahhh...get off me!" the guard barked. Then he back handed Letty. Letty flew off of him and crashed into the bushes. The guard looked down at the knife sticking out of his chest with a blank stare.

Della snapped into action and jabbed him in his hand before he could pull the knife out of his chest. "Ahhhh, somebody help me!"

Feeling overwhelmed with panic, Della continued to stab the guard. But the more she stabbed him, the more he screamed out in pain causing a stir in the calm night air.

Letty scrambled out of the bushes with a stick in her hand. "Move Della!" Letty barked, but she didn't wait for her to move. Letty came down on the guard's mouth with enough force to break his front teeth. The guard choked and gargled on his own blood as the two women stood back and watched him die.

"What are we going to do?" Letty asked after the guard fell silent.

"We should throw him in the bushes", Della suggested.

"Okay but let's hurry", Letty said, feeling the urge to get out of dodge.

Della took the guard's weapons and other useful belongings, then they rolled his body into a thick bed of bushes.

"Now come on, we have to make it to the west end of the camp", Della said, checking to see if the coast was clear. Then she led the way over to the meeting place for the rebellion

✶✶✶✶✶

Nipoly used a camp fire as her backdrop, as she stood front and center at the gathering that seemed to growing by the minute. People were arriving from all over the camp with stories of run-ins with the camp's patrols. Looking at the faces of the gatherers Nipoly got the feel of a people that longed for the opportunity to take back their freedom.

"More are coming!" someone shouted from the back of the small crowd.

"Tell them to step forward", Pham said from Nipoly's side. Standing at six feet five inches tall, Pham possessed the body mass the army loved to Industrialize and bring over to their way of life. But Pham was nursing a bad arm injury he received when the army invaded his land. Landing him on the servant's staff.

The crowd parted as the newcomers made their way up to the front. Nipoly recognized the people from the group, but they were accompanied by a face she didn't recognize.

"And who is that?" Pham asked stepping up, before Nipoly could ask the same question. Everyone in the crowd stared at the humanal with questioning eyes, while some reached for their weapons.

"I am Airman. I was sent here by my leadership council to assist you", he humbly stated.

"Leadership council? From where?" Pham asked. His voice as deep and threatening as his dark stare.

"The Brook", Airman said proudly.

Nipoly smiled. "You were sent by Lil Kay."

"Yes. The Dutchess is part of the Jungle City Council", Airman said.

"Thank you for coming", Nipoly said.

"You must be the songstress", Airman said with a slight smile.

"Yes, my name is Nipoly."

"Someone else is coming!" someone shouted from the back of the crowd.

"Tell them to step forward", Pham ordered.

The last group to arrive was the largest one yet, Nipoly silently noted. The group bought more electricity to her gathering with people openly greeting each other for the first time in years.

Della and Letty had run into another group on their way to Nipoly's rally, giving the two women a stronger sense of security, now that they weren't alone.

When Della and Letty stepped forward accompanied by a man named Jerome, Nipoly smiled. "I'm glad you could make it."

"I wouldn't have it no other way. Our freedom is the most important thing to us songstress." Jerome proudly said, looking over to his new found friends, Della and Letty.

"Yes. So what's next Nipoly?" Della asked, ready to get to the heart of their night.

"I was about to address that. I was waiting to hear word from the rest of the camp. And now that everyone is here, I think its time", Nipoly said. "The last time we spoke, you seemed to have your own plan of escape in mind."

"Yes. We are going back to Industriland to free our Queen", Della said.

"Okay. Like I said in the wagon, I welcome your decision to return to the city to free your Queen, but I have a different plan in mind. Since it is a dangerous one, I'm going to give everyone the opportunity to choose their own destiny."

Della silently nodded. "Okay."

"Can I have everyone's attention please?" Nipoly asked, ending the private conversations that were carrying on at the gathering. "I want to thank everyone for stepping into the forefront with me tonight. This step we have taken is a very large one toward our ultimate goal...Our freedom."

The small crowd roared its approval, then Nipoly continued, "You should be proud of what was done here tonight, but it doesn't end here. This is a new time in our history, so I ask you how do you want to proceed?"

"We can continue on with our fight and bring it to the backs of the army, as they fight the good people of The Brook...Or we can go back to Industriland and free our brothers and sisters from the dungeons in the city", Nipoly said, causing a stir of murmurs in the crowd.

"I know both plans sound dangerous, but that is all we have now my people...So with the show of hands, how many say we should go back to Industriland?" Nipoly asked.

An impressive amount of hands went up. "And who feels we should help the people of The Brook?" The rest of the hands went up in the air.

Looking over to Pham, Nipoly said, "I think those who want to go back should...And those who want to help the people of The Brook should do as they desire."

"I agree", Pham said as he stared out into the crowd. "Even though we will be stronger if we remained together. But the key to our independence is the freedom of decision."

"He's right", Jerome said as the murmurs continued in the crowd.

"Okay so its settled...Those who want to go back will do so...And those who will follow me to The Brook will do so", Nipoly said causing another round of discussions.

Nipoly looked over to Della, Letty, and Jerome and said, "Will you lead the people back to the city to free our people there?"

Letty looked over to Della and smiled. "Of course we would...Right?" Della said, looking over to Jerome.

"Aw, yeah", he said, surprised to be initiated by the songstress in this form of conversation. "Whatever you need me to do, I'm here with it."

"Good, cause they're going to need you to be", Nipoly told Jerome before she addressed the crowd and prepared them for the next phase of the night.

Chapter XXVI

The Industriarmy flooded the clearing in front of The Brook with front line soldiers, archers and catapults armed with heavy boulders. Through the ranks the tension was thick enough to suffocate the common civilian, but Industriarmy soldiers were bred for this.

High up top of the battlements on the fifty foot tall protective wall, The Brook's archers stood armed and ready for their order to fire on the mass body that idly surrounded their city.

"I'm going up", Major Zor said to Tmus, who simply nodded and continued to stare at the large wall. The Brook's flags flew high in the air, on top of the battlements giving the old city a respected look on the low mountain top.

The archers pointing their weapons at his army was the furthest thing from his dark mind. The only thing Tmus could think about was locking eyes with the big black bear he was there to skin, and use his fur as a rug at the foot of his throne.

"Alhotic, join me", Zor ordered as he rode his horse through the ranks. They rode up the hill and stopped one hundred feet from the closed portcullis.

"State your business!" D.Tiger growled from behind the gate.

Zor looked over to Alhotic as if to say, 'should I answer that?', then back to the red tiger. "I want a face to face with the head of your military", Zor stated.

D.Tiger looked over to Brendan and grinned. "They wish to speak with us."

"Let's do it then", Brendan answered, then gave the signal to raise the gate.

Brendan rode down the hill on his brown horse. When he was fifty feet away from Zor and Ahlotic, D.Tiger dashed out of the gate sending a nervous shock wave through Zor and his entire army behind him. They did not know how to react to the 450 pound red bangle tiger galloping down the hill. The last thing Zor and Alhotic were going to do was show fear. So they stood their ground.

Brendan and D.Tiger stopped five feet away from Zor and Alhotic. "If you think we are about to negotiate our peoples independence, you are sadly mistaken", D.Tiger growled, setting the tone for their little meeting.

"If you don't, you know this will turn bloody", Zor boldly predicted.

"And what do you think you will find on the other side of that wall?" D.Tiger snarled.

"I'm sure we will find a land full of people that would rather work this out peacefully, then to engage in a battle with the Industriarmy", Zor proudly boasted.

D.Tiger smiled. "I tell you what...I'm going to give you and your army five minutes to get off of our land."

"And if we don't", Alhotic said, fed up with the humanals tough talk.

"Then we will show you how far my people are willing to go in the name of High-Hop", D.Tiger growled.

"And what do you have to say to this?" Zor asked Brendan, to see if the human had more authority over the animal.

"Our brigade leader has spoken. Now you have three minutes left", Brendan said.

"You fools will wish you worked out a deal with us", Alhotic snarled.

"Times up", D.Tiger snapped, then in one jump he leaped into the air and crashed into Alhotic's chest knocking the man off of his horse. The horse whined and jumped out of the way as D.Tiger tackled Alhotic down to the ground.

"Awww...Get off of me!" Ahlotic barked as he wrestled with the large tiger. But his cries were cut short by a swift slap from D.Tiger's paw. Three claw wounds opened up on Alhotic's cheek, sending blood flying into the air.

Zor hopped off of his horse, drawing his sword. Brendan got his horse under control, then used it to ram into Zor, sending the Major flying through the air.

D.Tiger wanted to send a message to Tmus and his army. "RRROOAARRR!!!" he growled, then took a fatal bite into Alhotic's neck, killing the commander instantly.

Zor scrambled to his feet and tried to shake off the cobwebs, but it was too late because D.Tiger and Brendan was already making their way back up the hill.

The entire Industriarmy watched in horror as their beloved commander was slaugtered by the red tiger.

"Attack! Attack!" Commander Gossie ordered. "Archers Fire!"

Sekou stood atop of the tall wall watching the sea of approaching Industriarmy soldiers, waiting for the right moment."RRROOAARR!"

"Steady!" Sekou ordered, with his right hand raised high in the air.

Zor made it to his feet and looked over to his dead comrade. His blood immediately began to boil. The vibration of his troops coming up the long hill made Zor turn to face them. His eyes were full of fire and voice full of rage when he pointed to The Brook and screamed, "Kill Them All!!!"

The charging soldier's roared even louder, as The Major continued on with his raging rant. "You Will Make Them Kneel Before Me!! Their Souls Will Be Taken By Force!"

"Fire!"

The order came down with Sekou's arm, sending off a rain storm of poisonous arrows.

"AWWW! Shields Up!!!Shields Up!!!"

Screeching cries, mixed with shouting rang out as hundreds of Industriarmy soldiers dropped down to one knee and put up their hard wood and metal shields.

"Fire!" Sekou ordered, sending off another round of arrows. Bodies began to trample over bodies, giving the arrows the small window they needed to do their damage, cutting down the defenseless in mid-stride.

Feeling like they were slowing down, Captain Ishmael pressed the front line forward. "Let's Go!! Keep Moving!!!"

"Fire!" A round of torch lit arrows flew from the second tier of the army's formation. Lighting up the afternoon sky, the arrows pierced through the air striking flags, the wall and shields held up by brigade warriors.

The Industriarmy's front line made enough progress to set up make shift ladders against the wall.

"They're on the wall!" someone shouted down the track.

"Release the oils!" Sekou ordered, with his command echoed down the line. Big black kettles filled with bubbling black oil was turned over onto the heads of the unsuspecting invaders.

"AAWWW!! Help Me!"

"Light It Up!" Sekou ordered, then stepped back. A single torch was tossed over the wall and into the hot oil.

WHOOSH!

"NNOOO!"

Screams of agony echoed up and down the line, as the hot oil turned to fire. A protective wall of fire ignited around the city, setting everything in its path ablaze. The chaotic scene was too much for the Captain to take anymore.

"Pull Back! Pull Back!"

"Keep Firing!" Sekou ordered, as the archers released a fresh round of arrows down into the crowd.

Major Zor walked back to where Tmus was sitting patiently on top of his black stallion, watching the beginning stages of what looked to be a fierce battle.

"I see the legend is true about the red tiger. He looks like he will be a great asset to us", Tmus said.

Zor wasn't in the mood for Tmus' humor. His blood was boiling hotter then the fire that ran around the wall of the Jungle City. All he wanted to do was kill the red tiger. Now Tmus was talking about keeping it.

"That red savage will be dead by tomorrow", Zor spat. Then he grabbed the reins of a free horse and straddled it. Tmus simply grunted, and continued to watch the large fire hug the perimeter wall.

Major Zor rode off, barking orders at every commander and captain on the battlefield. They drew first blood by sending the red tiger to assassinate Commander Alhotic. Now it was Zor's turn to answer.

✱✱✱✱✱

"Poppa Big, the battle has begun", Diop said, dipping his head into the room.

"Okay. Go get P.D. the Wizard please. And you two meet us at the front of the castle", Poppa Big said.

"Yes sire", Diop said, then quickly ran off to fetch the wizard.

Poppa Big and Lady Light sat back watching the fire in the fireplace. Moments like these were priceless to the couple. Just the two of them, their thoughts, and silence around them. Lady Light took his paw and squeezed it.

"I guess this is it, huh", he said with a smile.

"You know I'm proud of you", Lady Light said.

"Why? I didn't do anything yet", Poppa Big joked.

"Oh yes you did", Lady Light said, looking into his eyes. "You made us as a people see that our freedom and independence is worth fighting for, no matter who the enemy is."

"Spoken like a true first lady", Poppa Big said. He stood up and pulled his wife to her feet. Then kissed her.

The beauty of Poppa Big and Lady Light privately happens when they connect with each other intimately. Something the rest of the world had the good fortune to see.

The moment Lady Light's lips touched the big black bears, Poppa Big transformed into a six foot five, three hundred pound black man. They kissed and embraced for a long moment before Poppa Big pulled back and looked into her eyes.

"My Lady Light, I love you."

"I love you too."

Poppa Big smiled, then his face and body slowly began to turn back into a bear. "Good. Now let's go...we have a battle to win."

Lady Light grabbed her powerful walking stick and together they walked out of the council room. Four guards waited in the hallway for them, and got right in step with their King and Queen as they marched down the hallway without saying a word.

Chapter XXVII

In the backlands of The Brook, the vegetation was full of color and wild life within the perimeter wall. An opening in the bottom portion of the wall allowed a stream of the Mona River to flow into the city and its wells. The stream was the jungle city's main source of water and fish. With an endless supply of tuna, mackerel, and other floating delicacies the city was never short when it came to having fish to grill for the night's meal.

Built deep in the woods, out of sight of the river and the rest of the city was one of the most secure structures in The Brook. With most of its body hidden underground, the jungle city shelter was built to protect the people from disaster and war.

Being new to the way how things worked in The Brook, Ms. Linda and Cory stuck close to Lil Kay's side so they wouldn't get caught up in the fray of the war on the outside of the shelter walls.

"Is this all of the children from your city?" Ms.Linda asked as they moved through the small and large groups to make sure everyone was getting along fine.

"Just about", Lil Kay answered. "There were a few people in the city who felt it was their duty to stay behind and defend their homes. This made them also keep their children close to them."

"Wow. Isn't that like worst then dangerous?" Ms. Linda asked surprised.

"Yes...Of course. But what can you do?" Lil Kay said feeling defeated. "People have the right to make their own decisions, no matter how dangerous we may feel it is."

Ms. Linda simply nodded, then stood back and watched Lil Kay squat down to briefly have some words with a group of young girls. Once she was satisfied, Lil Kay moved on to the next group of children.

The children were the most important prize of an invasion by the Industriarmy, because of the value in changing their way of life at an early age. The protection of the jungle city children was placed on Lil Kay's shoulders, making The Dutchess the last line of military defense down in the shelter. Her backup were most of the children's mothers, who were prepared to do whatever it took to keep their children out of harms reach.

Lil Kay was a natural at keeping people calm, but ready to move on a moment's notice if things got out of hand. She made giving herself to the women and children in the shelter, to help them feel comfortable in a bad situation look easy. Her individual words of encouragement always put a smile on a person's face. Making

The Dutchess a loveable figure amongst the people, and Ms. Linda could see why.

As Ms. Linda trailed Lil Kay around the shelter, she kept a steady eye on Cory. He had befriended three boys who looked to be in the same age range as him. It warmed her heart to see Cory interacting with other children, after she watched him go through three years of isolation from the children in Industriland. From a distance, Cory looked like he fit right in with The Brook children.

"Ms. Linda you want a snack?" Lil Kay asked, snapping her out of her trance.

"Ah…Sure", Ms. Linda answered after a slight hesitation.

Lil Kay smiled. "Don't worry, you'll still be able to see him from the storage room."

Feeling a little embarrassed, Ms. Linda said, "Was I that obvious? I'm sorry"

"Don't worry about that Ms. Linda. Even though I don't have any children, I still know how attached we get to them when we do have them. Especially at a time like this."

The two women went to the back of the shelter and Lil Kay opened up a large wooden door. Ms. Linda stood in the doorway with an amazed look on her chunky face at the stockpile of goods inside of the storage room.

"Wow, there's food inside of all these baskets?" Ms. Linda asked.

"Most of them. That's why we keep the door closed", Lil Kay said, as she dug out some wheat crackers. "We have to keep this room air preserved."

"Are those fresh fruit's?"Ms. Linda asked, walking over to a basket stacked with oranges.

"Yes...They were brought down here yesterday. We also have a lot of dry fruit, which will last down here much longer", Lil Kay said.

"And this thing pushes out fresh water?" Ms. Linda asked, as she inspected a metal pump that was built into the wall.

"Yes, it's connected directly to the Mona River", Lil Kay said, as she snacked on her crackers. "We've been blessed to have the best architects design this place."

"How long do you think we can survive down here Lil Kay?" Ms. Linda asked with some worry in her voice.

Lil Kay looked around the room, then she looked back to the woman who was fastly becoming a friend and said, "This place is built to hold us down here for a good amount of time, but something tells me your question was meant for our current situation."

Ms.Linda stared at the floor and kicked around a stem of hey that was on the ground. "I guess. I have a past that I just escaped...And I hate feeling like my past will come to reclaim my body, and this time take my soul."

Ms.Linda looked up and Lil Kay could see the hurt in her eyes. "I don't want your people to go through what me and Cory had to go through for the last three years."

"I don't either, but the important thing right now is keeping our positive thoughts going", Lil Kay said, as she closed the gap between them. "Right now we have everything we'll need to survive down here, and we have to keep our faith.

"I know, and believe the Gods of Song will protect us and those innocent children out there. So I'm going to need you Ms.

Linda to help me maintain that hope in this hard time", Lil Kay said taking her hand.

Ms. Linda smiled, "No problem Dutchess".

"Good...Now let's pray", Lil Kay said. Then she led them into a private moment with the Gods of Song.

✻✻✻✻✻

Wagons were packed with an abundance of supplies, and the horses were fed and watered before the large group of travelers began their trek through the majestic lands of Muzena, and back to Industriland.

A majority of the travelers wanted to take their chances trying to overpower a small group of guards back in Industriland, then picking a fight with Tmus and his army out on the battlefield.

A lot of the women were forced to leave their small children back in Industriland, and their return to reclaim their little ones was all the motivation they needed to choose the long journey back over the sneak attack Nipoly had planned for Tmus.

The further away from the camp the people got, the more comfortable they felt, and it could be heard in their conversations and laughter as they moved through the forest.

"How are you feeling?" Della asked Rose, snapping her out of her trance.

"Huh..Oh I'm okay."

"I know it must've been hard to separate from your friend", Della said.

Rose looked down at the grasslands as they continued to walk next to one of the wagons, and said in a low tone, "I have a lot of love for Tara. I understand how our imprisoned condition fueled so much anger inside of her. So I wasn't going to stop her from going with Nipoly and the rest of them to get some payback."

"I understand too", Della said with a smile. "Letty wanted to get a piece of the army too, for the way they treated us. But freeing our Queen is more important to us, than jumping on the backs of the army in the forest."

"Wow...Your Queen must be someone special for yah to go back and free her; instead of going in your own direction to free yourselves."

Della paused, then smiled. "She is special. Queen Taila would lay down her life for one of us. The people in Pakisound feel the same way about her."

"Our King and Queen died in the battle for our land", Rose said, then sighed. "That seems like centuries ago."

Della looked over to the hazelnut colored woman with salt and pepper hair and asked, "Rose how long have you been a prisoner?"

"Not as long as others," she said with a slight grin. "Maybe five years now. Why?"

"I'm just amazed at how well you kept yourself looking...And going. So what's your secret?" Della asked.

Rose giggled. "Della, I don't have any real secrets. I was always raised to keep myself looking and feeling like a lady. No matter what the circumstances may be."

"What are yah talking about?" Letty asked when she hopped out of the back of one of the wagons catching up with her partner.

"I was just asking Rose, what is her secret to looking so young?" Della said.

"Girl please", Rose said in between a chuckle. "I'm on the doorstep of being the elder of this group."

"Ain't nothing wrong with that", Letty said. "We going to need that guidance when its time to rebuild the city."

"Hey Della, when are we going to stop", Jacob asked.

"By night fall I guess", Della answered.

"You look like you forgot they were going to be coming to you for the answers now." Rose said with a slight giggle.

"I did. You know, when I thought it was only going to be me and Letty going back to Industriland, I didn't think much about when and where we were going to stop."

"Wait a minute. Are you telling me you two were going back to Industriland, by yourselves to, free your Queen?" Rose asked with a surprised look on her face.

"Good idea, huh?" Letty said sparking a round of laughs from the three women.

"I mean, yeah...If you had a knockout plan", Rose said.

"You're right", Della said. "So you think I should make up a plan for us?"

"Yup...And think of a good one...Because I'm not no spring chicken anymore. So I can't be rolling around in the dirt with one of them young soldiers."

"Yes ma'am", Della said, and they continued on their journey to make history.

The heavy downpour of rain seemed to be slowing down the more the large group ventured into the forest. There weren't enough swords to arm everyone in the group of escaped prisoners. So many of them picked up a strong club and a couple of rocks they could use to knock someone down and out.

Nipoly was feeling good about the fifty plus group of fighters she had as they made their way through the forest. But she was still feeling nervous about how they were going to take the fight to Tmus and his group of trained killers.

Nipoly was grateful Lil Kay had sent Airman to them. He had proven to be a great asset to them, flying overhead to get a look at the fight on the battlefield. Which was a hard thing for him to do, because once Airman arrived he immediately wanted to get into the fight himself. But he knew the group in the forest was counting on him, so he turned back around and headed back to the songstress and her group.

Airman glided through the trees and landed when he saw Nipoly leading the group. Nipoly had been up all night and it showed in her tired eyes when she gave Airman a warm smile.

"How did it look up there?" Nipoly asked, as Airman got in step with her and Pham.

"Songstress, it is quite a fight brewing on the field", Airman reported.

"How are they spread out up there?" Pham asked.

"Most of the army is out on the hill, while a unit is still trying to knock down the front gate", Airman said.

"Wow, they still haven't made it through the front gate?" Nipoly said surprised.

"We have a pretty strong defense in The Brook", Airman said proudly. "Also, at the edge of the forest is where Tmus and a group of knightsmen are sitting. They seemed to be watching the battle from the distance."

"How far are we from them?" Pham asked.

"About thirty clicks", Airman said.

"That means we're close", Pham said.

"Hey what's that up there?" someone asked out loud.

"I don't know", Pham answered, as he squinted his eyes in the rain.

Everyone was quiet as they got closer to the bloody scene. Bodies was piled on top of bodies in the most grotesque way.

"What's going on?" someone in the back asked as the procession began to slow down.

"Does this mean the battle began up here?" Jerome asked, once most of the group made it to the scene.

"They could have turned on each other", a woman named Rachel suggested.

"No. This was an ambush by one of The Brook brigades", Airman said, causing a circulation of murmurs to flow through the group.

"Come on...Let's keep it moving", Pham said, leading the way from the scene.

"If you see any weapons, pick them up", Jerome said. Causing the unarmed to pick up the swords and shields of the dead.

"We are close now", Airman said.

"Okay. Let's get everyone ready then", Nipoly said, taking a deep breath, before she said a silent prayer to the Gods of Song.

Chapter XXVIII

HEEE!

HOOO! Bang!

HEEE!

HOOO! Bang!

"How much longer do you think the gates are going to hold up?" Lady Light asked Poppa Big in a low tone.

"Not much longer", he said. Even though his words were meant for his wife's ears only, they carried on to everyone else in earshot.

The front line brigade stacked up in the court yard and braced themselves, as the archers on the top of the wall continued to engage in a heavy shoot out with the Industriarmy archers, who were now in close enough range to do some serious damage.

The rain began to let up as the smell of sulfur, smoke and death rose through the air. The vibration of the hungry army outside of the gates could be felt inside the city.

HEEE!

HOOO! Bang!

The portcullis began to bend inward, as stone particles rained down on the main walk way. With the strong metal whining under every hit, everyone knew it was just a matter of time before the army made their way in.

HEEE!

HOOO! Bang!

Big chunks of stone began to fall. Raising the anticipation level.

"One More! One More!" Captain Ishmael chanted with excitement in his voice. His eyes lit up as he gripped the handle of his sword. The one thousand man force Captain Ishmael had waiting behind him remained hunkered down under the shelter of their metal shields, as The Brook archers continued showering them with a rain storm of hot arrows.

HEEE!

HOOO! Bang!

The impact caused a large portion of the stone to crumble and the gate came free on one side. The portcullis was left hanging sideways and the Industriarmy smelled blood. The men handling the battering ram quickly stepped back, then rushed forward with all their might.

A loud bang froze in the air as the portcullis finally gave way, and flew up into the air. Everyone seemed to pause as they watched the battered gate crash land before the feet of The Brook brigade.

"CCHHAARRGGEE!!!" Captain Ishmael shouted with his sword pointed at the short tunnel.

RROOAARR!

The first twenty men on the front line brigade didn't wait for the Industriarmy soldier's to make it through the tunnel and into the courtyard. They rushed up into the tunnel and collided with the soldier's in the short tunnel.

"Ahhh!!! Men grunted and cried out in pain as swords clinked and sparked on impact.

To maximize his attack Captain Ishmael began to bark out orders. "Climb The Walls! Climb The Walls!"

His orders reverberated down the line as the anxious fighters saw the opportunity to get within the walls of The Brook now in reach.

"Get ready!" Sekou ordered as he pulled out his sword.

Long makeshift ladders wrapped up against the wall, with men running up them with reckless abandon. Some of them would make it halfway up the ladder, then end up flying through the air when the men at the top of the wall pushed the ladder off of the wall. But the Industriarmy's persistence began to pay off as the first wave of soldiers made it to the top and over the battlements.

"YAA!" Sekou shouted as he swung his sword and beheaded the first enemy fighter to step foot on the wall walkway, setting the tone for the rest of his men.

The battle on the ground was beginning to shape out like the one on the walkway with blood and bodies flying in every direction. War cry's carried through the air, as shouts for help tried to drown them out. The rain suddenly stopped making the battle a muddy one as the Industriarmy pushed on through the front gate of the city.

"Position 3! Position 3!" Brendan barked from the back of the crowd jammed up in the tunnel. The front line brigade shifted into three large groups as the battle raged on in the tunnel.

D.Tiger stayed close to Poppa Big and Lady Light, as a group of thirty men surrounded them.

"Get In There!" Captain Ishmael ordered, physically grabbing one of his men by his collar and pushing him into the crowd that was clogged up in the front gate way.

"Destroy Them!" Ishmael ranted, as the strong smell of death rode up into his nostrils. The motivational push gave the army the strength they needed to overpower the men who were trying to stop their advancement.

D.Tiger saw the army making its push, causing him to growl and grit his teeth. Poppa Big gripped his sword, and blocked out any thoughts of compromise. They were all in and ready for it.

On the other side of the wall Tmus was doing the same as he watched his soldiers overwhelm the group of guards at the front gate. Tmus could taste it. He could smell a victory rising in the air. It's been a long time coming and now he was about to get his just do.

Whhhhhnnn!

A horse in the back of Tmus' formation whined causing everyone to turn around.

✳✳✳✳✳

The rebellion fanned out and formed a semicircle around the unsuspecting Tmus and his personal guard. Jerome and Rachel were ordered to take half of the fighters over to the left side. While Nipoly and Pham were to lead the other half on the right side. Nipoly could smell tension in the air once the rain stopped and the humidity began to rise.

Tara stayed right on Nipoly's heels as they moved into position. The strong smell of the knightsmen horses began to seep through the bushes the closer they got to the stationed Tmus and his group.

Pham crept through the bushes with his knife armed and ready, sweat coming out the palms of his hands. When he was close enough, Pham reached out and snatched one of the knights off of his horse, and stabbed him in his chest. The loud thumping and the knight's screams caused a chain reaction of panic amongst the horses.

"Attack!! Attack!!" Nipoly ordered, then rushed the closest Industriarmy knight to her.

Some of the knights hopped off of their horses and immediately attacked by one of the hidden fighters. While others stayed on their horse, getting it back under control.

"Yah!" Nipoly stabbed the unsuspecting knightsman while he sat on his horse, causing the horse to whine and kick up in the air with its front legs. The knight crash landed to the ground taking the wind out of him. Tara wasted no time aiding Nipoly, as she ran out of the bushes and stabbed the fallen knight in his chest, killing him instantly.

Jerome and Rachel led the way out of the bushes on the left side with the same look of determination in their eyes, with close to fifty fighters following them. The war cry that rose up out of them when they made their presence known, scared the birds out of the trees. Further rattling the tension filled forest.

Tmus and Zor turned their horses around and were shocked to see their captives attacking one of the most elite units in the Industriarmy.

"What's This?" Tmus asked, looking at the mob coming out of the bushes. He looked over to his Major with confusion written all over his face.

"Tmus Get Back!" Zor shouted as he got his horse back under control, quickly assessing the situation. The mob spilled out of the bushes causing the tight knit formation to scramble. The elite knightsmen quickly snapped into attack mode, putting their swords to work on their attacker's.

"Destroy Them!" Zor barked. Then he took a closer look at one of the attackers and froze in his stance.

"Nipoly?" Zor mumbled to himself, with a dumbfounded look on his face.

Tmus heard the name roll off of Zor's lips, which didn't surprise the leader. Tmus knew if Nipoly was willing to lay down with his major for a position in his uncertain rulership of a new Industriland, then she could attempt a mutiny like the one before him.

Pham swung his sword like a man possessed, as he positioned himself two feet from Nipoly on her left. While Tara held down the songstress on her right side, together they laid down a one, two, three combo with nothing but red in their eyes.

Pham was going head to head with one of the knights when Tara jumped him from behind and stabbed him in his back. "AAWWW!" the knight cried out in pain as he crumbed to the ground, then cut down by Pham's sword.

Zor had seen enough. The major hopped off of his horse and went straight at Pham.

Nipoly saw Zor dismount his horse, then come across the small battlefield with an anger in his eyes she had never witnessed before. A large knightsman came from her blind side, smacking Nipoly back into reality, sending her flying to the ground.

"You Bastard!" Tara cried out as she ran to Nipoly's aid. Tara stabbed the knightsman in his forearm.

"AWWW!" he cried, then swung his sword wildly and connected with Tara's side.

"Taraaa!" Nipoly cried, then scrambled to her feet. She rushed the knightsman from his blind side and stabbed him in his throat, then in his shoulder. He crumbled to his knees gripping his throat, falling on his back gasping for air.

Nipoly disregarded the dying knightsman and ran over to her fallen comrade. "Tara, come on baby...You're alright...I'm here...I got you", Nipoly told the young fighter.

Tara coughed as blood continued to spill out of her side and said, "Save yourself...Freedom is a must", then died in Nipoly's arms.

Pham braced himself for the major's wrath by countering Zor's swing.

Their swords sang under the hard blows until Zor pulled a move the inexperienced Pham wasn't ready for.

Pham swung his sword with a body full of momentum. Zor blocked the blow with his gold forearm sending a vibration through Pham's body. Giving Zor one shot – one kill.

Zor dropped down to one knee, did a 360 degree spin and followed through with his sword cutting Pham across his stomach.

"AAWWW!" Pham cried out as he watched the flood waters of blood spill out of his open body. That's when Zor went in for the kill by punching Pham in his stomach.

"NNNOOO!" Nipoly screamed, as she ran over and jumped on Zor's back.

"Get Off Of Me!" Zor barked, spinning in a circle with Nipoly attached to his back. He tried to reach back and snatch her off of him, but she locked onto his neck.

"You Bastard!" Nipoly cried, stabbing Zor in his chest. The blow did not have the impact she wanted it to have, causing Nipoly to lose her grip and fall to the ground.

Nipoly gasped for air as Zor snatched her off the ground by her collar. "You Snake! You Dare Cross Me!" Zor spat.

"PPLEEASE!" Nipoly cried once she was face to face with Zor's fury. He wrapped his golden hands around her neck and began to squeeze the life out of her.

Nipoly fought him as their eyes locked. It was at that moment she knew if there still was a piece of love for her inside of Zor it was all gone now.

"FFFRRRREEEDDOOMM!!" Nipoly managed to squeal as he continued to squeeze the life out of her.

Zor dropped her lifeless body and stared at the dead songstress, baffled by her last word.

Zor looked around at the chaotic scene around him in a dead man's stare. Then his breaths began to get shorter. He dropped down to one knee and grabbed at the wound in his chest. His breaths became labored and he started looking around for help.

The fighting around the wounded Major got heavy and bloody, making his injury go unnoticed by all of his surviving knightsmen and the fighters they were chopping down. But it didn't go unnoticed by the man who always had his back out on the battlefield. Tmus snapped his reins and guided his horse over to his fallen major.

Tmus had watched the entire exchange between Nipoly and Zor, and he thought Zor was going to go soft on the songstress by letting her live. But he proved him wrong, making Tmus proud of his major for closing the chapter on the greatest songstress – and heart breaker Industriland had ever raised.

Now it was time to repay Zor by calling on the powers that be to save him. "Gods of Force...Heal My Son!" Tmus said, remaining on his black stallion. A bright light shot out of Tmus' hand and it hit Zor directly in his chest.

A hot surge of power burned into Zor's chest, then vibrated through his body. His gold arms lit up and he began to feel the air of life engulf his lungs.

"RRRAAA!" Zor roared. His cry rattled the trees around them as the birds scattered into the air.

"Retreat! Retreat!" someone began to shout. Slowly but surely the remaining fighters that could get away began to scatter. Airman grabbed a knight by his back, and lifted him high up into the air.

"Let Me Go You Freak!" the knight barked.

"Okay." Airman said, then let the knightsman fall to his death.

"Nnnnoooo!"

Airman stayed suspended in the air and saw the remaining fighter's running back into the forest. "Where are they going!" Airman snapped. "No! Keep Fighting!" he shouted. But his pleas fell on deaf ears as they continued to make their way back into the forest.

"Those cowards!" he spat. Then decided to fly back to The Brook once he saw Nipoly and Pham were amongst the dead sprawled out on the ground below. He knew once the leadership of the rebellion was gone, followers heart wouldn't be in it anymore.

Tmus caught a glimpse of the black birdman as he flew down the west end of the forest heading for The Brook.

"Your Excellency...They are in the main courtyard!" one of his men shouted, snapping Tmus out of his trance.

"Good. Then it is time", Tmus said with a newfound surge of energy flowing through his body.

Zor looked around until he came across Nipoly's dead body. He stared down at her for a moment, then reached down and retrieved his sword. He looked over to Tmus and with one swift motion Zor beheaded the dead songstress.

"Let's Move Out!" Zor ordered as he grabbed a horse's reins and mounted it.

Chapter XXIX

Poppa Big stood his ground with his first lady on one side of him and his red comrade on the other, watching his once beautiful courtyard turn into a place of carnage. The first tier of The Brook brigade had been defeated, and now the Industriarmy was working on the second tier.

"Fire Starters...Move In!" Brendan ordered, releasing a thirty man wave of Airmen armed with a bottle of liquid in one hand, and a torch in the other.

The bottles rained down on the advancing army men, breaking and splash liquid on every person in reach. Then the Airmen tossed the lit torches down onto the crowd.

Whoosh!

Pandemonium erupted with a fire quickly spreading from one man to the next. Flames shot high into the air followed by a series of screams and cries for help.

"Hit Em High!" Brendan barked.

"Hit Em Low!" his brigade responded as they covered all areas of escape from the burning Industriarmy soldiers. They staged a ferocious attack by breaking down in ranks, then fanning out to trap the burning soldiers in a semicircle. Burning body parts and blood soaked the main courtyard, turning it into a scene of horror.

✶✶✶✶✶

The fire in Major Zor's veins could be seen in his eyes as he lead the elite delegation from shadows of the forest and out into the open land. The sun began to disappear behind the 80 foot tall trees, giving the moon the open night sky.

Bodies laid in every walking lane, causing Zor to lead the way right over the dead. Tmus noticed his army did not fully take over

The Brook like he had expected at this time. He looked over to Zor and said, "They're stopping our advances on the wall Major."

Zor looked up and brushed it off as he rode up on Captain Ishmael. "Captain, are you ready for us to enter the city?" Zor asked.

Captain Ishmael had a frustrated look on his face when he tried to answer the major. "Ahh..Not quite Major..We are almost..."

Zor cut him off, "That is unacceptable! Make a way for us now Captain", Zor barked.

"Yes Sir." Andrew snapped. Then he quickly turned his horse around and galloped over to the crowd of soldiers clogging up the front gate in a fierce battle.

"Sergeant I want a full bum rush", Captain Andrew ordered.

The Sergeant of Arms looked at the clutter of soldiers waiting to get into the short tunnel to shed some blood, then back to Andrew and said, "Captain, there are a few scattered fires that are stopping our progress."

"I don't care! Just order the bum rush, before you end up in that pile of bodies", Andrew threatened.

Turning back to the crowd at the gate the Sergeant of Arms said, "Bum Rush! Full Industriarmy Bum Rush!!!Now!"

A loud roar rose up into the night as the mass body of Industriarmy soldiers began to push their way up into the tunnel. The sound of bones crushing was drowned out by cries from the injured.

On the other side of the wall P.D. the Wizard and Lady Light tried to use their powers to push the oncoming wave back out of the gate. The strong flash of light lit up the night sky, blinding some and burning others.

This didn't stop Major Zor from losing his patience. "Let's go", he ordered, leading the delegation over anyone and anything in their path. The air seemed to turn still as the group of black and brown horses burst through the crowd, trampling over anything and anybody in their path. Zor's gold forearms began to shine in the night, as the sinister look in his eyes sent a shock wave through the courtyard.

Poppa Big chopped down an Industriarmy soldier then turned his attention to the rush of horses that burst through the tunnel. "D.Tiger, they're here."

D.Tiger hopped off the chest of one of his victims, then suddenly locked eyes with Major Zor. "Yes they are." The red tiger growled, ready to mall down anyone who was ready to cross his path.

"Let's Get 'Em!" Poppa Big barked. Then he and his red partner went after the heads of the Industriarmy.

Zor wasted no time once he was finally in the courtyard. He hopped off of his horse and went right to work one two members of The Brook brigade. He chopped one man's hand off, then did a crouching 180 degree spin to chop the other man's stomach open.

Suddenly Tmus crossed the threshold of the jungle city with matching shiny red eyes as his black stallion. "Kill Them All!" he ordered igniting a roar from the wave of soldier who followed him into the city.

P.D. the Wizard knew it was time. He called on the Gods of Song to send down the God of War to assist them. "Gods of Song. Open up the gates of destruction on these enemies of High-Hop! Send us the strength of song", P.D. prayed with his hands raised high in the air.

A loud rumble echoed through the sky as lightening flashed through the night sky. Suddenly the sky began to open up. A loud eerie cry came down from the heavens. Followed by a group of black ghostly warriors, riding down on all white horses.

"I see this wizard wants to play", Tmus said. Then he called on his own spiritual reinforcements.

"Gods of Force! We are here to do the bidding of the most powerful!..Join us in the midst of this forceful takeover!" Tmus said. "Give us the Evil Orange."

The ground began to violently shake, causing everyone who was engaged in a fight to lose their balance. The earth began to crack and the ground split underneath everyone's feet. A fire shot up into the air followed by a loud roar.

A loud thumping sound echoed out of the ground as a large orange figure appeared to be walking up a staircase out onto the battlefield carrying a large mallet.

"RROOAARR!" the evil being roared loud enough to wake the entire Muzena.

"Get Back! Watch Out!"

"Very clever", P.D. the Wizard said under his breath.

Four white horsemen rode out of the sky and hopped off of their horses with fire red swords armed and ready. The fight with the living ceased for a moment, as the fight with the spirits began.

"Force them into submission!" Tmus barked with dry foam forming on the corners of his mouth.

"RROOAARR!" his creation responded, charging at the first spirit to touch the ground.

The white cloaked spirit braced itself and swung its sword at the large figure barreling down on him. His sword connected with Evil Orange's arm causing a bright flash on impact.

Evil Orange looked down at where the sword struck his arm and simply shook his head, with a sinister smile creeping on his bumpy face. Then he swung his large mallet, causing the spirit to put up his sword in defense.

BANG!

The sound of the mallet connecting with the spirit's sword was deafening. The other three spirits immediately jumped into the battle swinging their swords at every opening of Evil Orange's body they could get. Sparks and fire flew in every direction lighting up the night sky, but the damage was minor compared to what took place once Evil Orange grabbed hold of one of the white spirits.

Members from both sides were in awe as they watched Evil Orange grab the white spirit by the throat, then viciously slam him to the ground. The impact made the earth shift with the white spirit laying motionless.

D.Tiger took this opportunity to move through the crowd with the quickness and stealth of the jungle animal he was born to be. Before Zor could realize what was happening the red tiger was paw deep in his chest, knocking him to the ground. All of the air seemed to fly right out of Zor when he was slammed flat on his back. D.Tiger roared in his face, then cocked back his paw to smack the major.

"YYAAA!"

Suddenly one of his knightsmen came to his rescue, swinging his sword down onto D.Tiger's back.

"RROAAR!" D.Tiger cried out as he rolled off of Zor's chest.

Poppa Big rushed right in and without any hesitation beheaded the knight. Zor lit up his right arm punching the red tiger in his jaw. D.Tiger slid on the muddy grass and crashed into some bushes.

Poppa Big moved in quicker than the scrambling Zor and with the strength of ten men brought his sword down on Zor's left wrist. The impact was blinding as Zor's left hand severed from his arm.

"AAAWWW!"

The Major's cry hit Tmus directly in his bones as he turned around and saw his wounded friend grab his separated wrist, leaving himself wide open for Poppa Big.

Poppa Big went in for the kill and swung his sword at the Major's head. 'Pop!' 'Clink!'

Poppa Big was spun around in a 360 degree spin, then he lost his footing. He shook his head and quickly tried to figure out what just happened. When he looked down at his sword, he knew.

Looking over to where the shot came from his eyes landed on the man of the movement. "I know you didn't think I was going to let you do what your heart desired", Tmus said as he hopped off of his horse and sized he big black bear up.

The fighting around the two leaders continued to get out of hand as more Industriarmy soldiers made their way into the courtyard. The battle with the living was getting overwhelming for The Brook warriors as they tried to stand their ground.

The three remaining spirits decided to gang jump Evil Orange, causing a loud bang. They rushed him toward the opening in the ground and tried to push him back into the hole he climbed out of.

RRROOAARR!...EEEKKKK!!

Their screams were ear piercing as Evil Orange lost his footing and fell backwards into the hole. To make sure he wasn't going down alone, Evil Orange grabbed onto two of the white cloaks and pulled the spirits down with him.

EEEEKKKK!!!

Their cries echoed through the night as they all tumbled down into the eternal fire. Flames shot up into the night like a fire being fed lighting fluid. Taking no chances, P.D. quickly called on his powers and closed the ground behind them.

"Tell your people to join me, and submit to the will of the Industry, and I will spare them their lives", Tmus said as he continued to approach Poppa Big.

Poppa Big got to his feet, shaking off the cobwebs. "High-Hop is the word of our speech, the culture of Muzena and the will of our freedom. We will never submit our freedom to anyone but the Gods of Song!" Poppa Big spat as he raised his sword.

"Very well – Die your way", Tmus said.

Zap! AWWW!

Tmus was caught off guard by a shot that sent a shock wave through his body. Lady Light kept her powerful wand aimed at Tmus' back, as the strong ray of light coming out of it sent him to his knees.

Tmus' personal guard moved in on Poppa Big before he could swing his sword at their fallen leader. Three knight's-men moved on the big bear in a blitz, causing him to defend himself in a triple step block.

Clink-Clink-Clink! Whoosh!

Poppa Big swung his sword with so much force after the last block, that when he connected with one of the knight's swords the impact broke the man's arm. His scream from the sudden snap of his arm was agonizing.

Major Zor focused when he heard his leaders cry and locked in on the source of his pain. With his severed arm, Zor raised his limb and pointed it at Lady Light. A bright flash shot out of his missing limb and hit Lady Light in her cheek.

"AAAhh!"

Poppa Big felt his wife's cry run a chill down his spine. He turned around just in time to see her fly off of her feet and slide across the wet ground.

The beast in Poppa Big came alive; and so did D.Tiger who staggered to his feet and rushed Major Zor.

P.D. ran over to Lady Light and tried to get her up. "Come on Lady...Stay with me", he checked her pulse, then tried breathing air into her lungs. "Breath Lady...Come on...Breath!"

"She's gone", P.D. the Wizard looked up to see who said it, and his sad eyes filled up with surprise when he looked up into Fungi's face. The head knight brought his sword down with all of his might, splitting P.D.'s head like a watermelon. "Some wizard you are", he said as he moved on to his next victim.

Tmus remained on his knees trying to catch his breath, as Poppa Big went into a rage. He swung his sword one way and free paw the other, breaking up the three man group that jumped him. He then turned his anger to Tmus who was now back on his feet.

"RRROOAAARR!" D.Tiger roared as he tackled Zor and rolled him around on the ground. Zor tried to choke the red tiger with his good hand, putting up his maimed hand to stop D.Tiger from taking a bite out of his face.

Clink' Crack!

D.Tiger bit down so hard on Zor's gold arm that his teeth cracked in several places. "HHHWWWOOOO!" the red tiger howled in pain.

Zor punched D.Tiger in his jaw doing even more damage to his bleeding mouth. Then he gave the red tiger one more shot causing him to roll off of the Major. D.Tiger ran his front paws over his face as he laid on his back whining for the pain to stop.

"Let me help you", Fungi said in his deep ominous tone. Then he raised his sword and stabbed D.Tiger in his heart. The 450 pound tiger froze in shock, before his eyes faded away.

Fungi twisted his sword to make sure he was dead, then said, "That's it little kitty...Sleep well." He pulled his sword out of the dead tiger's chest, then looked over to Zor. The Major looked battered and bruised, but he was very much still alive. Satisfied with that, Fungi moved on to his next victim.

Poppa Big and Tmus collided, then wrestled with each other causing the ground to shake under their feet. Both man and bear grunted and growled as the wills of their respective strengths struggled to take the other one down. Tmus' foot stepped on a dead soldier's head causing him to shift in his stance.

Poppa Big took advantage of the opening and pushed all of his weight on Tmus. He slammed him hard onto the ground shaking the earth in his wake. Tmus kicked the black bear off of him, then quickly popped back on his feet.

Most of the fighting around them began to lean heavily in the Industriarmy's favor as they began to overpower the surviving members of the jungle city brigade.

"Enough of these games", Tmus spat as his face began to turn red and his hands grew two sizes bigger with long claws suddenly growing out of his finger tips. "You will knee before me!"

Poppa Big knew this was it. If he had one last call to his protectors of good, the same protectors that rewarded him the land of The Brook, the place he built under the love and traditions of High-Hop, then this was the time for him to use it to battle the more enhanced Tmus.

Poppa Big closed his eyes, "Gods of Song!..This is a call from your son of the Jungle City!...Give me your strength!"

The sky cracked and the wind sent a bone chilling howl through the land as the Industriarmy began to take control over the city. A sharp flash of lightening rolled down out of the dark sky and struck Poppa Big in his forehead.

"GGGRROOWWLL!!"

Poppa Big's growl could be felt by every animal in a two hundred mile radius, causing birds to burst out of the trees in fright, and animals scramble for cover. Poppa Big grew two sizes bigger, stretching his black fur and toning his body into a solid muscle mass. His face and mouth began to enlarge into a more menacing feature than the one he just had when he watched his wife die.

"HHHIIGGHH---HHOPP!" Poppa Big barked before he rushed across the short battlefield at his awaiting opponent.

Tmus outstretched his arms and welcomed the 700 pound bear that was barreling down on him and twisted his body in mid air once they connected. He slammed Poppa Big to the ground sending a shock wave down to the core of the earth.

As they laid chest to chest on the ground, the faces of dead souls from past campaigns began to appear on Tmus' skin. They began to bite into Poppa Big's fur, but the chunks of fur they was snatching off of the big bear's body was minute compared to the open paw smacks Poppa Big was administering on Tmus' face.

Poppa Big's claws cut open Tmus' red cheek and a condemned soul escaped out into the open, floating up into the night sky. Tmus pushed the bear off of him with all of the strength he could muster then climbed to his feet.

The two fighters gathered themselves, then engaged in a blow for blow fist fight in the center of the destroyed courtyard. Tired of taking so many punches, Tmus rushed in and grabbed Poppa Big by his fur. He dipped down to the ground and flipped Poppa Big over. Then he quickly flew up into the air coming down with a rib crushing stomp.

Poppa Big momentarily lost his breath, then rolled over to avoid a second stomp from the airborne Tmus. When Tmus landed back on the ground, Poppa Big rolled back into him knocking him over. He then hopped on Tmus with an open paw swipe across his chest. Two more condemned souls howled, as they were set free from the body of their oppressor.

Tmus had enough of this. He kicked Poppa Big off of him, then hopped back to his feet. "Fungi, Your Sword!" he said to his top knight's man.

Fungi gladly tossed his leader his weapon, and then Tmus went right at Poppa Big.

Poppa Big quickly looked around for a weapon of his own and saw a sword wedged in the body of a dead soldier. As he went to pull it out of the dead man, Tmus swung his sword and sliced Poppa Big on his left bicep. Poppa Big stumbled sideways, but still managed to grab a sword of his own. Raising the sword Poppa Big was able to block the second blow Tmus came at him with.

Clink-Clink-Clink!

The two traded sharp blows after powerful swings until Tmus took a deep breath and blew out air full of fire into the black bears face.

"AAWWW!" Poppa Big cried out as he dropped his sword and tried to brush the flames off of his face.

Tmus seized the moment by dipping low, then cutting open Poppa Big's stomach. Blood spilled out of him, but Poppa Big wasn't trying to go down. He let out an energizing roar, then rushed Tmus going straight for his throat.

Poppa Big was able to grab Tmus by his throat, allowing his claws to cut into his thick red skin. However, his move came with a price as Tmus jammed his sword into Poppa Big's stomach.

Poppa Big's grip slowly began to loosen up as the two stared into each other's eyes. Tmus watched the light slowly fade out of the big bears eyes. Suddenly Poppa Big's body spasmed and his mouth snapped taking a bite out of Tmus' cheek.

Tmus took the final blow to his face as he twisted his sword in Poppa Big's gut – turning out the last spark in the big black bear eyes.

Tmus then stepped to the side and let the dead body drop to the ground with the sword still wedged in his stomach. The sound of Poppa Big's body hitting the ground was deafening, as all breathing throughout Muzena seemed to be suspended in time.

Tmus took one last look at Poppa Big, then he looked at the large crowd of spectators and raised his fist high in the air.

"INDUSTRYYYY!"

His follower's roared their approval, as the surviving jungle city warriors were taken hostage, with their heads held down in defeat.

Chapter XXX

"What do you think happened out there?" Ms. Linda asked as she and Lil Kay made their way around the large table. They were handing out fruit to each child for their morning breakfast.

"I don't know", Lil Kay answered in a low tone. "Elisha make sure you don't waste none of that flat cake today like you did yesterday."

"Yes Lil Kay", the little girl replied.

"Did you fell those shock waves last night?" Ms.Linda asked sticking close to The Duchess

"Yes", Lil Kay replied, trying to keep it short. "Octavious, no playing at the table."

"Yes Lil Kay", the chocolate faced boy said, feeling like he was just scolded by his own mother.

Lil Kay moved with grace around the table, greeting every child with a smile, a touch on their shoulder, or a caress on their cheek.

"Let's go to the storage", Lil Kay said to Ms. Linda when she finished making her rounds at the breakfast table.

When they stepped into the room Lil Kay turned to her and said, "Ms. Linda we have to keep our conversation around the children limited. They are holding onto a lot of hope out there that

Poppa Big and the rest of the brigade will get us through this. So I don't want to discourage them with talk of the war outside."

Ms. Linda nodded and said, "I'm sorry Lil Kay...It's just..."

Lil Kay tried to fill the void. "I know what you're feeling Ms. Linda...And I'm sorry for bringing you and Cory into this situation, but we have to hold it together. Those children lives depend on it, okay", Lil Kay said taking Ms. Linda's hands into hers.

"Okay", she said, then suddenly hugged Lil Kay. "Thank you Lil Kay."

"No, thank you", Lil Kay said with a bright smile.

Bang!-Bang!-Bang!-Bang!

The loud thumping made both women jump. "What was that?" Ms. Linda asked with a nervous look in her eyes.

"Come", Lil Kay said, grabbing Ms. Linda's hand. They shuffled out into the main room.

All of the children had stopped eating, while the adults stood stock still not sure of what to do next. Everyone stared at Lil Kay and Ms. Linda as they hustled into the room and made their way down the aisle to the big steel door.

Bang!-Bang!-Bang!-Bang!

Everyone nervously jumped, except for Lil Kay.

"Please help us", a faint voice said from the other side. "Someone please help us."

Ms. Linda looked at Lil Kay who continued to stare at the door. Making up her mind, Lil Kay took two steps back. There was no way she was going to open the door.

"Please. we need you", the pleas were persistent, but convincing enough for Lil Kay to take that chance.

✷✷✷✷✷

The stench of death was heavy in the air as the sun rose in the jungle city. The Brook looked to be in near ruins with Industriarmy soldiers now covering every section of the large metropolis. They had search parties out looking for survivors, food, and any valuables left behind for the taking.

Tmus ordered the bodies of Poppa Big and D.Tiger put into boxes and placed on the back of a wagon. The boxes were placed under heavy guard until the wagon was transported to Industriland, where their bodies would be put on display for all the world to see.

Then Tmus, Major Zor, and Fungi set up camp inside of the jungle city boardroom. Basking in their victory as they received first aid for their wounds.

"Gentlemen, this is one of our proudest conquests in our history", Tmus began, once he shooed the man away was stitching up his face. "And your loyalty to me...Industriland, and the Gods of Force will be rewarded."

Tmus stood up and poured three cups of wine. Shocked by the gesture, Zor looked over to Fungi who returned the same confused look. For as long as Zor could remember Tmus has never poured anyone a drink. Tmus handed each man a cup, then raised his own cup.

"To Industriland!"

"To Industriland!" Zor and Fungi repeated, then they all took a large swallow of the red liquid.

"When Muzena is divided up, you two will possess a section of it to rule", Tmus said with a slight smirk in the corners of his mouth.

"Thank you Tmus", Zor said, feeling pleased by his leader's words. Zor had worked hard all his life for this moment and now it was going to pay off.

Fungi on the other hand never thought his services to the army would ever pay off to anything more than the position he was already holding. Surprise was written all over his face. "Yes your Excellency...I want to express my thanks as well."

"You two have earned the right to govern your own land", Tmus said as he took a seat in Poppa Big's huge chair. "And I think it's time we prepare the army for the transition."

Both men nodded in agreement as Tmus continued. "I know we have one more city to go before we can call ourselves the true rulers of Muzena, but in the meantime, bask in our victory gentlemen. You deserve it", Tmus said giving his to two military leaders their well earned praise.

Zor and Fungi saluted Tmus, then continued to hammer out the details of the Industriarmy's future, while their men continued to loot the city and lock down any survivors they could find hidden in the city.

"Any sound from inside?" Captain Ishmael asked when he reached the bottom landing of the jungle city shelter.

"No Sir."

“You sure he isn't lying to us?” Captain Ishmael asked, then cut his eyes at the man they had standing off to the side under knife point.

“No man! I'm not lying. I'm telling you, they're in there”, the man pleaded.

Captain Ishmael looked at him with nothing but disgust in his eyes. Then he went back to watching his men work on the big steel door. “How much longer?”

“He should be in there in a few Captain”, one of the Industriarmy soldiers said over his shoulder.

“Good...Once you’re inside, kill all those who resist”, Ishmael said.

“Yes Sir.”

The Captain then turned and left the shelter thinking the man was only buying himself some time. If there was someone on the other side of that door, they couldn't have possibly had any plans of staying in there without any food and a water supply. Ishmael laughed to himself, thinking the man was going to die anyway, no matter if someone was on the other side of that door or not.

*****

Lil Kay stood front and center with her two trusty daggers in her hands, and Ms. Linda close to her side with a metal pipe in her hand. Behind them ten mothers stood armed and ready with knives, clubs, and metal pipes of their own.

The tension in the air was thicker than the smoke from their burning city on the other side of the door. The women stood stock still for hours waiting for the people on the other side of the door to break into the shelter. The door finally shifted, then it was rocked back and forth, as the stone around its edges crumbled to the ground. Lil Kay closed her eyes, and said a silent prayer.

When she opened her eye's the pounding stopped. Then all of a sudden a loud bang made all of the women jump out of their shoes.

Bang!-Bang!-Bang!

The loud banging sent stone chips flying into the room until one loud bang knocked the door off track and it swung inward into the shelter. An Industriarmy soldier stuck his head into the shelter and locked eyes with Lil Kay. He slowly smiled revealing his rotten teeth, as dust particles hung heavily in the air.

"They're here!" he reported before he could pull his head back into the corridor.

"YYAAH!" Ms. Linda's cry of strength was felt throughout the entire shelter, as she swung her metal pipe and connected with the soldier nose.

"AAAWWW!" he fell back into one of his comrades, then crumbled to the ground as blood rained down out of his nose like a waterfall.

Ms. Linda's sudden burst of anger set the tone for the rest of the women in the room, as the grip around their weapons tightened.

Bang!-Bang!-Bang!

The door was suddenly pushed in far enough for two men to climb over the fallen rocks and push their way into the room. The first man in ran right into the waiting Lil Kay and her five inch dagger.

"YYAHH!" Lil Kay stepped to the side and stabbed the soldier right in his chest. When he buckled to grab at the dagger, one of the pipe welding mothers attacked him like a wild cheetah.

The second soldier through the door stepped over the fallen rocks and, managed to swing his sword once before he was attacked by the shelter's protective mothers. The soldier cries sent a chill up the spine of every child held up in the back room.

Cory snatched open the door just enough for him and Dorus to get a peep of the action. The nervous children hovered behind them and tried to catch a small view of the next room, but were quickly pushed away by Tola and Elisha.

"Get Back!"

"What's Happening?"

"We want to see."

"No, Stay Back!"

When Cory saw the fifth and sixth Industriarmy soldier make his way into the chaotic shelter, he knew it was time to make his move.

Cory quickly closed the door and turned to the group behind him, "Okay yah...It's time to go".

"Go? Go where?" someone blurted out.

Cory ignored the question and made his way over to the spot Lil Kay showed him when they first came down to the shelter. Lil Kay knew Cory would be able to keep the spot a secret, and when it was time to use the secret spot, he would be their best choice to lead the rest of the children to it.

"Come on. Help me", Cory ordered, then turned back to the wall of baskets.

Octavious and Tola hurried over to help Cory move the baskets as the rest of the children looked on. When Cory cleared out the area he was looking for, he pulled up a drop rug revealing a trap door in the floor. Cory pulled it open releasing a cool air breeze from the underground tunnel.

"What's down there?" Elisha asked nervously.

"Our escape. Come on Dorus, you lead the way, and I'll bring up the back", Cory ordered over the screams that seemed to be getting louder the longer they stayed in the room.

Dorus hesitated. "But where am I going? I can't even see in there."

Cory turned around, grabbed a torch from off the wall, then lit it with some sulfur and a spark next to it.

"Here..Now Go!"

"We need reinforcement's!"

The scene in the shelter's main room got bloodier by the second as a team of Industriarmy soldiers made their way into the shelter, only to be met by the same welcoming the soldiers before them received.

Ms. Linda watched Lil Kay's blind side, as Lil Kay showed how she earned her respect as The Duchess of the Jungle City, by sweeping one soldier and pitching a dagger in the neck of another. Giving Ms. Linda the time she needed to swing her now bloody pipe at anyone in range.

In the midst of the fighting Lil Kay lost count of the soldiers coming in through the door, and the brave mothers who were losing their lives; until she looked up and took a quick survey of the room.

The only ones remaining were Lil Kay, Ms. Linda, and two other women. Five Industriarmy soldiers moved around the dead and tried to gain position on the surviving women, causing two of the soldiers to lose their lives, while the last three cut down the last two mothers standing.

Lil Kay gathered herself, then cried out in anger as she ran at one of the waiting soldiers. "NNNOO!"

Lil Kay stopped short of her run and turned around to face the voice that just stopped her from taking the Industriarmy soldier out.

"Sekou?" she asked with a confused look in her eyes.

Sekou looked haggard with fresh blood on his face, hands, and the front of his ripped shirt. He was holding a long sword with blood dripping off of its blade, and he had the look of murder in his eyes.

"Look at this Owen, the rat is coming to the rescue", one of the last three surviving Industriarmy soldiers joked as he aimed his sword.

"Rat? What is he talking about Sekou?" Lil Kay asked.

Sekou looked at the woman he had a secret love affair with for several years now and felt at peace with his decision.

We've been defeated Lil Kay", Sekou said as everyone in the room seemed to freeze for their exchange. Lil Kay looked at his eyes and tried to read what he really was trying to tell her, but her thoughts were quickly interrupted.

"That's right ladies...It's over...So surrender now, and I promise we'll let you live", one of the soldiers spat, as he moved closer to his prey.

"You brought them here?" Lil Kay asked not wanting to believe she had to ask that.

Everyone stood stock still as her question hung in the air.

"Trust me Lil Kay", was all Sekou could say before he charged at the closest soldier to him.

Clink-Clink-Clink!

Their swords popped and snapped as the soldier tried to defend himself against the heavy onslaught. One of his partners flexed to jump into their fight, but he was quickly cut off by one of Lil Kay's daggers.

Aaaww! Lil Kay's dagger slammed him in his stomach. Ms. Linda wasted no time sliding in to put the soldier out of his misery. She hit him in his head, cracking his skull before he hit the ground.

Sekou used his experience as a brigade leader to cut down the last two Industriarmy soldiers in the shelter, then he turned to Lil Kay and said, "You have to go. Reinforcements are on the way."

"But why Sekou? Why did you bring them here?" Lil Kay asked. Her voice cracked at the mere thought of her only love turning her over to the army.

"To give you and the children time to get out of here", Sekou said. "Lil Kay, we might have lost the battle, but as long as those children make it out of here and avenge The Brook when the time comes, then we will be able to win the war."

"What? What are you talking about? What about Poppa Big and Lady Light?" Lil Kay asked.

"Dead...They're all dead", Sekou said with a grim look on his face. "But not you. You will be able to teach the children their history, and give them the strength they'll need to return here one day."

Lil Kay softened up and walked toward him. "What about you?"

Sekou smiled, "Maybe one day we will see each other again, but for now, you are to follow the escape plan we designed and take the children to the Kingdom of Soul."

"Come with us", Lil Kay said feeling her love slowly slipping away.

A mixture of voices and footsteps could be heard coming down the steps. "No. I will hold them off. Now go!"

Lil Kay ran to Sekou and kissed him hard on his lips knowing this would be the last time she would see him alive. When she pulled back, tears began to dribble down her cheeks as she said her last words to him.

"I love you Sekou."

The footsteps got closer.

"I love you too. Now go", he said, giving her a light push away from him. Then he ran straight for the broken down steel door to cut off anyone that tried to enter the shelter.

Lil Kay grabbed Ms. Linda's hand and led the way to the back room. Lil Kay closed the door behind them and locked it, blocking out the screams from the other side. "Down there", Lil Kay said, grabbing a torch and lighting it before the two women headed down into the dark tunnel.

When Lil Kay and Ms. Linda came out on the other side of the tunnel they found the children waiting for them in a twenty foot long boat that was stashed on the edge of the river.

"Look. Its Lil Kay!" Tola shouted, catching everyone's attention as the boat floated away from the shore. Cory got the rest of the children into the boat, then got it to float out into the river. But he didn't know how to stop it or turn it around.

That didn't stop Lil Kay from getting to the boat. She ran out into the water, and began to swim for the boat with Ms. Linda hot on her heels.

Ms. Linda thought she was going to have a heart attack from all the running and swimming. She was relieved when the children reached down into the water and pulled her and Lil Kay safely onto the boat. The boat quickly turned into an emotional scene as some of the children began to cry. While others bombarded Lil Kay and Ms. Linda about what happened and where they were going.

"Children claim down."

When they all settled down to hear what Lil Kay had to say, she looked into the eyes of them all and said, "We will make it through this if we stick together, and pray to the Gods of Song for our safe journey to the Kingdom of Soul."

"Yes Lil Kay", the children answered in unison as the boat continued to float down stream into the sun light.

To Be Continued

Dedicated to

Grand-Ma Trinidad Attles, your strength and drive to keep working will always shine threw me.

www.ingramcontent.com/pod-product-compliance
Lightning Source LLC
Chambersburg PA
CBHW071149020726
47502CB00002B/343